PRAISE FOR ANDREW MAYNE

"In Mayne's exciting second Jessica Blackwood novel, the cunning FBI special agent applies her magician training to investigating a bizarre explosion . . . A fast-moving thriller in which illusions are weapons for both good and evil."

—Publishers Weekly on *Name of the Devil*

"Science supersedes the supernatural in this action-packed follow-up . . . With snappy prose and a smart protagonist, this is an adrenaline-fueled procedural with an unusual twist. Great reading."

—Booklist (starred review) on *Name of the Devil*

"Mayne, the star of the A&E show *Don't Trust Andrew Mayne*, combines magic and mayhem in this delightful beginning to a new series . . . Readers will look forward to Jessica's future adventures."

—Publishers Weekly on *Angel Killer*

"Professional illusionist Mayne introduces a fresh angle to serial-killer hunting . . . Mayne forgoes gimmicks, instead dissecting illusions with human behavior, math, and science without losing sight of the story's big picture."

—Booklist on *Angel Killer*

LOOKING GLASS

LOOKING GLASS

ANDREW MAYNE

Text copyright © 2018 by Andrew Mayne
All rights reserved.

Published by Thomas & Mercer, Seattle

www.apub.com

Amazon, the Amazon logo, and Thomas & Mercer are trademarks of Amazon.com, Inc., or its affiliates.

ISBN-13: 9781542047999
ISBN-10: 1542047994

Cover design by M. S. Corley

Printed in the United States of America

LOOKING GLASS

PROLOGUE
MUTT

Tiko kicked the deflated soccer ball down the alley, laughing as MauMau, the tan puppy with the chewed-up ear, chased it into the puddle, his too-big paws splattering mud and droplets everywhere.

He loved that dog. It wasn't quite his; it was more a village dog that sniffed around looking for scraps and chased after rats when there were none to find. But he was Tiko's best friend.

An outcast like the puppy, Tiko had been turned away by his mother when he was three and she realized his white skin and reddish eyes weren't going to go away.

She'd prayed for him and even had the woman from the next village, who people said could heal, try to cast out the evil. But it hadn't worked.

As others began to scorn Tiko's mother for giving birth to a witch child, she sent him out for longer periods at a time, feeding him when she had to but making him take his meals outside and eventually sending him off on longer errands, not caring when he got back.

He was four when he heard his mother explain to another woman that he wasn't really her child; he was actually some friend's poor child she looked after.

Tiko was pretty sure this wasn't true but didn't blame her. He knew he was different, and it couldn't be easy for his mother.

When she was pregnant with a new child, Tiko's mother had stood on the doorstep and kicked him out in front of all the neighbors. She renounced him, telling everyone that he wasn't hers.

From that day, he'd never been allowed back inside. At night if he came to the doorstep and cried from hunger, she might give him something. But if his mother had a man with her, she'd yell at him to go away, pretending she didn't know him.

Tiko learned to survive by staying out of everyone's way and learning that some people would help him—but only if nobody saw them do it.

There was the old lady with no sons, who would give him half a bean cake or some jollo when her friends made extra. There was Mr. Inaru, who had the repair shop and yard filled with rusted car parts. He let Tiko sleep there at night and slide between the bars to hide when other children chased him.

They chased him a lot. And when they caught him, they punched him, pulled his hair, and called him a witch child.

The reason he liked MauMau so much was that the dog didn't hate him or merely tolerate him—he'd lick his face and cuddle next to him when it rained or it was cold.

Tiko knelt down, patted MauMau, and picked up the soccer ball, curious whether Mr. Inaru might be able to fix it so it could hold air. Of course, he knew that it would be only a matter of time before the other children took it away from him.

As he stared at the ball, he noticed a reflection in the puddle. A man—a very, very tall man—was smiling down at him.

Tiko looked up at the kind man. He was dressed in black slacks and a white shirt, like men in his village wore when they went to work or needed to look important.

"Are you Tiko?" asked the man in a voice so strong yet warm that Tiko would have answered yes no matter the question. But he merely nodded, too nervous to speak.

The man's large hand grabbed Tiko by the chin and turned his face from side to side. Instead of revulsion, he looked at him like Tiko looked at MauMau.

"You're a very good boy. Would you like to go for a ride in my truck?"

Tiko had never been in a truck but had watched them roll through his village as men with guns headed to some far-off place, and sometimes he'd watched as they raced back with men lying across the beds, their eyes shut or screaming in pain as they clutched bleeding stomachs or limbs.

Tiko nodded. Riding in a truck sounded exciting. Especially with this man.

The man held out his hand for Tiko to take and led him down the alley toward the green vehicle parked at the other end.

When Tiko looked back at MauMau, the puppy was sitting at the edge of the puddle, his head cocked to the side, trying to make sense of something but too young to understand.

Tiko waved goodbye. For a brief moment, he could have sworn that he saw his mother's face poking around the edge of the alley, watching. But when he looked back again, she was gone.

The man opened the door to the truck, and Tiko climbed up into the seat. A smile spread across his face at the thought of how jealous the other children would be when they saw him riding in this truck.

But the man didn't drive through the village—he drove Tiko straight out of the community, using a smaller road that passed only a few huts, then a path that led deeper into the brush, far away from the other townships.

As Tiko watched his town get smaller in the dusty rearview mirror, he saw something out of the corner of his eye: the nice man's smile was no longer there.

This was a different man from the one he'd seen in the reflection in the puddle.

Tiko never would have gotten into a truck with this man.

This was the man the other children teased him about—the man who took witch children away, never to be seen again.

CHAPTER ONE
1-Up

I'm playing a video game in which someone could actually get killed. They don't call it that, but that's exactly what the Virtual Tactical Field Theater is. It's a series of connected rooms with video projected on all the walls, creating a virtual space that's the exact replica of a real place elsewhere in the world.

Right now the virtual theater is an apartment in Houilles, a suburb north of Paris. The apartment's tenant, Yosef Amir, an IT worker for a French bank, is across town at his sister's birthday party. While he's away, we have two men in the actual apartment in France. One is scanning the interior with a high-resolution camera, turning blocky pixels on our walls into images that are too good for the eye to tell the difference. Meanwhile, the other man—whom we call Blurry Man, because the cameras catch only his trail as he moves around the apartment—is using a small device that resembles a flashlight to scoop up hair from the shower, fibers from the furniture, and dust from the bottoms of shoes and the doormat.

Every few minutes, he pops a cartridge from the scoop and hands it to a third man, who runs back and forth between the apartment and a FedEx truck outside, where about $20 million worth of equipment that would be the pride of any university laboratory sends us real-time data as it decodes DNA, searches for matches, and tries to build a model of everyone Yosef came in contact with. It's a god-awful amount of data. Thankfully, we have software that helps us sort through it to achieve our intended goal: to learn whether a bomb will go off in a soccer stadium in the next twenty-four hours.

Yosef's name came up in an intercepted phone call between a known ISIS operative in Yemen and another in France. Normally, authorities would simply call Yosef in for questioning and run down everyone he knows, but lately that's become problematic. Terror groups have been using the names of innocent civilians in their communications, causing far more people than the news has let on to get pulled into interrogations and have their lives upended while the real bad guys stay underground.

"Dr. Cray, Dr. Sanders?" asks Emily Birkett. She's our government liaison from the Defense Intelligence Agency. Late thirties, chestnut hair pulled into a ponytail, Birkett is a former air force officer who went to work for the spookiest of all the spooky government intelligence agencies.

Kerry Sanders and I are civilians. Sanders is an anthropologist about my age, in her early thirties, who spent several years helping Facebook figure out your social graph—whom you know and what they mean to you—before coming to work for OpenSkyAI.

On the surface, OpenSkyAI seems like any other Austin, Texas, technology firm in a bland office park filled with video-game companies and health-care businesses.

What OpenSkyAI is, really, is a private contractor for the Defense Intelligence Agency that helps them sort through thousands of data points, deciding who should be renditioned to some black site to find out if they know something or are about to commit a crime that poses a clear and present danger to national security.

Sanders is looking at a grid of all the faces pulled from the photos in Yosef's apartment. "Facial recognition isn't coming up with a match."

"Theo?" Birkett asks me again, this time a little more impatiently. "Yosef's heading back now. Can I pull the team?"

I'm walking around the apartment—well, the virtual version—staring into the open cupboards and closets, trying to see the unseen, while something in the back of my mind wonders how the hell I found myself in this situation.

"I think he's clean," says Sanders.

I want to agree with her. The thought of Yosef going through a life-changing ordeal because some asshole in Yemen pulled his name from a Google search sickens me. But I also know that just because it sickens me doesn't mean I should call it before it's time.

I walk back into the kitchen. Yosef's refrigerator is covered with photographs. Most of them are him and his girlfriend or his friends, smiling at the camera, laughing at a table filled with drinks. It's the kind of thing you'd expect a typical Parisian millennial to have.

We'd already searched his online presence. Every Facebook post, every like, every friend who liked his posts: it's all been through our system.

There were no red flags. That's not to say there weren't connections. We're all three or four degrees of separation away from someone awful. Yosef has an uncle in Qatar who went to the same mosque as a man who is active in ISIS, but in this interconnected world, that's tenuous at best.

The problem with digital footprints is that the terrorists have gotten smarter. They know how to separate one life from the other. We can track Yosef, but if he has an alter ego and is smart enough never to link the two, catching him is next to impossible. Fortunately, most slip up at some point. Unfortunately, the ones who don't are smarter than our systems for finding them. We've built a trap that breeds smarter rats.

"Cray," says Birkett. "I'm going to pull the team."

"No," I say a little more forcefully than I intend.

"What have you got?" she asks.

"Hold on . . ."

"What does your gut say?"

"I'm a scientist. I've trained myself not to have a gut. I need a few more minutes."

"We've got everything here," says Sanders. "We can let the team go and spend more time going over everything."

"We don't . . ." I've tried to explain this to them a hundred times. A simulation, even one based on real data, is still a simulation. I know there's a peanut butter jar on top of the counter, but I don't know if that's actually peanut butter inside until we have someone take a look. It could be C-4. I'm sure it's not, but it's a hypothetical.

On the surface—and it's all surface—this so-called noninvasive forensic examination is useful, but it's no substitute for good lab work.

"If it's critical, I can stop him when he gets out of the subway station. But you have to tell me now," says Birkett.

I kneel to look at the photos on the refrigerator more closely. Most of them are printouts.

Sanders is standing behind me. "We have all the photos. We sent all the faces through image rec. No connections."

I reach out to grab one, forgetting it's just a simulation. "That one. Ask Blurry Man to get a closer look."

Yosef is smiling into the camera next to a pretty young woman of Middle Eastern descent with green eyes. She appears to be in her early twenties—a stunner.

"Who's she?" I ask.

"She's not in our database. We can extend it and probably get a name. But she's not in our filter."

Blurry Man turns the photo over. There's a date stamp from March and the name Most Special Events printed on the back.

"Grab him," I call to Birkett.

She calls something into her headset. "Intercepting now."

"Who is she?" Sanders asks, repeating my question.

"Hell if I know. It's the photograph. It's from a disposable film camera. The kind they have at weddings where they send them off to be developed, then mail the photos to you with a digital copy."

"We don't have a wedding on Yosef's graph," replies Sanders.

I stand and turn to her and Birkett. "That's the problem. They usually give you digital copies of those photos. Yosef clearly didn't use a digital copy to make this print. He chose to go analog, making sure there was no electronic trace." I call to the operator controlling the visualizations, "Bring up Mosin Kasir's apartment."

Instantly we're virtually teleported to an apartment in Yemen that a field team searched four days earlier. On Mosin's wall, over his desk, hang dozens of photographs.

"She's not in any of them," says Sanders. "The computer would have flagged that."

I point to a photograph of Mosin with an older woman who has the same green eyes. "Who's that?"

Sanders checks her tablet. "An aunt, twice removed. Did we get the back of the photo?"

I shake my head. "No. But it's the same size and lens distortion as the other."

"Mosin's cousin was married in March. And it says here that Yosef was in Bahrain. Maybe he was actually in Yemen."

"Got you," says Birkett. "Good work, Cray. We've got Yosef in a van now. We'll find out soon enough. We're also going to pull the photos from the camera company. Who knows what else we might find."

She's beaming. If Yosef pans out, then it justifies this whole expenditure to her superiors.

"We need to be sure we get the backs of any photographs we find," says Sanders, making a note of it.

I want to explain that's not the point, but I know it's useless. They're all congratulating themselves on a success when all we have is a correlation.

I step out of the office and into the Texas sun glaring off the shiny asphalt parking lot, trying to tell myself this was a good thing but worrying that the tools and the process might do more damage than good—or at the very least, should be in the hands of better people doing smarter things.

As I drive back to my apartment, I try to reconcile how a trail of dead bodies led me here.

CHAPTER TWO
COWBOYS AND INDIANS

A year ago I was a college professor who specialized in computational biology. I tried to build predictive models of the world around us. My work was interesting to me and had far-reaching implications, from the spread of infectious disease to understanding why the Neanderthals went extinct. Then a serial killer named Joe Vik and I crossed paths, and everything changed.

He murdered one of my former students, and for a brief moment, suspicion fell upon me because the victim had happened to be in the same part of Montana as I, doing her own research—which to local authorities was too much of a coincidence.

After my exoneration, the authorities decided that Juniper Parsons had died in a bear attack—a deliberate ploy by Vik, and not the first of his victims that he'd disposed of in that way.

In trying to understand what happened to Juniper, I found more victims and more law-enforcement people who couldn't see what was in front of them. Eventually enough bodies piled up that I was able to find Joe.

In the end, his rampage took the lives of his family and seven police officers. I was a millimeter away from being killed myself.

Some people think I'm a hero because I found the Grizzly Killer and helped end him. Law enforcement has a mixed view. All I know is, when I go to bed at night, I can imagine a thousand different ways I could have played the case out—and in many of them, good men and women would still be alive.

For me, the troubling part is that I don't feel any guilt—only an empty compartment where it should be. I think I have a number of empty compartments where similar emotions should reside.

Jillian, the woman who saved my life and the person who really ended Joe, visited a week ago. We were trying to see if there was something more between us. The problem is, I can clearly see the compartment marked Jillian, but I can't say whether she belongs there—or if anyone does.

I was this fucked-up before Joe, so I don't blame him for that. He just brought it to the surface. I don't even know if I blame Joe in the same way you blame another human.

After our ordeal, while sitting through endless inquiries and explaining my methods for finding bodies to still-skeptical law enforcement, I sequenced Joe's DNA and searched for my own answers.

I found one, a gene related to APOE-e4, the so-called risk gene. Joe had a variation I hadn't seen before. Roughly speaking, in a manner that I'd never commit to paper or let a colleague overhear, Joe was wired for risk taking but also had a predisposition for a kind of obsessive-compulsive behavior not unlike what makes a professional golfer great or a neurosurgeon brilliant. Joe got the same thrill from extreme risk taking that a chess grand master gets from a brilliant opening gambit. Calculation, followed by euphoria.

Whereas you or I would (or should) feel bad if we got away with some infraction, Joe would feel elation and seek out more of those encounters. He got high not only from doing evil things, but also from taking actions to keep from getting caught.

His killing pattern was like that of a great white shark. As I peered into his DNA, I realized those correlations were more than circumstantial. The same predatory algorithm that drives a shark can also drive a software system taking over a network or a killer who finds the right kind of prey.

When Birkett recruited me, it was with the promise that I'd be able to hunt other killers like Joe. That ended up being half true. While the war on terror remains urgent—and while I'm even more resolute that people who drive explosive-laden trucks through crowds of civilians or convince teenagers with Down syndrome to strap on a bomb vest need to be stopped—I'm not always sure about our methods.

On one word from me, Yosef Amir was yanked off the street and pulled into a van and probably taken to some secret site where French intelligence, the Americans, and maybe some interrogator from a third country will force him to spill his guts.

They don't tell me what or how they do it. Lately, though, I do know that there's been a black hole in research relating to psychotropic drugs and the speech system. In the same way that a dip in research papers on quantum computing tells you that the NSA, CIA, NRO, and their private contractors have been on a massive hiring spree, snapping up anyone qualified to work on some super-advanced encryption breaker, a publishing gap in this niche tells me that the intelligence community has been making great strides in producing so-called truth serums and other drugs to make people cooperative.

People like me, and companies like OpenSkyAI and its Virtual Tactical Field Theater, are being given far more credit than we deserve. While I may be getting results, I'm not so sure if it's because my methods are so brilliant or because the previous tactics were so bad.

My phone makes a buzz. I set my beer down on the kitchen counter next to the empty Panda Express containers and check to see if Jillian has texted me back.

It's Birkett: **Win by 7**

That's code—Yosef led them to seven other conspirators. Officially, I'm not even supposed to know that. I'm a civilian contractor with a moderate security clearance, but Birkett likes to keep me happy—or at least do things that she thinks will make me happy.

She sends one more text: **Meeting with boss at 9**

Our boss, Bruce Cavenaugh, not the head of OpenSkyAI, but the DIA supervisor who authorizes our budget, scares me. He's a genial man in his early fifties. The kind of guy who volunteers at his church on Thanksgiving to feed the homeless and helps strangers change flat tires.

What scares me is the kind of power he has. A few weeks into working at OpenSkyAI, during my first visit with him, I offered up some of my concerns about our profiling methods.

When he asked what I would do differently, I thought of Joe Vik and mentioned the notion of looking for certain risk-factor genes in potential terror recruits.

"Would nine hundred thousand dollars do it?" he asked.

"Do what?" I replied.

"Help us build out the tech to do that. I need authorization to go above that amount. But I can green-light a lab on that right now. We'd need a field kit in five months."

Based on one passing comment by me, Cavenaugh was ready to give me almost a million dollars to build them some gadget to pinpoint DNA markers that might correlate to behavior related to terrorism.

Might. Causation and correlation are not the same thing, although they often live in the same neighborhood. I was aghast at the thought of putting some borderline pseudoscientific gadget into the hands of a CIA or DIA spook in the field looking for an excuse to justify his gut. I imagined how DNA gathered from "collateral casualties" might be used as evidence that maybe they got the right guys. One more excuse the government could use to downplay the civilian deaths in the war on terror.

Cavenaugh didn't see any of that. He just wanted to catch the bad guys. The real danger isn't what the *Atlantic* articles or the *New York Times* editorials would have you believe: that good guys become bad guys.

The real danger is that the good guys will blindly keep doing bad things that they don't see as bad. It's why people who would give the shirt off their back to help the poor and the hungry will then march against genetically modified food, even if such food products could save millions of children from blindness or starvation. It's when people who want democracy in the Middle East find themselves building military bases instead of schools and hospitals.

It's when guys like Bruce Cavenaugh offer people like me unlimited budgets for gadgets and programs that could cost even more lives by wasting time and misdirecting resources when the real answers are less sexy and far more unlikely to get a senator aroused.

I've since learned to keep my mouth shut around Cavenaugh. Unfortunately, Birkett has him thinking I'm some kind of analytical genius. While the academic world has all but shunned me for what happened with Joe Vik, in defense-intelligence circles, apparently I'm supposed to be some kind of Dark Knight avenging scientist.

Jillian tells me I'm overreacting, but there are things she can't ever know: for instance, that the Yemen drone strike that's all over the news tonight happened because of something I said earlier today.

Or that the photo of one of the victims being pushed all over Arab media is the same green-eyed woman I saw on Yosef's refrigerator.

Collateral damage.

CHAPTER THREE
PREDOX

Bruce Cavenaugh gives me a broad smile as I enter the conference room where he's encamped during his visit to OpenSkyAI. Birkett is sitting across from him, along with Trevor Park, the CEO and founder of the company.

Park worked in video games and imaging before he started selling technology to the government. Rumor has it the Virtual Tactical Field Theater—or VTFT—came about when intelligence agency officials started complaining about having to go into the field to do intelligence gathering and wanted a way to make it more "dronelike." In drone operations, a commander watches over the shoulder of a remote-control-aircraft jockey in an air-conditioned room in the middle of Nevada instead of being anywhere near the place where they're planning on doing some damage.

While I'm far from being an intelligence expert, the scientist in me says you want to get as close to the data as you can get, because it's the questions you don't know to ask that will make all the difference.

Being able to flip the wedding photo over made all the difference in the world—for better or worse. Still, not long ago, the DIA wouldn't let a low-level analyst like me into the VTFT, instead reserving that honor for the top brass.

That policy changed after the first run-through I was involved with, when I pointed out literally forty different places their scoop guy didn't collect useful samples and that the imager ignored details like making sure the books on the shelves actually were what their jackets represented. The VTFT had some spiffy software that would pull up data on a book found on a potential terrorist's shelf and tell you whether it tended to correlate to radicalization, as well as whether it had been found in the possession of other suspects. What it didn't tell you was if the book had been hollowed out to hide a burner phone we didn't know about.

Everyone seems pretty happy with themselves as I sit. Birkett is watching Cavenaugh, waiting for what he's about to say.

He pushes an envelope toward me with "Classified" written across it. "The French DGSI sent these over. I thought I'd let you know what you did."

I warily slide the photos out, expecting them to be from the strike in Yemen. Instead they are photos of a soccer stadium filled with people. A circle has been hand drawn around one hundred people.

"That's the blast radius of a bomb we found in Nice. It was built into the fabric of a jacket that belonged to a colleague of Yosef Amir. He had tickets for that game and that section. This photo was taken last night after they raided his apartment."

I study the faces of my colleagues and am suddenly conscious of an alternate time line in which I'm reading about a tragedy that happened, spending eight seconds to feel bad about it, and then clicking to read something that will make me feel better . . . a pattern that Kerry Sanders made me aware of.

I set the photo back down. "What about Yemen?"

"Pardon me?" says Cavenaugh.

I can see Park is tensing up. He doesn't like it when I'm confrontational, but he also knows I could have my own lab and my own budget based on one word.

"There was a strike in Yemen on the news. It took out some ISIS commanders but also some family and staff. What about that?"

"They've been in a civil war for over a year. This happens all the time. I'm not sure what you're getting at."

"This wasn't done by their government or the rebels. This involved French or US assets."

Cavenaugh turns to Park. "Could you and Sanders give me a moment with Dr. Cray?"

They awkwardly shuffle out of the room. Park gives me a backward glance, pissed that I just got him kicked out of his own conference room.

Cavenaugh waits for the door to shut. "Dr. Cray, I can't even fathom how your mind works, but the problem with the view from the ivory tower is that you don't know how things work on the ground."

I would agree with him, but I don't want to interrupt.

"Was that attack related to what we discovered yesterday? I genuinely don't know. What I do know is that rules of the game are different than what you're accustomed to. If they try to push their conflict onto our soil, we can't just try to deal with the poor sons of bitches who are sent to do those things—we have to go after the bosses and the masterminds. And not weeks or months after they pull it off. We have to punch back hard."

"Did we hit the right guys? What about the woman?"

"The woman?"

"The one all over Arab news. The woman whose photo I found on Yosef's refrigerator."

Cavenaugh nods. "Her? The civilian? I pray for her. I pray for all the children that get hit by our bombs. I wish it wasn't that way." He stabs a finger onto the photo of the people at the stadium. "One hundred people lived. Half a dozen died. You do the math."

God knows I've tried. How do you weigh the known versus the unknown? You can't. It all comes down to what statistics you choose to believe.

"Dr. Cray, I would love an alternative. I've offered you a budget. I already put your terror-gene idea into place. We've got a lab in Maryland working on it."

"Terror gene?" I blurt out. "What the hell is that?"

"The idea you mentioned about risk factors in genetics that lead to radicalization. You didn't want to pursue it, so we got an outfit that was willing to work on a profile and a field kit."

I strain to keep my voice measured. "That's bullshit. We don't even know if there's a correlation, and even if there was, we don't know if the gene is switched on or off. There are a million other factors. We can't just criminalize an entire group of people based on their genotype."

"A majority of all terrorism-related deaths are committed by adherents of a religion followed by one-fifth of the population. Is that just a coincidence?"

"And homicides in Chicago are responsible for fifty percent of the increase in the United States' murder rate in the last year. Do you think the problem is deep-dish pizza or that it's become a shitty place to live?"

This gets a chuckle from Cavenaugh. "That brain of yours. I'll bet you just thought of that comparison and it wasn't something that was just laying around. We need more of that. I'm here to congratulate you on saving over a hundred lives and to tell you that if you have a better way to do it, let's make it happen. A while ago you mentioned some new version of that AI software you used to catch the Grizzly Killer. What was it? Predox? We'd love to see that happen. Have you made any progress?"

"No. I ran into some technical problems and stopped working on it when I came here."

"That's too bad," he replies. "If you could do for hunting terrorists what you did for finding serial-killer patterns, the world would be a better place."

I wish that, too, but increasingly I find myself in the middle of something so dark I can't even see my moral compass, let alone figure out which way it's pointing. It's one thing to catch a terrorist before he bombs a bunch of civilians; it's another to know that your success will be used to justify retaliation against someone who may or may not be innocent. This is why I fear what well-meaning men like Cavenaugh would do if they had a tool that could tell them exactly who had the potential to be a bad guy.

"Just think about it," says Cavenaugh. "Also, at the very least, think about teaching again."

"College?"

"No. Military and intelligence agents. Maybe we could rub some of your smarts onto others."

"I'll think about it."

He has no idea how tempting it is to have my own lab and the ability to teach again.

Or maybe he does. What would I compromise for that? What lie would I tell myself?

CHAPTER FOUR
Fan Club

Your life takes some unexpected turns after you catch one of the most prolific serial killers of all time. The first turn is that the law-enforcement officials who didn't even believe there was a killer on the loose suddenly manage to create an entirely new narrative about how they'd been tracking him and were close to capturing him. That's fine—let them tell the media their task forces were actually working on the case and on the verge of nabbing the killer.

The other twist is that you go from being a lone person shouting into the wind, with almost no one hearing you, to a quasi celebrity with more incoming inquiries and requests than can be humanly managed.

My in-box is flooded with missing-persons reports from families, conspiracy theories, and at least every few weeks some new nut job telling me that they're the real Grizzly Killer and they're coming for me.

I send them all to the FBI and make sure my conceal-and-carry permit is filed in every place I visit.

Amid all the noise are lots of desperate voices, people who've lost someone and have nobody to turn to. Mothers of missing children, husbands of wives who never came home, and every other conceivable loss you could imagine.

I used to e-mail responses to almost everyone, directing them to a national missing-persons organization and the appropriate law-enforcement channels.

Then one day I stopped responding. I was spending hours trying to reply and there simply wasn't enough of me left.

The problem is that everyone sees their case as special. Like autograph seekers hounding a celebrity, they think their situation is unique; they imagine their interaction will feel as special to their idol as it does to them.

At any given time there are ninety thousand missing persons in the United States—and those are only the reported ones. In the Grizzly killings, we discovered an overlooked category of missing but not reported. Because of this, Joe Vik's real death count is probably in the hundreds, if not higher.

While everyone who reaches out to me feels their case is special, they can't understand that theirs is only one case in ninety thousand. A mere statistic, to misquote another serial killer, Joseph Stalin.

Today, as I arrive home and see a man sitting on my front porch holding an envelope in his hand, I already know his story.

If he'd been pacing back and forth, compulsively smoking a cigarette, I'd suspect he was a conspiracy theorist, there to tell me that Joe Vik was a CIA plot and, by the way, the earth is flat.

I have a ready response for those people: What amount of evidence would convince you that you are wrong?

For the truthers, moon-landing hoaxers, and extremists on both sides of any issue, the answer is simple: nothing.

When no amount of evidence can convince you that your worldview might be inaccurate, then we've exited the realm of reason and entered religious territory. This is why I laugh at the notion of reconciling faith and science. Science is based on the premise that logic and reason can tell us the true nature of reality. Religion is based on the idea that when logic and reason don't support a predetermined view of reality, they are at fault.

The next time you get into a political discussion, stop and ask yourself what amount of evidence would change your mind. If the answer is none, then realize you're actually in a religious discussion, one more zealot arguing with another.

Have I mentioned I'm not on Facebook?

I abandoned social media a long time ago, when I observed my scientific colleagues rejecting the concepts of empiricism for emotional arguments, polemics, and outright embarrassing leaps of logic to support things they had arrived at through emotion, not reason.

While I can turn off social media and send the conspiracy nuts to go harass someone else, the hardest person to deal with is someone who has lost a loved one. Their grief is real. Their reality is more certain than my own.

When I get out of my car, I can already tell what's going to happen next. This middle-aged African American man in the blue sweater and blazer is going to pull a photo out of his folder and show it to me. It'll be his wife, his daughter, his son. They're missing. The police can't help. He looked me up online. I'm the only one he can turn to.

I turn the ignition back on and pull out of my parking spot. If I never see the photo, then I won't make a connection. I won't have a face. I can just wait for him to go away, and if he persists, I can call the cops.

I'm allowed to do this.

I head toward the exit to my apartment complex and convince myself that I can go grab a beer and a steak somewhere with a free conscience, ignoring the man on the porch.

I've done more than any man should ever be asked to.

There's only so much Theo Cray to go around.

But then who the hell is Theo? What part is left? The part that doesn't care?

When I was cowering in the ambulance, waiting for Joe Vik to come for me and Jillian, it was Detective Glenn who was outside trying to give us cover.

Sure, I found my courage. So did Jillian . . . god, did she ever. But Glenn had it all along. He died. We lived.

Would Glenn turn away and leave this man on his doorstep? This grieving man.

Fuck me.

I turn my truck around and head back to my parking spot. I take a deep breath and try to figure out how to at least listen to this man patiently, offer him some solace, and maybe help him find some peace and accept what he already knows: the person in that envelope is dead. They're never coming back. And if someone took them, if it's been weeks or months, he's not going to find the killer.

How do I know this? Because if it weren't a hopeless case, he wouldn't be waiting for me on my doorstep. I don't get the low-hanging fruit, the "It was the handyman with the criminal past" type of cases. I get the ones where there is no evidence. No clues. Not even a body. Just an empty place where a person used to be.

I can't fill those places. I can't even fill the emotional compartments in my own head for the people who are supposed to be close to me.

"Dr. Cray?" asks the man as he sees me walking up the sidewalk.

"I got an hour. That's all I got."

He's already sliding the photo out of the envelope.

Fuck. He's got me. The boy has green eyes. Just like the girl in Yemen. It's a coincidence. I've been shown thousands of missing-person photos. Lots have green eyes.

But this one had to be today.

Instinctively, I know that I'll be spending a lot longer than an hour on this one.

CHAPTER FIVE
THE ACCOUNTANT

"Dr. Cray, I appreciate your taking the time. I'm a big fan of what you did."

I'm not sure if vigilantes should have fans, but I take the compliment. "Let's have a beer while you tell me about . . ."

"Christopher. My son's name is Christopher. I'm William. William Bostrom."

Now that I have a face *and* a name, Christopher is becoming more real, not simply an envelope I can ignore.

I let William inside and invite him to take a seat at my kitchen table. He sets his envelope down and looks around the apartment. There's a couch and a television and not much else.

"Did you just move in?" he asks.

"About six months ago."

"Do you live alone?"

"Do you realize that's a creepy question to have a stranger ask you?"

Bostrom makes a small laugh. "Yeah. I guess you're right. I could just be some crazy guy. I bet you get a lot of those."

"Indeed." I take two beers from the fridge and twist the caps off. "Here you go."

"Uh, thanks." Bostrom takes the smallest sip from his, and I realize he's not a drinker. He might even be a recovered alcoholic.

I slide the beer over to me. "I got Diet Coke. Want one instead?"

"Yeah. Thanks. Again, I appreciate you helping me out."

We'll see how appreciative he is when I tell him there's nothing I can do and ask him to leave.

I bring him his drink and sit again. "Before we start, it's important that you understand the only reason you even heard about me is because I noticed a particular way foliage would grow in parts of Montana around areas where bodies had been recently buried."

"Yes. Ecotones? Was that it? Areas where different plants were growing while one tried to starve out the other? Also because Joe Vik buried his victims on the lowest-lying area near a kill site so erosion wouldn't expose the bodies."

William had done his homework. It was still surreal to hear people mention Joe Vik's name in the casual way they'd talk about Charles Manson or Ted Bundy.

"Basically. The FBI has my system now. Local law-enforcement agencies have started adding it to their forensic investigations."

"I'm sure that'll bring peace to a lot of families."

And grief. Many of them are still holding out hope that their loved ones will come home. That's the hardest part about these kinds of cases. They want me to tell them there's hope. I have none.

"Chris was a good kid. Real good kid. I know they all say that. But he had good grades. He stayed out of trouble. I'd come home and the house would be clean. That kind of boy. We'd go to the toy store and he'd throw his allowance into the Salvation Army bucket. That kind of kid."

You're killing me, William. I wanted a drug addict runaway. But I don't see any of that in Chris's photo. He looks about nine years old. Big cheeks. Goofy smile. So earnest.

"What happened?" I ask.

"Chris didn't come home."

"How long before he went missing was this photo taken?"

"A month, maybe."

"And the police?"

William shrugs. "They did what they were supposed to. Talked to neighbors. Put up flyers. Chris's photo was even on the news. And then nothing. I'd call the detectives, but they'd take longer to answer my calls. The flyers came down and something else would be on the news. Some white girl in Colorado or something." He pauses when he realizes what he just said.

I nod. We all look at white crime and black crime differently. The reasons are complex, some of them biased, to be sure, others more basic in-group and out-group perceptions. Whites will ignore the daily death toll in black inner cities, but when a gunman kills nine Christians in a church, who all happen to be black, they're as outraged as anyone else. That's because suddenly the victims become relatable.

"Were there any leads?"

William shakes his head. "Nothing. At least nothing the police told me."

"And this was where?"

There's a noticeable pause. "Willowbrook. It's near Los Angeles."

"South of Los Angeles?"

He nods.

I remember something about the area. It's known as South Central Los Angeles. Near Compton. Gang territory—at least as far as I know from the movies I watch. I don't have a clue beyond that. But I understand his hesitation. It's an area with an extremely high homicide rate.

"Chris was a good boy," he says defensively, assuming I'm jumping to some prejudicial conclusions.

"I believe you. So he was snatched? Just like that?"

"Yes. No ransom note. No warning. He was just gone."

The mere mention of a ransom note raises a flag. I'd heard that every day there are hundreds of drug-related kidnappings in which family members are held hostage because one party wants something from another. The families of the victims are in no hurry to tell the police that their son got kidnapped because the father failed to pay back a cocaine debt.

"Well, I'm afraid there's not much I can go on. I don't even know the area. I wish I could be more help. Are the mother and you still together?"

"She's dead. And no, her family didn't take Chris," he adds, assuming I'm thinking this might be a child-custody matter.

"And you know this because . . . ?"

"Because Chris is dead."

"Why are you so sure?" The conversation has taken an odd turn.

"Because Chris has been gone nine years. I know he's not coming home."

"Nine years?" That trail isn't just cold; it's paved over.

"I know the statistics, Dr. Cray. I'm an accountant. I can do the math. Chris didn't run away, and he isn't lost. Someone took him and killed him. God knows what else . . ." He eyes the other beer bottle in front of me. I'm not sure if I should push it to him or go dump it in the sink.

"So now that it's almost ten years later, what do you want from me?"

"I want his killer. I want the man that took my boy."

"That man could be long gone."

"Or he could be someone from the neighborhood. Someone I pass every day. He could be right under our nose. Like Lonnie Franklin."

Lonnie Franklin, aka the Grim Sleeper, was a serial killer in South Central Los Angeles who was active for three decades. His victims, primarily prostitutes with drug addictions, were the invisibles. Their murders were written off as drug related and cynically blamed on the dead. Dozens of women, already victimized by life, were ignored, all under the nose of the police and Franklin's neighbors.

"Do you have any suspects?"

"No. I've walked on every sidewalk, knocked on every door. I've seen some shady things, Dr. Cray, but no sign of what happened to my boy. Nobody I could point a finger to and say they could be the one. I talked to his teachers. Every adult he could have come in contact with. Nobody."

I take a sip and think my response through. "I don't think there's anything I can do." I stop myself from saying the data set is too small. "Have there been other missing-children reports in the area?"

"A handful. The police say there isn't enough for a pattern. Of course they also told the families of Franklin's victims there was no reason to believe there was an active serial killer." He raises a hand preemptively. "I'm not saying that's what happened to Chris. But somebody that would do that to a child, would they do it just once? Would that really be the end of it?"

"I'm assuming the police pulled up names of known child predators," I say.

"I knocked on those doors, too." He leans back, shaking his head. "Lots of perverts. None that I could tell you took Chris."

"I don't have the tools or resources to really look into this, Mr. Bostrom."

"Did you have them in Montana? Did you know what you needed for that?"

"I had DNA. I'm a biologist. I had blood and hair. I had something to work with."

"But you're also a math guy," he says. "A computer scientist. You know how to see things in the data that other people don't."

"I'm not psychic. All I know how to do is ask questions."

Bostrom stands up. "You've been more than kind hearing me out. All I ask is that you let me know if you think of a few questions to ask that nobody else has."

We wait outside for his Uber to arrive to take him to the airport. He tells me Chris's favorite movies. He tells me about the time Chris tried to make him a birthday cake in the microwave. He tells me with great pride about the projects Chris worked on and his ambitions to be an astronaut.

The kid wanted to be a scientist. He wanted to invent things. He wanted to help people.

As Bostrom's Uber drives off into the night, I am chilled by the thought that the man who snuffed out this bright, little shining light is still out there.

Statistically speaking, Chris wouldn't be the only one or the last. Statistically speaking, I have a better chance of finding a living, breathing Al Capone in Chicago than I do of catching Chris's killer.

CHAPTER SIX
NUMBER THEORY

Kerry leans over the top of my cubicle and watches me. She's realized that sometimes I need a second to shift from the reality in my head to the one around me. "What are you working on?"

"Just running some numbers. What's up?"

"Just a warning. Park is pretty pissed at you. He was ranting earlier about how you interact with clients."

"Clients?" I reply. "We're not an advertising agency. We're a quasi-legal consulting group given far too much power by people looking for an excuse to pull a trigger. I'm pretty sure Cavenaugh's not going to give us a bad Yelp review, if that's what he's afraid of."

She drops into an empty chair and slides next to me. "He's afraid you'll take Cavenaugh up on his offer. Park knows that DIA knows you're the one that's making this work."

"Your graphs have been helpful."

She groans. "That's BS work I came up with so I could leave Silicon Valley and not be expected to pull eighty-hour workweeks. Your Predox system has them all excited. That could be a billion-dollar ticket."

"To what?"

She gives me a funny look. "You really are a weirdo."

"Because I don't want to be a snake-oil salesman like Park? It's bad enough that I'm working in the factory."

"Maybe if you owned the factory, things would be different. Birkett would back you in a heartbeat. I'd follow you, too."

"What are you saying? Tell Cavenaugh to shovel some antiterror money my way, just so we can go into some other office and stress over doing the right thing while knowing lives are at stake?"

"With better parking spaces," she adds.

"I'm not the one Park should be worried about. You don't even hide the knife."

"No need to when all eyes are on you." She gives me a wink, then goes back to her cubicle.

It's a tempting thought, to be sure, but I'm still not ready to throw away my moral compass, even if I can't read it.

A few minutes later I get an instant message from Park asking me to come to his office.

"What's up?" I ask from the doorway.

"Close the door and have a seat."

You can tell the really important office in an intelligence-contracting company, because it's the biggest one with no windows.

Park has dozens of screens on his walls showing all kinds of bullshit stats meant to impress whatever government spook who comes in here curious where all their money is going. What they don't know is that Park can flip a switch and play Overwatch on them when he thinks nobody is watching.

He leans back and wipes his eyes. "What am I going to do with you?"

"How about my own office so I can play my games in privacy, too."

This gets me a sharp look. I clearly pushed the wrong button.

He jabs a finger at me. "That's the problem. That's why no university will hire you right now."

"Actually, I had that attitude before. The reason they won't hire me is because campus-safe-space snowflake types are a little uneasy with a professor who was acquitted of stealing a corpse and accused of shooting a man in cold blood." Did I mention the Joe Vik thing was complicated? It was Jillian who shot Vik, but I took the heat. I may have denied Red State America a female vigilante hero, but I also spared her more drama than either of us could have imagined.

Park is in a weird position. He knows DIA values me more than him. His project is just a video game if it lacks good players. Birkett told him to hire me, and he did so reluctantly. Now he's stuck with me if he wants to keep this enterprise going.

For me, the game is seeing how he takes his frustration out on me. There are only so many ways he can maneuver. The smart one would be to ask me how he can stop acting like an asshole and turn this sham show into something useful. Which is the last thing he'll ever do, and that's because Park is under the delusion that he's smarter than me.

He doesn't realize that brilliance is a kind of binary thing. You either got it or you don't. If you do, a 130 IQ and a 170 aren't that different, so long as you know how to apply what you got.

Richard Feynman, my personal hero and one of the greatest physicists who ever lived, scored a 128 on his army IQ test. That wouldn't have gotten him into Mensa. Meanwhile, the guy with the highest IQ on record is a bouncer at a nightclub and spends his free time reading fantasy novels. Tell me that guy is smarter than the man who corrected Stephen Hawking's science papers.

"If you're not happy, you're welcome to leave any time you want," says Park.

"If I take you up on that right now, how long before you text me? Will I make it to the front door? My car?" I'm not one to enter dick-measuring contests, but I've been on edge.

"You don't know the kind of power I have here," Park replies acidly.

I glance at his gaming monitors. "What? Your video-game league?"

"Cavenaugh may like you, but you don't know how they work. You're one fuckup away from their shit list. If you make them look bad, things could be even worse. If you make me look bad, you have no fucking idea what I can bring down on you. I know things about you. I didn't just hire you because Birkett wants to fuck you. I looked into you. There are things about that whole serial-killer fiasco that don't add up. Things involving people close to you."

He's talking about Jillian. Does he know she pulled the trigger? Does he know something else?

I can only imagine what kind of data he has on his terminal. That's not quite true—I got him to give me special privileges without realizing it—but I've never actually probed around.

What I do know is that threatening me is one thing, but mentioning Jillian is something else entirely. I owe that woman more than just my life.

Ever since she picked me up off the pavement of her diner when a meth-head hooker and her boyfriend beat the shit out of me, she's been the bright, shining beacon in my life, even when I'm not so sure what I'm supposed to do with that light.

I stand up. Park's eyes widen. I take my company phone from my pocket—the secure one that costs more than my truck—and throw it into his TV wall, smashing a plasma screen and sending out a small shower of sparks.

I then lean on his desk, knuckles down, and push my face into his.

"The last guy to threaten someone I cared about? I shoved a lethal injection needle into his neck."

I realize two things in that moment. One is what I already suspected: I am not the same man who went into that forest to hunt Joe Vik. The other: I've just made Park piss himself.

"I can have you arrested!" Park yells at me as I head for the door.

"And I can have Cavenaugh bail me out and kick you out of here by tomorrow."

It's an empty threat, but next to me coming for him in the middle of the night, it's what he fears the most.

I'm halfway home when I get a call from Birkett on my personal phone.

"What the fuck did you say to Park? He's on the phone yelling at Cavenaugh that you should be put into custody."

"He made a threat."

"Like what? He was going to fire you?"

"No. Like he had intel on someone I care about."

There's a long pause. "Shit. That just doesn't fly. I'll look into that. Maybe you should stay away from the office for a little while."

"You think?" I reply sarcastically. "I wasn't planning on coming back. Plus, Park would probably have me arrested."

Birkett laughs. "That ain't gonna happen. The only reason he has his little project was so I could get my hands on you . . . for the DIA. Cavenaugh isn't the only one who wants whatever is up your sleeve."

"It's empty."

"Don't let them hear that. And bullshit. Anyway, just go out of town while I work on this."

"Already planning on it."

"Any place in particular?"

"Yeah, somewhere I can take my mind off this: Compton."

"Hilarious." She doesn't hear me laugh. "Oh, shit . . . You're one weird son of a bitch."

I'm an angry one, too. I've realized that all those empty compartments aren't so empty. They're filled with rage. I need to channel it on something other than some douchebag like Park. I need to catch a killer.

After the Grizzly Killer case, I realized Joe Vik wasn't the only one with a troublesome, risk-taking gene. My own DNA told me what I already knew: I'm as much of an outlier as he was. Different in my particulars, perhaps, but still apart from most humans on this planet.

Like Joe Vik, I need to hunt.

CHAPTER SEVEN
COMMUNITY WATCH

William Bostrom greets me at the door with a broad smile. His house is in a working-class neighborhood in Willowbrook. The cars in the driveways aren't all new, but the yards are nicely kept and it's a far cry from the image most people have of South Central Los Angeles. That's not to say we aren't a half mile from gang territory, but it's not some urban dystopia filled with burned-out cars and constant gunfire.

"Before we get started, I don't want to raise any false hopes," I explain.

"Understood." He guides me over to his dining room table, where he's laid out stacks of folders in neat rows, exactly what you'd expect from an accountant. "I've got every missing-persons report I could get over here. I've got folders of all the registered sex offenders over here." He points to a map covered with red *x*'s. "This shows Chris's route home, all the possible places he might have gone, and I put *x*'s over all the offenders."

"That's a lot of *x*'s," I reply as I sit down.

"Most of them are guys who picked up hookers. But I needed something to start with."

I looked at all the documents. "Normally I like to work with electronic data. It's easier to sort that way. I know a twenty-four-hour scanning service."

"I've got that covered already. I made my own database." He points to a laptop at the far corner of the table. "Started it a few weeks after Christopher went missing. I can e-mail you the files."

"Please do." I drop my bag and pull out my own laptop. "The first thing we want to do is to take all of the missing-persons data and look for some kind of anomaly."

"Like what?"

"Are there more missing children in this area than a city with a comparable demographic? Like Atlanta?"

"You mean where black people live?"

"More or less. White victims get more coverage and are handled differently, or at least that's my perception."

"And black folk don't talk to the police when something goes down." He thinks for a moment. "How do we look for anomalies?"

"I have a piece of software."

"MAAT? The thing you used to get Joe Vik?"

"More like MAAT 2.0. It's designed to find predator patterns. I call it Predox." Other than Jillian, William is the first person to whom I've admitted that Predox is real. After my encounter with Cavenaugh's overzealous enthusiasm for any half-baked tool that could be used for better or worse by the military, I decided to keep it on the down low.

To be totally honest with myself, when William brought me this case, somewhere in the back of my head I started thinking it was time to field-test Predox.

"I've read the paper you wrote on MAAT, but explain it to a simple accountant," says William.

"Do you know how they beat Garry Kasparov in chess with a computer?"

"Raw numbers?"

"Not quite. There are more possible game-board configurations five moves into chess than all the particles in the universe. That's why even though you can win chess in a handful of games, chess masters can still give computers something of a run for their money.

"Deep Blue, the computer that beat Kasparov, was designed to evolve strategies. It didn't calculate every possible move—just the ones that would beat him. If a different chess master sat down that day, one that Deep Blue hadn't been programmed to beat, then the outcome might have been different."

"So there's still a chance for humans," replies William.

"No. Not a prayer. Computers are getting better than we are at chess, go, and a hundred other things. And when they catch up, they still keep getting better. Our only hope is figuring out how to work with them and put enough of ourselves in them that they stay our friends.

"The way Predox works is that I taught him to think like a scientist. When I give him a set of data, he uses part of it to build a hypothesis based on a correlation: all redheaded people are Irish. After he has his hypothesis, he tests it with the other set of data. If it confirms the hypothesis, then it becomes a theory until he encounters a Lebanese girl with red hair and has to modify his theory."

"Kind of like Bayesian statistics?" asks William, who works with numbers all day.

"Very much. What makes Predox special is that he also gets better at understanding data. He can take an image and recognize it's probably a woman and start making certain inferences—even ones that are nonobvious. He can tell you with a high probability if the photo was taken by a stranger you handed the camera to or a friend. Friends stand closer. It can also tell you how tall the photographer was by the angle of the photo. That's not even counting what he can read in facial expressions."

"Have you thought about selling this?" asks William.

"There are other tools out there." I don't tell him I've had offers, or that that's what I'm most afraid of. "Predox makes the best tool only for its intended purpose."

"Finding bad guys."

"No. Helping me think."

"Predox is you."

William catches me off guard. I'd never thought about it that way. While I'd tried to make an all-purpose research tool, what I'd really done was program a computer to follow the same steps I would to solve a problem.

"Something wrong, Dr. Cray?"

"It's Theo, by the way. Just Theo. And no. Everything is fine." I'd gone silent because I had a realization that Predox might not only think the way I do; in some fashion, it might also have my own biases. There might be better ways to solve a problem that I was ignorant about. I needed to be mindful of that.

We spent the next few hours entering data from the Department of Justice's statistics database and the FBI's public ViCAP data set, setting Predox up to look for correlations and anomalies. Nothing stood out immediately above the statistical noise.

This was what I was afraid of. In Montana, the population was far smaller and a serial killer stood out like a sore thumb if you knew where to look.

Los Angeles has a population twenty times that of Montana. That means you could hide twenty Joe Viks there, or a hundred slightly less prolific serial killers.

If Christopher's abductor didn't have a very high rate of activity, he'd be impossible to detect with my system.

I spend the next several hours trying to massage the data and get the most out of the missing-persons reports. I even flick through the photos, looking for something that Predox can't find.

In the end, it's my worst fear as a scientist: nothing. Not even weak conclusions to calibrate. Just an empty data set.

I find myself staring into space, vision blurry. William puts a hand on my shoulder. "It's okay. Get some rest and I'll show you where Chris went to school in the morning. If nothing hits you, then I'll take you back to the airport."

This man accepted his loss a long time ago, now he's just trying to make sure it's okay to put it all to rest.

There's one more thing I can do. It'll put me in more hot water, but right now I'm in the "zero fucks to give" zone.

I'd bet anything that Park hasn't pulled my clearance yet. That means I can do a records search and have a request sent to LAPD and the FBI for anything they have relating to Christopher or other abductions. It's bending the rules and possibly illegal, but hell.

I log in to the data acquisition request system and put in a pull request.

Tomorrow I'll find out if it went through or if I'm going to jail.

CHAPTER EIGHT

LATCHKEY

"Chris would usually get himself up and make breakfast before heading to school," William tells me as we stand in his driveway. It's a cool Los Angeles morning, and children ride by on bicycles as they head to school.

"Did he walk or ride?" I ask.

"Ride. Most of the time." William unlocks his garage door and raises it to show me the interior.

The walls are lined with secure metal cabinets. He notices me eyeing them. "Accounting records."

"Don't you use a service to store them?" I ask.

"Most of them. But for some clients I need to be able to have easy access." He walks over to a bicycle leaning against a stack of file boxes.

It's a BMX bike with Transformers stickers. "They found it where he was abducted." He sighs. "Just yanked off the street."

I take a photo of the bike with my phone. There's nothing unusual about it, but the ordinary is where the extraordinary likes to hide.

"And nobody saw anything?" I ask as William locks the garage door.

"Not that the police told me. And nobody I spoke to. Any luck on getting those files?"

"I have a request in. We should know later today."

We start down the sidewalk, heading toward Chris's elementary school, which has the rather uninspired name 134th Street Elementary School.

Cars are pulling out as people head in to Los Angeles traffic and off to work. William's neighbors are mostly a mix of black and Hispanic people, although I notice a few older whites.

"Did Chris have any friends he went to or from school with?"

"Nothing on a regular basis. Kids at that age are always changing alliances. Chris was also a bit of a loner. It's easier to be a black nerd now . . . maybe not so much then."

I was a solitary kid even before my dad died. Having one more excuse to retreat into my head only made me that much more of an introvert.

As we walk along the sidewalk, I glance into open windows and take note of the houses with extra-thick bars and security cameras.

We reach a large, open field that's a greenway for the tall electrical towers connected to the power plant that snake their way through Los Angeles. William points to a patch of weedy grass near the sidewalk. "That's where they found his bike."

There's a fair amount of traffic, but not a lot of houses nearby. It's easy to see how afternoon commuters wouldn't think anything of a car that slowed down to talk to a boy riding his bicycle along.

"Was Chris the kind of kid that would talk to strangers?" I ask.

"He knew better. But he was a friendly kid. He'd talk to anybody, but he'd never get in a car with them."

Which suggests that Chris may have been pulled from the street and off his bike. But out here in the middle of the day, that would attract some attention. It's one thing to ignore a kid talking to the driver of a car, but to not tell the police you saw a child dragged into a vehicle?

Chris's abductor must have been very lucky that day or had a vehicle like a van that would make it easy to shield what he was doing from drivers.

But a van or some other premeditated way to snatch a kid implies some forethought, bolstering William's fear this wasn't an isolated incident. I won't know about that until I have more data.

We finally reach Chris's school. Children are out in the playground and on the courts running laps, kicking a red ball around and laughing and yelling, making all those delightful sounds we forget when we become adults.

William has his back to the fence. I can tell it pains him to be here. God knows what he's feeling.

I take some photos of the school through the fence, then walk over to a boxed-in cage.

"This used to be the bike cage," says William. "They don't let the kids ride them to school anymore."

"Because of Chris?"

"No. Bad drivers. Plus, kids' bikes were getting stolen all the time."

From behind us a woman's voice calls out, "Can I help you?"

I turn around and see a sturdy African American woman in a Los Angeles Police Department uniform striding toward the fence that separates us from the school.

William still has his back to the fence. I decide to use the honesty approach—or a form of it, at least.

"I'm Theo Cray." I slide my federal ID out of my pocket and show it to her. It's given to certain civilian contractors who need access to government facilities. "I'm just doing some background work on the Chris Bostrom abduction."

She glances at it for a moment. "Well, you have to talk to Principal Evans if you want to be on school property."

I don't bother to point out that I'm standing on public property. There's no point to winning an argument when it might cost you the war. "No problem. We're just leaving."

She catches a glimpse of William's face. "And he has to leave right now or I will have him arrested."

This takes me by surprise. I'm about to ask why, but William grabs me by the sleeve. "Let's go."

The officer watches us until we reach the corner, then heads back into the school. I stop at the intersection. "What the hell was that about?"

William won't look me in the eye. "After Chris was taken, I . . . I came by here a couple of times and yelled at some of his teachers. I was given a warning."

Ah. Got it. Understandable. "I see."

"Let's just go back," he says, visibly shaken, and starts to cross the street.

"Hold up. Isn't the faster route this way?" I point toward the end of the block.

"Yeah. But this is the way home Chris took. I thought you might want to have another look."

"How do you *know* that was Chris's route?"

"It's where they found his bicycle." As he says this, I can see something awaken behind his eyes. "Wait . . ." His gaze turns toward the shorter path. "Could he have?"

For him it means his years of canvassing and knocking on doors may have been concentrated in the wrong area.

"I don't know. But let's assume that the location of the bike doesn't confirm the path he took. Why don't we just take the shorter route and have a look?"

He nods and we head down the block back toward his house.

As we retrace Chris's possible alternate path, William eyes every house with renewed suspicion and each person we see with a sense of barely held malice. To him, any one of these people could have seen what happened. One of them could even be Chris's abductor.

I take photos and stare into houses when possible. I also play a mental game that I learned hunting Joe Vik and that I have since found helpful with my work at OpenSkyAI: it's called "think like a predator."

Instead of projecting myself into Chris's head, like William is probably doing, I imagine that I'm the abductor looking for the best place to snatch him while evading detection.

If the bike was dropped away from the actual abduction location, then Chris's abductor was directing attention away from something. Something that might still lie along this path.

CHAPTER NINE
THREAT ASSESSMENT

By the time we make it back to William's house, I've developed three possible scenarios, each with its own corresponding variables, relating to Chris's abduction.

In the first scenario, Chris was snatched by an opportunist who happened upon a vulnerable young kid and literally yanked him into his vehicle exactly where the bicycle was found.

In the second scenario, Chris's abductor didn't live locally but had been following Chris, perhaps for days. He waited for the right time to grab him and then moved his bicycle to hide the place from which he'd been observing Chris in case a witness could provide a description.

In the third scenario, Chris's abductor lived on the path, either the one we initially believed Chris took or the shorter one. In this case, he moved Chris's bike to draw attention from himself and his residence.

There are dozens of other permutations based on the known knowns, and an infinite number if some of our core assumptions are incorrect. For now, though, we have three theories to work with, each with its own drawbacks.

The first scenario is almost impossible to investigate without any additional data.

The second relies upon witnesses from almost ten years ago being able to recall something from a specific date—which, given that the investigation did canvass those areas, makes it unlikely that any big breakthrough remains to be found. Smaller details, such as a spooky green van near the 7-Eleven in a police report, would be useful, but I'm not holding out any hope for that.

The last scenario, and perhaps the most chilling, is the one that has the abductor living along the path. As police knocked on doors and talked to neighbors, Chris could have been alive and still unharmed, only a few dozen feet away.

"What are you thinking?" William asks me as we reach his doorstep.

"The alley seems a likely shortcut for Chris. I mean, if I was a kid, I'd take that route. The area by the Baptist church looked unobserved. And the corner by 117th had no houses directly facing it. Those would be my primary spots."

"I don't suppose we're going to find anything there now."

"I took photos. But other than that, it's been too long to expect anything. If I can get the police reports, I can see if there's anything that connects them."

He nods.

"Also, we can do a background check on everyone who lived on the streets between here and there."

"Like home-owner records?"

"I can get police records, too. We just need to make a list of addresses."

While my government access puts a frightening amount of personal data at my disposal, the kind of information we're looking for could be purchased relatively inexpensively from private companies that specialize in providing information to loan companies and prospective employers.

I've found that a lot of government records are routinely inaccurate— except when there's a financial connection. That's why the IRS or a creditor can track you down faster than the police can.

As William makes a list of houses to research, I check my e-mail and find a response to my police-records request.

The good news is that they can provide me with what I requested; the bad news is that they need four to six weeks to gather the information.

William is leaning over a map spread across his kitchen table, taking note of all the houses. "It kills me to think he could be here . . ."

"Yeah. We got a problem. I can get the records, but they say it'll take at least a month." In my head I've already accepted the fact that a month isn't going to make much of a difference on a case that's already a decade old.

He sits back and folds his arms. "A month?"

I point to his map. "We can still follow up on the houses, see who lived in them at the time. There might be something there."

He nods, tacitly accepting that this is just one more disappointment that life has decided to throw at him.

I shove my hands into my pockets, and my fingers touch the hard plastic of my ID. William takes a moment to acknowledge the situation, then goes back to making notes and putting together a list of addresses.

"Fuck it," I reply. This could cost me my job, if I haven't lost it already. It could mean jail time. I hold up my ID. "I might be able to go to the LAPD and just have a look."

"Are you allowed to?" asks William.

"Until somebody stops me." I might be able to come up with some bullshit excuse that I was working on a DIA research project or something. The truth of the matter is that I can get away with it if nobody makes a stink. If, on the other hand, I piss someone off, I could have problems. So . . . better not let Park know what I'm up to. "Do you have a scanner?" I ask.

"A document scanner? I got a portable one in my office. Hold on."

William goes down the hall and pulls out a key to unlock a door at the end of the house. Since I started working in the intelligence world, I've encountered several people with secure rooms inside their houses. For an accountant, it's probably the same thing. His clients probably want to know that nobody else could go snooping through their records.

"Here you go," he says as he shuts the door. "It uses a smart card to store the documents in PDF. Will that work?"

It's about the size of an extra-long bread stick. "Perfect." I could use my phone, but having a specialized scanner makes things much easier and will make me appear less fly-by-night to the records custodian—assuming my pass gets me through the door.

CHAPTER TEN
COLD CASE

In what will go down as the most boring heist in history, after presenting my ID to the woman at the desk of the records office, I was led
through a secure door, given a map of the labyrinthine maze of tunnels
and storerooms under the city of Los Angeles, and sent on my own
merry way without an ounce of skepticism or even a second look.

I chalk this up to two things. The first is that all my ID did was
give me access to records that could be obtained through a Freedom of
Information Act request. I was not being given access to LAPD's current case files and wouldn't be able to pull so much as a parking ticket
if it was still working its way through court—at least that's what was
explained to me on the flyer that the woman gave me with my map.

But as I passed a room that said ACTIVE RECORDS, I got the impression this was more of an honor system than a series of actual barriers
blocking prying eyes from ongoing investigations.

Content with simply having access to Christopher Bostrom's case,
I found the room where the missing-persons case files were stored and
a completely uninterested clerk who could be charitably described as
"retired in place."

He grunted some general directions toward the row that included a cabinet that held a folder containing Christopher's case. I had to check with him to make sure I wasn't missing anything, because the file I found was thinner than the paperwork I'd had to file to get my apartment.

The police work didn't appear sloppy. The initial report was concise. Interviews with neighbors, teachers, and others that took me by surprise but made sense once I put myself into the cop's head: like talking to bus drivers who ran the routes near where William's son went missing, postal workers, and even utility and electrical work crews. The detective, Ted Corman, even went so far as to reach out to FedEx and UPS drivers in case they'd seen anything.

He had a solid, street-level view of who might have seen something. Unfortunately, nobody had seen anything.

As far as forensics were concerned, there were none. Only a photo of Chris's bike. I checked through the file, and it didn't even appear that the bike had ever been fingerprinted. I'm not a cop, but that seemed like a big mistake.

I understand how they wouldn't think their suspect had ever touched the bike if they thought Chris had dropped the bike to get into the car, but there was no reason to make that assumption. I send William a text message telling him not to touch the bicycle.

Hopefully the bike had gone straight from the police cruiser to his garage and he hadn't handled it much. While lifting a regular fingerprint after nine years is unlikely, if the abductor touched any bicycle grease, then it made for an increased possibility—remote, yet possible.

Getting that print would probably require a really good state lab or the FBI—which brings me to another odd thing about the file: there were only two calls placed to the FBI.

Even though a standard kidnapping wouldn't be under FBI jurisdiction in most cases, there would be a lot of contact between LAPD and the Los Angeles FBI office. Informally, there's often even an agent on scene in a case like this, to make sure of jurisdiction.

Corman's report mentions getting a call from the FBI—they reached out to him—and a return call from him, updating them on what the LAPD had found: nothing.

Another confusing aspect of the report is that it mentions conferring with two agencies. One's the FBI; the other isn't mentioned.

If I had to go out on a limb, maybe it was the IRS, since William was an accountant. Did they want a character witness who could tell them if the disappearance might have been caused by a domestic disturbance?

The last interesting bit of information is the fact that Chris wasn't reported missing until 11:00 p.m. While William told me that Chris got abducted after school, there was an eight-hour window between when his last teacher saw him and the 911 call William placed to the police.

The transcript was about as matter-of-fact as an episode of *Dragnet*:

> 911: Nine-one-one, how may I assist you?
> W. Bostrom: My boy, he didn't come home today.
>
> 911: How old is your son?
> W. Bostrom: Eight. Nine. He's nine years old.
>
> 911: Is it possible he's at a friend's house or with another relative?
> W. Bostrom: No. He doesn't have a mama anymore. When I got home, he wasn't here. He should have been home.
>
> 911: Okay, sir, we're going to send a patrol car by. Is 1473 Thornton your correct address?
> W. Bostrom: Yes, ma'am.

911: Okay. Please stand outside so the officer can
see you.
W. Bostrom: Thank you.

The police car was there eight minutes later. Detective Corman arrived on the scene almost two hours after that.

According to the responding officer's report, they called the parents of Chris's classmates and sent out extra cruisers to look for him. His bicycle was found that night by a uniformed cop with a flashlight.

Besides the length of time it took William to report his son missing, the only other unusual thing about his actions is that he mentioned to the uniformed cop that he'd called someone named Mathis and asked him if he knew anything.

Corman didn't follow up that line of inquiry in his report, but he did everything else he was supposed to: sent out an AMBER Alert, contacted other departments, and put Christopher into the appropriate databases. Beyond that, there wasn't much else in the file.

In biology, you can tell how tightly bonded a community is by its degree of response to danger. Packs and herds will rally around their young. Distant relative whales will protect a young calf when an orca is nearby. Other animals, mainly nonmammals, are indifferent. If a predator snatches a child, their evolutionary calculus tells them they're lucky it wasn't them and life goes on. The reaction to Chris's abduction doesn't quite feel as if a strong pack response—at least from the leaders—was demonstrated.

But we're talking about people, and many of the authorities involved were black, so it couldn't simply be a racial thing—not all of it. I'm missing something here.

Did it look like Christopher ran away? Was he not so happy at home? Was there a suspicion regarding William that the cops couldn't substantiate enough to put into a report?

Why didn't anyone seem to give a fuck?

CHAPTER ELEVEN
PERSON OF INTEREST

I suspect I could build a computer profile that could guess your occupation with a better-than-random outcome based upon posture and eye gaze. Doctors tend to look around you, kind of like a farmer sizing up a heifer. Scientists look into the space next to you as they think about your words or, more likely, their own precious thoughts. Cops look right at you. They don't look away when you make eye contact. They maintain the dominance stare because they've got a gun and a license from society to intimidate you. If you stare back and threaten that dominance, they're only one radio call from a bunch more cops with guns.

As I step out of the records room with my digital files and a head full of my own precious thoughts, I'm being given the dominance gaze by a cop. Which shouldn't be a surprise in a building full of them, but this one is staring directly at me.

He's middle-aged, bald, with a thick black mustache flecked with gray, dressed in a black LAPD polo shirt, badge on one hip, gun on the other; this man is about as cop as you can get. For a fleeting moment, I wonder whether that's what decides academy admission.

"Find what you were looking for, Mr. Cray?" asks the man.

I used to be much worse at these kinds of encounters. That was before the forest. I'm not saying I'm the smoothest operator now, but I've learned to not just stand around with a slack jaw.

I give him a wide grin and reach my hand out to shake his. "How you doing?"

Reflexively he shakes mine. There's a slight change in his demeanor. The eyes still stare right at me, but now they're trying to read me, not telling me how to react.

"I apologize, what was your name?" I'm pretending we are friends. "Did we meet at the San Diego counterterrorism conference?" This is me signaling to him that we're in the same field. "Were you at my talk?" Now I'm telling him I'm a peer, if not a superior.

He regains his composure. "No. We've never met." There's a small pause. "And you know that."

My social-engineering skills exhausted, I only have one option left as I try to figure out the real purpose of this encounter. I'll have to be Dr. Theo Cray. "Well, in answer to your question, no. I didn't find what I was looking for. And what is it *you're* looking for?"

He softens his expression. "I just wanted to have a friendly chat. My office is across the street. Mind if we head over there?"

"Is this the kind of discussion where I should have legal counsel?"

"Do you normally need to have a lawyer when you talk to someone?"

"Considering what happened the last time a police officer surprised me and told me they wanted to talk, it may have made a lot of difference."

"I get it. To be clear, you're not in trouble. I want to help you avoid it."

"Well, that sounds ominous."

"It's a courtesy, trust me."

In my brief experience being under the watchful eye of law enforcement, I have learned that the vast majority of cops are good people doing a very difficult job. Even the assholes I've had to deal with were looking out for everyone else. Unfortunately, they saw me as the threat.

Another thing I learned from the late Detective Glenn, who laid down his life so Jillian and I could live, was that really good cops work on two levels.

Like an actor who's recited Shakespeare a million times and is actually onstage thinking about what to eat for dinner, or a surgeon who can suture you up in their sleep while they dream of the golf green, a skillful cop can go about asking you questions, getting you to talk, while behind the scenes he's guiding you somewhere. Maybe it's not to get that one little clue or slipup. Often it's to suss you out and decide if you're hiding something and *how* you hide things.

Like scientists, they gather data points. They ask you questions they already know the answers to. They ask you embarrassing questions. They give you the chance to tell small lies so they can see how you handle the bigger ones.

There's a reason lawyers tell you to shut up when a cop talks to you. If you're lucky, that's the first and last time a cop ever speaks to you. It's your only good guy/bad guy conversation. As for the cops, they do it every day. They've met a thousand liars and heard a million lies. Yours ain't gonna fly. They won't tell you that you're full of crap—they'll keep you talking, getting you to lie about a bunch of things, making notes in their head while you tell yourself that you're the most persuasive motherfucker on the planet. They want you to walk away thinking you got away with it, or so panicked you screw up in front of them. It all depends on how they read you.

As I follow him back to his office, a realization hits me, one that should have been obvious the moment the cop stopped me. This is Detective Corman. The one who wrote the reports.

This is a surprise to me, because I'm fairly positive the woman in the records office didn't call and tell him some guy was digging around in a nearly decade-old case of his.

Corman was aware of me even before I set foot in the building. Probably even before I decided to come here. And that's what has my mind racing.

CHAPTER TWELVE
ACCOMPLICES

Corman sets a water bottle in front of me and drops a stack of folders on the conference-room table before taking a seat on the other side. Through the glass window, cops in uniform and in plain clothes go about their work, talking on phones, typing at computers as staffers move from cubicle to cubicle, delivering messages and making idle chat. Take away the uniforms and it could be just about any other office except for the toned forearms and percentage of mustaches.

"Your experience in Montana. I read up on that. That sounds like one hell of an ordeal," says Corman.

"Yes, it was," I reply drily.

"How much do you know about William Bostrom?" he asks, no doubt getting ready to tell me something I don't know.

"He's a grieving father, a widower, and an accountant. Nice guy."

"William is. Most of them are."

"Them?"

"Did William happen to tell you who his biggest client is?"

"We didn't talk about his business," I reply.

"His biggest client is a man by the name of Justice Mathis. He owns a dozen laundromats around Los Angeles, three check-cashing stores, and several used-car dealerships."

"Sounds like quite the entrepreneur." I don't add that it also sounds like more work than one accountant can handle.

"Oh, he is. Justice used to have another name back in the day. They used to just call him Master Kill. He was the head of a Crips offshoot called the Ninety-Niners. That was the number of rival gang members they claimed to have killed after the head of the Crips and Bloods went to jail and there was a fight for control.

"The funny thing about Justice was that, although he grew up near here, he wasn't quite from here. His father was a lawyer. Justice went to USC to play football and was a little smarter than the rest of the clowns. He knew how to act street but think like a businessman.

"Instead of giving his money to his thug friends, he sought out a more educated crowd, guys without a record, and had them put the cash into property and businesses—avoiding the kind of red flags that usually draw attention."

"So what are you saying?" I ask.

"William is a crook who works for another crook. A dangerous one. A man that gets people killed."

"Then why aren't you arresting him?" Bostrom's locked office and sealed cabinets are starting to make a little more sense to me. But still . . .

"Well, that's not my department. These things take time."

I suspect the reason he's talking to me is because William is under surveillance and someone pulled a file on his out-of-town, white-guy visitor.

"This is all . . . troubling, but I really don't care what he does for a living or who he works for. I'm here to help him find out what happened to his son."

"Right." Corman pulls an envelope out of a stack and pushes it toward me.

The last time a cop did this to me it was the picture of a body. "Who's the victim?" I ask, not touching the envelope.

Corman gives me small smile as he nods. "You've been spending time around cops. It's William's wife. Did he tell you how she died?" He stares at me, waiting for me to reply or to open the envelope.

As restrained as I'm trying to be, there is a zero chance a guy with my curiosity is not going to look at the photo. I slide the picture out and immediately regret it. It's an image of a young black woman on her side in a pool of blood with bullet holes in her head and torso.

"That was a year before Christopher went missing. The photo was taken in the back room of a janitorial supply company in Lynwood that was actually a count room. The newspapers reported that it was a rival gang pulling a rip-off."

"And what do you say?" I ask, taking the bait.

"The count room was one of Justice's, we're pretty certain. But we have a theory that he was actually the one that ordered the hit, killing three people."

"Why would he do that?"

"Because they were stealing from him."

"William's wife was ripping her husband's biggest client off?"

"Brenda. That was her name. And yes. We suspect William was in on it."

I'm trying to put this sordid theory together in my head. "But you say that William still works for him."

"Yep. William knows that could have been him in the photo. He screwed with Justice and was taught a lesson. How could he keep working for him—fear? Maybe. It could be that he hasn't quite accepted the fact that his boss is the one that ordered the death. Hell, maybe William was on the outs with Brenda. They both were using and fucking around back then. Could be *he* pulled the trigger." Corman watches my reaction to that.

I can't reconcile the man I've been helping with a cold-blooded killer. Corman's given me a lot to process, but none of it is relevant to why I came to Los Angeles. "And still there's a missing boy. Do you think he was stealing from Justice, too?" I ask sarcastically.

"I think that kid had two very fucked-up parents that are the reason he's not around."

While I don't know what to make of the idea that William would have been involved in his wife's murder, I can't see the man sticking by Justice if he thought he killed his boy. Underneath the calm accountant is a man perpetually on the brink of rage. I don't think he'd go quietly if someone took the last important thing from him.

"You have kids?" asks Corman.

"No." It's still a strange notion to me.

"Well, you can probably assume that if someone hurt your child, you'd do everything you could to get revenge. There's one exception to that: guilt. If you knew you were the reason it happened. You'd spend your time chasing your own tail in a guilt spiral. William's a man looking everywhere for an explanation except the one place he doesn't want to. His own actions."

"So you're saying it's gang related?" I ask.

Corman nods. "That's the prevailing theory."

"Then answer me this question . . ."

"Go for it."

"What the fuck happened to Christopher? Putting a label like 'gang related' or 'drug crime' doesn't solve the case. The facts are still the same. Someone took that kid, and we don't know who."

Corman doesn't flinch. He simply slides over a stack of folders about eight inches tall. "Take your pick." He yanks one out from the middle and opens it to a mug shot of a rough-looking young man with a face tattoo of a hand grenade. "How about D'nal Little? He's killed at least three men we know of, plus been involved in at least a dozen drive-bys between here and Las Vegas." He yanks out another folder.

"This is Chemchee Park. Nice guy. He'll even kill your goldfish. Or Jayson Carver? He shot two ten-year-olds at a party. Some of them work for Justice. Others are thugs for hire. Any one of them could have killed Christopher."

"And the body?"

"It could be in an oil drum in Bakersfield or ashes in the bottom of some incinerator in one of Justice's chop shops. Chances are there's not an atom of that boy left. Or maybe it wasn't even Justice that did it. He's got plenty of enemies that wouldn't hesitate to strike close to him. My point is—"

I interrupt him. "You've got every excuse in the world not to give a fuck. I get it. To you it's solved—just not processed and convicted." I drag the folders of would-be suspects in front of me and stare at the faces. "Let me ask you another question: Do any of these gentlemen strike you as intellectual giants?"

"Clearly, no. What's your point?"

"His bike was found nowhere near his route home from school."

Corman shrugs. "He was gone for eight hours before he was reported missing. The kid could have been in Anaheim by then."

I pull my phone from my pocket and load the image of Christopher's bike. Something was bothering me when I first saw it, but I couldn't put my finger on it until now.

"Take a look." I push my phone in front of him.

"It's the bike. And?"

"Did you fingerprint it?"

"The bike wasn't missing. The kid was."

"Okay. Sounds a little sloppy to me. But that's your call. I'm just a scientist. But take a look at it again."

Corman glares at me. "What?"

"You found the bike, but you know what you didn't find? And maybe the reason you should have had it fingerprinted?"

"You're testing my patience."

"The bike lock." I point to my phone. "There's no bike lock. I can't imagine there's a kid in South Central that doesn't keep one on his bike." I zoom in to the shaft under the seat. "You can even see the scrape marks from the metal chain."

"That's not exactly what I'd call a eureka moment. Maybe in the movies."

"Nope. It's not. But it's proof to me of one thing: you guys did a half-assed job and threw away the one piece of forensic evidence that was right in front of you. I don't know if any of the suspects you just tossed at me are the kind to plan ahead or cover their tracks by moving a bike. Maybe I'm wrong. But Christopher isn't his father or Justice. The kid deserved better."

"Okay, hotshot. You're clearly enjoying telling us how to do our jobs. I figured that was coming." He slaps another stack of folders. "Why don't you have a look at these, too. Over a hundred missing children in the last ten years. But I suggest you take the files back to Texas and keep clear of Mr. Bostrom. And by all means, tell him we spoke."

The fact that Corman offers this up freely tells me that they're watching Justice and William very closely and something may be coming to a head soon.

While I don't doubt the broad strokes of what he told me, Detective Corman clearly only sees what he wants to believe. There's something more going on. Something I can't yet pick up on.

I have some questions for William, but I need to get some more information on him first.

CHAPTER THIRTEEN
FOLLOW THE MONEY

Who is the real William Bostrom? Grieving father or banker for South Central's version of Pablo Escobar?

Corman left me with a lot to think about, not to mention, inexplicably, a pile of file folders of other missing children. I can only interpret this as an attempt to show me that he's an overwhelmed man. I get the sense that it's his ready excuse if I do find something—although that seems even less likely, given what he just revealed to me about William.

Now it's time for me to gather some Bostrom information of my own.

I rented a car and parked down the street from his house right before I called him and explained that I would be running a few hours behind.

In an experiment, you want to eliminate the effect of the observer as much as possible. Whether it's measuring wolf populations in Alaska or trying to find out which path a photon takes through a gallium arsenide grid, you want your subject to behave as if you weren't there.

Twenty minutes after I make my phone call, William pulls out of his driveway and heads away from my position.

As he drives into Compton, I try to keep a block back so it's not obvious that he's being followed. His first stop is one of the laundromats Corman mentioned.

William spends about fifteen minutes inside before getting back into his car. He doesn't carry anything in or out.

Eight minutes later we're at another laundromat. Again, he's in and out in about fifteen minutes.

This continues for two hours as he stops in at ten more laundromats, same routine. As I watch William dart in and out of these businesses, I wonder how many of them are legitimate and how many are fronts for moving drug money—if any. The small bills and coins used at a laundromat wouldn't seem like the best place to mask the twenties and hundreds used to buy drugs.

If I had to guess, he's making random visits to check the counts. Laundromats are almost all-cash businesses, making it easy for dishonest employees to steal from the till.

I suspect that William and his employer, Justice Mathis, are clever enough to put hidden cameras in their businesses so they can watch for the little tricks like resetting machines and exchanging cash for tokens out of their own pockets.

After visiting a string of laundromats, William takes us to a check-cashing store, where a line of people, mostly Hispanic, stretches out the door, all of them waiting to cash their checks or get an advance on their next payday.

This part of the economy is fascinating to me. It's been a target of regulatory reform, as the government has tried to shut down payday-loan stores that offer advances with rather exorbitant interest rates. While I understand the urge to protect the little guy, I'm not quite sure if turning them away from a legitimate business and into the arms of illegal lenders is in their best interest. But I'm a biologist, not an economist. All I know is that where one system subsides, another, more predatory system will swoop in.

In any event, the check-cashing store seems to be doing brisk business. The exterior's as clean and professional as that of most banks; it doesn't look like a front for something else. Maybe that's the point and why I'm not a cop.

William gets into his car, and a minute later I get a text: I'll be running errands for another hour. Won't have access to my phone.

Well, this got interesting, unless he's heading to a massage parlor.

I keep a discreet distance between us as I follow William into a neighborhood north of Compton. He reaches the end of a cul-de-sac and pulls through an electronic gate in front of a two-story house.

It's dusk, but the house is brightly lit and I can see an older black woman walking past an upstairs bay window. She's dressed in a fashionable blouse and is wearing the kind of capri pants my mother likes.

I type the address into my phone and do a search to see who lives there. Property records say it belongs to Ocean Dream Holdings. A search for that company leads to the name of a Los Angeles law firm.

Staring at my phone has completely shot my night vision, to the point that I don't even see the man with the gun approaching until he taps on my window and tells me to get out of the car while shining a flashlight in my eyes.

My first instinct is to drive off, but then I see another man standing directly in front of me with a phone to his ear.

I decline to get out of the car but roll down my window. That's when I see that the man who knocked on the glass is wearing a security guard's uniform.

"Can I help you?" I ask, trying to play it as calm as possible.

"May I ask what you're doing here?" he says politely, still keeping the flashlight in my face.

Meanwhile, the other man, dressed in jeans and a baggy shirt, shoves his phone in front of me and snaps a photograph before walking away.

I check the guard's uniform again just to be sure he's a rent-a-cop. "I'm minding my business. If you don't mind taking the light out of my eyes, I won't call the cops and accuse you of assault." It's mouthy, but it's a public street.

"We had a complaint that someone was peering into windows."

"Then I suggest you stop doing that." While I banter with him, I keep my eyes on the other man. Clearly there's something going on here. "I'm happy to leave."

He reaches a hand into the window and grabs the steering wheel. "Not so fast."

Fuck. This just escalated.

The other man whispers something into his ear that sounds suspiciously like, "Not a cop."

A moment later there's a gun to my head. "Out of the car!"

I decide it would have been easier for him to shoot me inside the vehicle, so there's some small chance there's a misunderstanding. I'm an optimist.

He pulls open my door while the other man puts his hand behind his back, presumably to reach for a weapon if I decide to break free.

The guard spins me around and pulls my wallet from my pocket. "Let's see who this fucker is."

I'm not sure if my federal ID will be a good thing or a bad thing. My gun is in my bag and almost within reach, but nowhere close enough to make a difference if the guy behind me decides to use his first.

I'm spun around and the flashlight returns to my face. "What are you doing here, peckerwood?"

"Check his arms," says the other man.

"Pull up your sleeves!" the guard yells at me.

I try to play it calm. "I'm not sure if you're allowed to do this . . . ," I say as I pull back the cuffs on my jacket.

He scans them with his flashlight. "Nothing," he says to the other man.

The light goes back in my eyes. "You a fed?"

"Would that be good news or bad news for you?"

"Did he have a PI license?" asks the other man.

"Nope."

"Then I say we work his ass over."

"Stop!" William shouts from the other side of the street. "Let him go!"

"You know this mouthy asshole?" asks the guard.

"Yeah. He's with me."

"Does Mathis know?"

William comes running over to me. "Yes. Yes. He wants to talk to him. Theo, I'm sorry. I didn't uh . . . remember that I told you to meet me here."

He knows I followed him, but he doesn't want them knowing that. I don't know if that's for his benefit or mine.

"Come on," he says. "Let's go inside so you can meet Justice Mathis."

CHAPTER FOURTEEN
PUBLIC ENEMY

Detective Corman's public enemy number one is drinking a Smartwater on the other side of a coffee table with a James Turrell art exhibition book resting on it as his teenage daughter sits in the kitchen with her grandmother working on her AP European History homework.

Athletic, dressed in a formfitting black sweater, he could be a wealthy attorney or an on-the-rise politician. It's hard to reconcile a man whose enunciations are more pronounced than my overly educated ones with a South Central gangbanger who ruthlessly killed his way to the top.

But I don't doubt it for a millisecond. Mathis is intelligent, watchful, and one of the most charismatic people I've ever met. You hear how some people swooned when Bill Clinton entered a room or Brad Pitt flashes a smile; Mathis has that kind of charm. So did Ted Bundy.

So did Joe Vik, from what people described. Although my altercation with him was less than charming.

That's not to say that I think Mathis had anything to do with Chris's disappearance. But I think it explains his ascendancy to power and why a guy like Detective Corman is infuriated that this man is sitting here in a multimillion-dollar home prepping his daughter for the Ivy League.

"First off, Professor Cray, please don't pay the fellas outside any mind. I still have some enemies from my rowdier days."

Rowdier days. That's how he spins it? "I hope they don't look like me."

"You might be surprised. Some boys watch a little too much *Sons of Anarchy* and get some idea in their head."

I vaguely remember that being a television show about a gang of white bikers. Could that really be what his welcoming committee thought I was? If so, then it doesn't exactly make it look like Mathis's rowdy days are all that far behind him.

"Second," says Mathis, "I want to thank you for helping William out. He's like a brother to me, and the loss of Christopher . . . well, it was like losing one of my own."

Was it? How much effort did Mathis put into finding him? Or did he do anything at all?

"I'm not sure how much help I can be. But William's . . . or rather Christopher's, situation seems rather frustrating."

"Yes." He nods sympathetically. "William says you were at the LAPD going through records about Chris's disappearance. Did you find out anything?"

Loads. But maybe I don't need to share everything. "Yeah. It looks like it was a half-assed investigation." I turn to William. "I even spoke to the investigating detective."

"Corman?"

"Yeah. That's the one."

"He stopped taking my calls years ago."

"I think he gave up . . ." Suddenly, I'm not sure what else I should say.

"Did he blame me?" asks Mathis. "Did he say this happened to Chris because his daddy was in with a gangster?"

Well, that was on the nose. "In a roundabout way."

"Did he lay out a file and tell you I was the Al Capone of Compton?"

"I got more of a Pablo Escobar impression."

Mathis nods, then turns to William. "How many times have we been audited?"

"Nine times," he replies. "None ever successfully prosecuted."

"And how many times have we been raided?"

"Five times."

"And did they ever make a case?"

"Yes. Once."

Mathis's face changes. "What?"

"Health violation. Your cousin Stacey was putting raw meat on the prep counter. They shut us down."

Mathis raises his hands in mock protest. "Well, then I guess I'm guilty of hiring my idiot cousin to run a burger joint she wasn't qualified to operate."

I smile. It's a great show. I bet he's done it for politicians, celebrity friends, and his rich friends at Soho House when the subject comes up.

I buy the innocence bit even less because he's let me know how smart he is. Of course cops used to busting dumb asses who never graduated high school aren't going to have an easy time getting a guy like Mathis.

Maybe he's done, maybe he's not, but I'm pretty sure he's pretty far removed from all that right now and never touches something outside his lawyer's office.

I learned everything I needed to know when the thug outside took my photo and told the guard I wasn't a cop. Anyone clever enough to have a database of police officer head shots is already too many steps ahead.

None of that matters to me. What I need to know is if he was involved in Chris's abduction. Corman and the LAPD can worry about everything else.

"I was doing some research," I tell Mathis, "and I came across a statistic that said most kidnappings go unreported because they're drug related. Corman suggested that maybe one of your rivals took Christopher. Maybe to get to William. Maybe to rattle you."

Mathis's voice lowers. "Do I look like I rattle? Let me ask you a question: Why are you here?" He raises a large hand before I can respond. "I don't mean helping William. I mean why are you talking to me instead of dead back somewhere in Montana?"

He's clearly been talking to William. "The real reason? Because that asshole took someone I cared about."

"Some seven-foot hillbilly giant who killed seven cops was about to hurt someone you loved. So you ended him. What do you think a so-called gangster like me would do if somebody tried to rattle me or go after someone close to me? You think that wouldn't be in the papers the next day?"

"I see your point. Unless *you* did it."

"Me?" He stares at William incredulously. "Why me?"

"Why isn't Chris's mom here?"

I can see Mathis's neck muscles tighten and hear the sound of William inhaling.

Mathis locks eyes with me but doesn't say a thing.

"That had nothing to do with Mathis," pleads William. "Nothing. Why would you bring that up? You can't say stuff like that."

"That's low, man. Real low," Mathis finally replies.

I may be on a one-way trip to one of his chop-shop incinerators, but I need one more reaction to confirm my theory. "What did the papers say the day after she and the other two people got killed? Which of your enemies did you smite?"

There's a long, uncomfortable pause. Finally he replies, "Retributions were made."

Fuck. He killed her, and William knows this. I catch the pained look on Bostrom's face out of the corner of my eye.

I take a deep breath. "Let me be clear. I'm not a cop. I'm a scientist. I find patterns. William showed up on my doorstep because he wanted me to find out what happened to his son. That's all I care about. I want to know who took the kid. I want to know if the man who did it is still out there."

Mathis's gaze intensifies as he reads my face. He nods, then holds out his hand for me to shake. "And I want you to find him."

CHAPTER FIFTEEN
FATHER FIGURE

William is sitting across from me in a booth at a bar where I'm pretty sure I'm the only white face, but nobody could give a damn.

"Brenda and I were pretty messed up back then. I was using. She was using. It's a miracle Chris was such a good kid. That boy raised himself. And then—"

I raise a hand. "No offense, but I don't need or care to know what happened to your wife if it doesn't relate to Chris's disappearance."

William has a hurt look on his face. He wants to confess something to me. He wants me to try to understand. There's only one problem: I'm pretty sure there's no version of the story I would believe in which he didn't look bad.

"I just wanted to say that Mathis—"

I cut him off. "Mathis is a special kind of sociopath."

"You don't know him. He's a great guy. He's funded community centers. He'd give you the shirt off his back . . ."

"Unless you took it from him. Look, you can convince yourself all you want, but you know what he is. One minute he's father of the year, the next he's making someone an orphan."

"You don't know what it's like to grow up out here."

"I don't. But neither does he. Mathis came from money. He came here because he knew he could get away with the evil things he wanted to do a little more openly."

William shakes his head. "You judgmental—"

"I haven't judged anyone. Have I said something that isn't true? Mathis isn't like you or me. He's a particular kind of sociopath. The kind that makes a great politician. He makes you think he loves you until you stand in his way. And then when he does something to fuck you over, he makes you think it's your fault."

"And you know this from experience?"

"I've spent a lot of time this last year trying to understand those kind of minds. There are even genes that correlate with charisma. Some of them overcompensate for a lack of internal empathy. They make you feel like they care more than anyone else while you're nothing to them."

"So it's all just genes to you?"

"No. Not always. I think you can teach yourself that, too." Like you can convince yourself it's okay to continue working for your wife's murderer.

William nods slightly. "But you don't think he had anything to do with Chris?"

"I don't think so. Not directly."

"What does that mean?"

"With Joe Vik, there was a pattern to his victims. Many of them were girls on their own with drug problems."

"Like Lonnie Franklin? The Grim Sleeper?"

"Yeah. Easy prey."

William crosses his arms defensively. "And my son was easy prey?"

I don't know any other way to put it. "Christopher's father worked for a reputed drug kingpin who was rumored to have murdered his mother for revenge. In the cops' eyes, you guys were tainted. They did the bare minimum to find out what happened to Chris because they were pretty sure he was already ashes in one of Mathis's furnaces. They knew they'd never be able to prove it, so they didn't bother looking."

"You're one cold motherfucker. At least Mathis doesn't make you feel like shit."

"That's so you don't see the knife coming. I'm honest. I never met your kid, but everything you told me about him makes me like him. I lost someone who was closer to me than I realized. I didn't go after Vik because he threatened someone I loved. I went after him because he took someone from me I never even got to know. I understand guilt. I know pain. The only antidote I have is brutal honesty."

William starts to speak, but I raise a hand to stop him.

"I can lie to you and pretend that your past doesn't matter. But it does. You and I both know that you and your wife were playing with fire. I have zero judgment on what happened. It's not my place to forgive you or make you feel guilty. The only monster I'm concerned about is the one that took Christopher. Not just because of what he did, but because of what he might be doing."

"You think he's still out there."

I nod. "Why would he stop? He figured out how to get the cops to not care. That's where I look next. For some reason Corman gave me a stack of missing-kid folders. I suspect he knows there's something out there. I also suspect he thinks he's still out there because he discovered Corman and the other cops' blind spot."

"Families like ours."

"Yep. Invisibles."

William takes a long sip of beer and watches me. "You're still judging me."

"I'm going to help you find out what happened to your boy. Does it matter what I think?"

William shakes his head. "What I'm saying is, Mathis is smart. Real smart. He could help us. All we have to do is ask."

"Personally speaking, I plan on staying as far away from him as possible."

"So you think you see through all that charm?"

"No. I don't. That's the problem. My gut says to like him. The rational part of my brain tells me to pay attention to the obvious. Your boss is a crook and—"

"I'm a crook," he puts in.

"But not a child killer." I tip my bottle toward his. "Let's finish up and go find one."

CHAPTER SIXTEEN
OUTREACH

Corman's files aren't just a random collection of missing-children reports. They're the hard cases, the ones where it was difficult to gather any evidence because the kids came from broken homes. In some cases, when the police went back to get more information, the families had left in a hurry.

At least half of the files were from households that appeared to be filled with illegal aliens. I get a chill thinking about how many cases of abducted children go unreported because the families are too afraid to talk to the authorities. I can't even fathom what kind of nightmare it is to be too afraid to go to the police in a situation like that.

When I put the data into Predox, I get a purple band stretching across a map of the city, indicating areas where a predator might be at work. I could have gotten the same map if I pulled up the records for where people buy prepaid phones and long-distance calling cards to Mexico, Central America, and South America.

I decide to start with the point closest to where Christopher went missing and work my way outward.

Andrew Mayne

A year ago, the grandmother of Ryan Perkins reported him missing to the police. He left an after-school care program and never made it home.

The police report mentioned that his father was at large and there had been custody issues. A follow-up report from Corman pointed out that the father was in county jail in Henderson, Nevada, at the time of abduction, suggesting that it might not have been so simple.

A pleasant older black woman greets me when I step inside the community center. She's laying coloring books out on tables for when the kids arrive.

"Hello, young man. May I help you?"

"Hi. I'm Theo Cray. I'm doing some background work on some missing-children cases."

Her face turns sad. "Oh, dear. Is this about Latroy?"

"Latroy?" I check the name on my note. "Who's Latroy?"

"He went missing three weeks ago. I called his house and nobody answered. When I spoke to the police, they said his mother had been arrested. But his grandmother had no idea where Latroy was. She thought maybe child services got him."

Jesus Christ. What a mess. "Actually, I'm here about Ryan Perkins."

"Ryan Perkins?"

I show her the photo of the boy. It was taken from a distance, so his eyes are red and his features hard to make out.

"Oh, yes, him. Didn't he go off with his father?"

"It would appear not."

"My . . ." She puts a hand to her heart. "We get so many in and out of here. It's hard to keep track."

No kidding. Two missing kids in one after-care program for disadvantaged kids? I think I'd rather send mine out on the street.

Easy there, Theo. The whole reason this place exists is because of the broken homes these kids fall in and out of. This lady is doing her best to give them a stable environment.

"Can you tell me anything about either of the boys? Did they know each other?"

"Oh, no. Latroy Edmunds had only been here a week or so. Talented boy, though. Wonderful artist. Very pleasant." She walks over to cabinet and unlocks it. "He left this behind. Which struck me as odd. It was his favorite thing. He wanted me to hold on to it for safekeeping. It seems his mother had a habit of selling his things."

She hands me an Iron Man action figure. It's well used. I take a couple of photos, then hand it back to her.

"Was there anything else you remember about Latroy? Did anyone ever pick him up besides his mother or grandmother?"

"No. This is a walk-in program, so we don't have the same kind of control over the children as a school does."

"What about Ryan Perkins?"

"I don't think so, either. I try my best to keep track of them."

"I'm sure you do. Kids are lucky to have someone like you looking after them."

I look around the colorful room, and my eyes fall upon the back wall filled with children's drawings. I walk over to have a closer look.

There's the typical illustrations of crudely drawn superheroes. Lots of green for the Hulk. Giant robots and loving renditions of dogs and cats. A number of them show idealized versions of family life with everyone holding hands.

One drawing stands out among all the rest. It's an all-black figure with a bag of toys. It reminds me of a bizarro Santa Claus. I lean in for a closer look.

"Oh, you know Latroy's work," says the woman.

"Pardon me?"

"Latroy drew that. It's a little urban legend; I guess you'd call it that."

"What urban legend is that?"

"The Toy Man. He's supposed to drive a big Cadillac around and give toys to the good boys and girls."

"That sounds pleasant enough."

"Yes. It does. I wouldn't let Latroy put the other drawing up."

"Why is that?"

"It was . . . disturbing. It shows what the Toy Man does to the bad boys and girls."

I don't know how long I stood there before she asked me if I needed help.

CHAPTER SEVENTEEN
SIGNAL

The assistant principal of Garvin Elementary School guides me down the hall and points to the school library. "We have a wonderful tutoring program here. Kids from UCLA come in and work with the children on their schoolwork."

"That's great," I reply, peering into the library and pretending to be interested. Children sit around tables as a teacher reads to them from a book.

Ms. Dawson is a nice woman, proud of her school and the impact they have on students coming from challenging backgrounds. "You said your daughter is in the fourth grade? Transferring midyear can be difficult, but we handle a lot of transient students here. She'll be able to make friends quickly."

"I hope so. Gracie has had some difficulties. Nothing behavioral."

Dawson nods, understanding that I'm telling her my imaginary daughter might be a problem learner. "Let me show you our achievers program. We're able to help kids get fast-tracked into regular curriculum."

We head down another hallway, passing more classrooms. I peek through the windows, looking for drawings like the one in the after-care program.

Most appear to be schoolwork related, none resembling the free-form art I saw before. My hope was that a school that focused on first-generation immigrant children and served problem learners might be a vector for more Toy Man drawings.

It's a real long shot, but the fact that Latroy, a kid who hadn't even made it into Corman's files, was making such creepy drawings has my curiosity piqued.

If the children weren't abducted by a complete stranger, then it may have been someone who knew them or interacted with them prior to their abduction. The way in which these kids were targeted suggests that he had some knowledge about their family life. One way to find that out is to ask. Another is to have access to their records, which might reveal that he works in one of the schools or public services that look after children.

It sounds paranoid, but Ted Bundy worked next to a former police officer at a crisis hotline who described him as kind and empathetic. This is the same man who in one night attacked five separate women, killing two of them.

The school district here has had no shortage of monsters preying upon students. The scary part is that several of them, teachers who abused and molested their students, had complaints going back decades. The most egregious involved a teacher whose students were primarily the children of illegal aliens too afraid to say anything.

Besides having a large number of potentially at-risk children, Garvin is where Latroy went to school. I want to find out if any of his classmates also had experiences with the Toy Man.

"Here's our achievers class," says Dawson. "It looks like Mrs. Valdez has taken the kids to the activity field."

At the back of the room is a wall full of drawings. Too far away for me to see in detail.

"Can I take a look?"

"Uh, sure." Dawson holds open the door for me. I catch a slightly suspicious look in her eye. "What did you say the name of your company was, Mr. Gray?"

"I didn't. I work from home. I'm a software analyst."

I couldn't exactly walk into the head office and tell them I was some concerned citizen who wanted to inspect their school for evidence of a fourth-grade Freddy Krueger.

"Right. And what does Mrs. Gray do?"

"She's a waitress," I reply as I make a beeline through the tiny tables and chairs toward the drawings in the back of the classroom.

There's the same collection of animals, families, and things kids see on television. Dawson is trying to figure me out as I scrutinize the pictures. I get the sense she's suddenly afraid that I'm not who I say I am.

"I have to take a phone call; we should be heading back to the office."

"Of course." I don't move. I'm trying to process the kids' sketches. They're a little abstract.

Far to one side, I see a slender man in black with a bag of toys. I point it out to her. "Do you know what this is?" The name at the bottom says Rico, not Latroy.

She bends down for a closer look. "A black Santa Claus?"

"One of my daughter's friends mentioned something about the Toy Man. Have you heard that?"

"No. I think we should be going."

"Of course. Let me text her mom and ask." I pull out my phone and take a photo.

"Mr. Gray, I can't allow you to take photos in here."

"I'm sorry." I drop my phone to my side and spot the teacher's open planner on her desk. "Let's get you back to the office."

She turns to the door, and I head straight to the desk.

"Mr. Gray?"

"I need to spit out my gum." With my back to her, I take a photo of all the student names.

"All right. I'm calling school security." She's got the walkie-talkie from her hip at her mouth in a blink of an eye.

"Great." I stare her down. "Ask them what happened to Latroy."

She freezes. "Pardon me?"

"Latroy Edmunds. He went missing a month ago." I point to the drawing on the wall in the back. "He was drawing pictures of the Toy Man, too."

"I have no idea what you're talking about. You need to leave before I call the police."

I raise my hands in surrender. "I'm here to help."

"Did anybody ask you to?"

"The father of another missing child."

She's trying to decide how to wrap her head around what I said. On one hand, I've acted like a suspicious asshole; on the other, I'm talking about missing children and parents trying to find out what happened.

Finally she says, "If you have any questions, then you need to take them up with our principal. In the meantime, I have to ask you to leave our campus."

It's a tense walk back to my car as she follows me closely, trying to decide if I'm a threat or just some lunatic she let wander around the school.

It's a valid question, one that I'm not sure even I can answer.

CHAPTER EIGHTEEN
EMERGENCY CONTACT

Deciding how far I'm willing to go to track down the origins of the Toy Man means deciding how far out of bounds I'm willing to step. Right now I only have two drawings—one from a missing kid, the other from a child who is presumably not missing. I haven't asked William yet, because I want to make sure I'm not going to send his already-stressed mind down another blind alley.

Tracking down the artist behind the second drawing, fourth-grader Rico Caldwell, may be more difficult than getting the LAPD records.

I can't exactly call up Ms. Dawson at the elementary school and ask if she'll give me Rico's home address. Standing outside the school when class lets out and yelling "Rico" as kids get onto their school buses isn't exactly a great idea, either.

One option is to use a piece of phishing software, pretending to be the district IT department and calling someone in the school office and instructing them to click on something—a criminal tactic with a frightening success rate. The problem with that approach is that it's a federal crime. I'd rather find an approach that won't have me doing time.

There's another approach that's risky in its own right but could get me an answer in hours. Although it would be slightly more hazardous to my health.

One of the side benefits of consulting for intelligence agencies is that you get access to all kinds of interesting workshops. I took one on social engineering because my own natural skills were nonexistent. Besides learning the typical ways that nefarious people can convince you to load virus software or talk their way through to the head of a company, I learned a remarkably easy way to get access to secure buildings.

After parking my car down the street, I walk around the back of the LA Unified School District administration building until I identify the area at the edge of the parking lot that's the highest point of vulnerability: where people go take their smoke breaks.

I see two women and a man dressed in semicasual business attire, all three puffing away under a tree the appropriate distance away from the building according to California code.

With my ID on my hip but "accidentally" facing in, I pull my just-bought pack of Camels out, give them a friendly nod, and light up as I join them.

"Look, a new guy," says the man. He's Hispanic and about my height, with a full head of hair and a cheery expression.

"I figured this is where the bad kids hang out."

"I'm Corrine," says the black woman to my left, giving me a polite nod. "This is Jackie and Raul." She indicates the other black woman. "Who the hell are you?" she asks with a smile.

"Jeff. Here from the governor's office for a meeting that I've been in for two hours and still couldn't tell you what it's about."

"Sacramento?" asks Jackie.

"And Los Angeles. I commute."

"More importantly," says Corrine, "single? Straight? We're suffering a Y-chromosome shortage around here."

"Divorced. Adjusting to single life."

The women look at each other and share a smile as they both say, "Pauline."

"Oh, buddy," Raul sighs. "You have no idea what you just walked into."

Likewise.

I carry on for the next ten minutes with my newfound friends, feeling slightly dirty. When it's time to stub out our cigarettes and head back inside, I start a conversation with Corrine as Raul swipes his badge on the sensor and lets us all through.

"Do you remember where you're headed?" asks Raul as we make our way to a bank of elevators.

"The conference room with all the sleeping people."

"Floor two. You'll have to take your pick," he says as we step into the elevator.

As I get off on the next floor, Corrine points to me. "Stop by the fourth floor afterward. We have someone we want you to meet."

Raul rolls his eyes as the doors close.

And, just like that, I'm inside the school district's administration building and have a prospective date—all because I signaled to a group of people ostracized for a particular habit that I am one of them. The hardest part was not coughing as I pretended to smoke.

Although I'm in a building full of records, my goal isn't to try to get access to a computer or riffle through their files. What I actually need is an open phone.

I walk down the hallway, looking through the windows of conference rooms until I find a small, unused one. I drop down into a chair, spread out some papers from the folder I brought with me, and make it look like I own the place.

Satisfied that nobody is about to boot me, I pick up the phone and call Garvin Elementary, hoping that Ms. Dawson won't be the one to pick up.

"Garvin Elementary, how may I direct your call?"

"Hello, this is Showalter from Unified records. We're trying to process a parent emergency-contact form from one of your students and having trouble reading it. I was wondering if someone there can clarify the information."

"I can do that. What's the name?"

"Rico Caldwell."

"Okay. I can't give you that information over the phone, but I can clarify it for you if you want to read what you have."

I was expecting this. "Unfortunately the image is too pixelated. But I can give you my extension here if you want to confirm."

"That will work as long as it's at the 818-434 number."

I check the number on the phone. "Yes. Extension 3874. Just ask for Showalter if I don't pick up."

"It should only be a second."

Actually, it takes twelve.

"Showalter," I answer.

"Sorry about that. Sometimes they check to make sure we're not giving out student information. I think we already had a call about Rico. Is everything okay?"

"Yes, I think so. Do you know who called?"

"Three days ago someone from his pediatrician's office called, but they didn't leave a return number."

Well, that's interesting. I wonder if someone was circling Rico?

"Have a pen?" she asks and then gives me Rico's home address, the name of his mother, and everything else on the contact form.

I thank her and then get out of the building as quickly as possible.

While following up with Corrine and company on the fourth floor could make future access easier, it also runs the risk of them mentioning the guy from the governor's office to somebody who knows better.

While the chances are almost zero that anyone would care, they're not nonzero. And more importantly, I need to make sure that Rico isn't in harm's way.

CHAPTER NINETEEN

Outreach

Rico lives in an apartment complex called Lincoln Gardens—a string of two-story yellow buildings with chipped paint surrounding a park showing more brown than green.

Black kids are bouncing a basketball around while Hispanic teens chase a soccer ball out in the spotty field—reinforcing every stereotype already in my head.

Mothers stand outside trading gossip while men lean on cars talking to one another in Spanish and English.

Rico's apartment is toward the back of the complex, and I make my way there, never getting as much as a second glance from anyone.

I can hear a television set blaring through an open door on the second floor. When I get to the top of the steps, there's a little girl, maybe two or three, playing with a broken doll and a saucepan lid.

Inside are two teenage boys, both around thirteen, draped over the couch, watching a movie involving cars racing through streets.

I knock on the open door. "Hello?"

The boys glance at me for a moment, then turn back to their television.

"Is your mother home?" I ask.

One of them shouts, *"¡Vete, gringo tonto!"*

I shout back at him, *"Bájate del sofá, cucaracha perezosa."* This gets his attention. But only enough to flip me off.

I knock on the door again, hoping to get the attention of an adult.

Frustrated that he can't hear the sound of the cars revving, the brat yells into the other room, *"¡Abuela! ¡Hay un maricón en la puerta!"*

An old woman no more than five feet tall comes waddling toward the door in a housecoat. *"¿Qué?"* she says, looking up at me.

I show her my ID, hoping it conveys some kind of token credibility. *"¿Dónde está Rico?"*

The woman shouts into the house. "Rico! Rico!"

A small boy wanders into the room and stares at me skeptically. Wearing only a pair of shorts, he looks a little too skinny for his age.

"Rico?" I ask.

The boy nods.

"¿Hablas Inglés?"

"Yes?"

He gives me a wary look, then steps closer, still under the protection of his grandmother. I kneel so I can be eye to eye and get a friendly smile from the little girl who had been playing at my feet.

I pull the printout I made of his drawing out of my pocket and unfold it. "Did you draw this?"

He stares at it for a moment, not sure if I'm going to get him in trouble.

"It's fine. I just wanted to know."

The two teens from the couch have suddenly become interested and crowd the doorway behind Rico.

"Yes," says Rico.

"Do you know who that is?"

He nods.

"What's his name?"

Suddenly there's fear in the boy's eyes. Not at the drawing. Not at my question, but of me.

He runs through the others and back into the house. The two teens start laughing.

"*Hombre de juguete* is going to get you!" one of them yells at him in broken English.

I stand up. "You know who this is?"

"*Sí,*" says the other. "Toy Man. Everybody knows who he is."

"Have you seen him?"

"*Sí,*" he says, stealing a glance at the other boy.

"Where?"

"Guzman Park. He's there all the time."

"White man?"

"No," he shakes his head. "*El negro.*"

"Do you know when he'll be there?"

"He's there right now."

There's an earnestness in the way that he replies without even conferring with his friend that tells me he's certain of that. Everything else, I'm not so sure about.

While I'd like to press little Rico for more answers, I get the feeling he's in no mood to talk to me. The kid went white as a sheet when I brought up the Toy Man. His older friends thought it was a joke but seem very convinced of where he is.

"Thank you." I give their confused grandmother a smile. The little girl waves to me as I walk back down the steps.

Walking away, I can feel the eyes of the teens on me as they watch from the balcony at the top of the stairs.

Something is up, but I can't quite figure out what.

Guzman Park is a two-minute drive away. It's between Lincoln Gardens and Rico's school and a likely spot Rico would pass every day if he didn't take the bus.

I park my car and walk around the park, trying to act like I'm just out for a stroll. Kids are playing on the basketball court while a group of teen girls sit on a concrete bench chatting with one another.

I see at least two families pushing strollers and holding hands with their ambulatory children.

It's a pleasant evening, and everyone seems to be enjoying themselves. There's a group of young men off to the side, smoking some pot, and two others standing near a corner, engaged in what looks like some kind of illicit commercial transaction that everyone else is ignoring.

I don't spot a white Cadillac or a black man dressed in dark clothes with a sack of toys. Not that I was expecting exactly that.

I finish walking around the perimeter and take the path into the park that reaches a small circle of benches in the middle. Sitting there, I watch for anything suspicious.

I'm starting to feel had when I hear the sound of footsteps on grass behind me. When I look over my shoulder, I see Detective Corman striding toward me.

CHAPTER TWENTY
MISSING CONNECTIONS

"I hear you're thinking about moving your family out here," he says sarcastically as he takes a seat next to me.

"I would, but you have a reputation for losing track of children," I reply.

"The problem is that when people find whoever was missing, they don't always tell us."

"Is that the problem?" I ask. "Or is it that when someone goes missing they don't tell you?"

"Can't help them if they don't ask."

"What about Latroy Edmunds?"

"Who's that?"

"A lady at the after-care program says he went missing."

"If we had to file a report for every kid that left with their parents back to Juárez or off to Nevada without telling anyone, I could build a border wall with the paperwork."

"What about Ryan Perkins? Are his parents heading back to Mexico?"

Corman shrugs. "Probably not. Maybe Atlanta. Maybe Houston. Who knows? Hard to keep track. People want a police state without the police. So what brings you out here? Looking for a place to take your kid?"

"I had a look at those files you gave me."

"I was hoping you'd read those on the plane back to Texas."

"I'm more of a field researcher. Anyway, I have a theory. But I suspect I'm not the first one to have it."

"And what's that?" asks Corman.

"That there's an active serial killer in the Los Angeles area."

"Well there's a shocker," he says drily.

"More specifically, one that targets at-risk children. Someone who moves around, not a lot, but maybe a few miles away every couple of years to break up a localized pattern. Maybe changes the demographic of his victims a little, but not by much. He seems to focus on young boys."

He folds his arms and tilts his head. "Intriguing. You picked all this up from the files?"

"Well, it wasn't explicitly in there. But I could see how an LAPD detective with little more than this would be in a bind. Of course, the problem is that even he doesn't want to see what's out there. Maybe he hastily draws some conclusions on a few cases, writing them off, and then a few years later has some regret."

"Well, that sure as hell isn't me," says Corman. "I gave you those files because there might be something in some of those cases. But I assure you, the vast majority have very boring explanations or tragic ones we already know the answer to."

"Maybe so. But there's one connection that might link them." I hand him a printout of Ryan Perkins's and Rico's drawings. "Our missing kid made this. And a classmate of Latroy's drew the other."

Corman takes the pictures and stares at them for a moment, then chuckles. "The Toy Man."

"You know the story?"

"Yes. He's Compton's Freddy Krueger—or what is it my sons talk about? Slenderman." He hands them back to me. "I've heard the stories. Is that why you're here? You're staking out an urban legend? Should we get the *Mythbusters* guys out of retirement?"

I put the drawings back into my pocket. "I know. Pretty silly. But here's the thing: I did an Internet search for the Toy Man. I've got some pretty useful tools that let me do deep searches into social media and that kind of thing."

"What did you find?"

"Basically nothing. There's only a handful of mentions."

He waves to the park. "And yet you're out here trying to get the drop on an imaginary character."

"While this stakeout may be a bust, my research turned up one very interesting bit of data. The mention of the Toy Man only came up in this area. All those files you gave me are within the range of the meme. Which strikes me as kind of odd. If it's just a story and nothing more, it seems like we'd also be hearing about it in places without missing children."

"Have you asked Bostrom if his son saw the Toy Man?" asks Corman.

"Not yet. I wanted to see if it was more than a neighborhood legend."

"Does it even go back that far?"

"I don't know. Like I said, there's hardly any online footprint. Plus the fact that it's an elementary-school story, and they're not the most prolific tweeters. Especially these kids."

Corman gets up and checks his watch. "Well, good luck on that. It's something to think about on your flight home."

"Is the sheriff kicking me out of town?" I reply as I stand as well.

"I don't know about the sheriff, but this cop says that if I find out you've been on school property again under false pretenses, you'll be able to talk to some suspects firsthand at the LA County jail."

"You're not bothered by the Toy Man connection?"

"Two kids, maybe one is really missing, make a drawing of a boogeyman? No. I'm not bothered. That's less than circumstantial."

"Ever hear of John Butkovich? His parents called the cops over one hundred times asking them to look into a man they suspected killed their son."

"Let me guess, that man killed him."

"Yep. And at least thirty or forty others that we know about. But even John Wayne Gacy lost track."

He groans. "Well, I promise you, if someone calls me about a killer clown on the loose, I'll take it seriously."

"Would you?" I take out the drawings and hold them up. "What if these kids are calling?"

"Good night, Dr. Cray. Have a nice trip home. I'll let you know if the Toy Man says hello."

I stare past him as a car's headlights illuminate something I hadn't noticed before. I was too busy staring into the park to see what was right there.

"You okay there?"

I point to something past his shoulder. "The little fuckers weren't lying to me after all."

CHAPTER TWENTY-ONE
TAGGED

I press my face up to the metal bars blocking the back side of an air-conditioning repair shop that doesn't look like it's seen any business since the start of the last ice age. A collage of graffiti with a thousand different cocreators stretches across the wall. But in the middle of them, seemingly given a certain amount of reverence for the artistry displayed, is a figure of a man with a dark suit and a void with red eyes and a sinister smile where a face would be. At his feet are the severed limbs of children scattered among bloody dolls and action figures.

He looks almost as if he's stepping through the wall into reality. A caption above his head says THE TOY MAN IS WATCHING.

It's a sinister nightmare that clearly means something to the artist. I take several photos while Corman looks on, unimpressed.

"Do you think a nine-year-old made this?" I ask.

"I think that was made about ten years ago. Have you considered the notion that maybe this little nightmare is what started all the other kids talking?"

"Maybe." I take my phone out and call William.

"Hey, Theo. How are things going?"

"A quick question." I try to play it nonchalantly. "Did Chris ever mention anything about an urban legend involving someone called the Toy Man?"

"No. I don't think so. Why?"

I feel a sinking feeling as a lead slips through my fingers. "Nothing. Just curious."

"Sorry. I never saw the movie. So I wouldn't know."

"The movie?" I reply.

"Yeah, wasn't the Toy Man a movie or something, maybe a TV show?"

"Why do you say that?"

"I don't think Chris said anything about an urban legend, but I think he mentioned something about seeing the Toy Man. I thought maybe his auntie took him."

Seeing the Toy Man . . . "And what did he say about the movie?"

"I guess he was some kind of black Santa Claus. He drove a white Cadillac and gave presents to good kids. You know how kids get obsessed with a movie and start thinking it's real."

Jesus. Christ. I have to take a deep breath to collect my thoughts. I don't even know where to begin with telling him that the Toy Man wasn't a movie, but an actual man his son may have spoken to—who may have killed him.

"Let's talk later. I got to check on something."

Corman is leaning against the fence, watching the exchange. He can read my reaction on my face.

"So I guess Chris Bostrom heard about the Toy Man, too?"

I nod. "He told his father something about seeing him."

"Well, Dad never told me," Corman replies a bit defensively.

"His father thought it was a movie."

Corman shakes his head and stares at the ground. "Do you know why his dad took so long to tell me Chris was missing?"

"You've given me a lot of reasons."

"When I met with him, his eyes were bloodshot and he was coming down from something. I don't know if he has any idea what his son was up to or what he thinks he saw or who he knew."

I hold up three fingers. "Three kids. Three Toy Man sightings."

"I'm sure they all know who Magneto is, too. That's not even a correlation. It's a local folk story the drug dealers tell their little brothers and sisters to keep them in line." Corman waves off the idea. "If you find him, let me know. I've gone down every alley, every side street. There's no Toy Man waiting around the corner."

After he leaves, I take a seat on the bench facing the mural and zoom in to the image of it on my phone.

There's so much detail in the blood and the way the eyes gaze into you. It's not the kind of thing a teenager spray paints because it's fun—it's the kind of thing they do to cope with something that's haunting them.

I don't get the feeling that the artist heard about the Toy Man. I sense that he encountered him, the artist's graffiti almost a kind of therapy.

I zoom in on the lower right-hand corner of the image and notice a signature: *D. Rez.*

I'll bet anything he has a story to tell. Maybe it's how he and his buddies made up this crazy urban legend ten years ago. Maybe it's what my gut is telling me.

My gut . . . I can't ignore it. I have to either disprove or confirm it.

I call Corman's cell phone even though I can see him from here as he gets into his car.

"Yeah?"

"Can you give me the number of someone in the gang unit? Whoever works on graffiti?"

I can hear him groan. "If it will make you go away. You want to talk to Marcus Grenier. Just call LAPD direct."

"Thank you."

"And do me a favor? Don't tell him I told you to call him."

Ten minutes later a rather laconic-sounding man answers the phone. "Grenier speaking."

"I was told you were the one that I could call and ask about graffiti."

"You want OCS, Operation Clean Sweep. They'll help you clean it up."

"No. I'm trying to find out the identity of a tagger," I reply.

"If you tell me you're from an art gallery, I'm going to punch you through this fucking phone. We don't need to encourage the little fuckers."

"What if I was a rival and wanted to give him a beatdown for tagging my art?"

"I'd say you're full of shit, but I like your ideas anyway. Some asshole get your building?"

"Basically."

"Well, I can give you a name if you want to contact a lawyer to sue him. Ha-ha. Or I can put you in touch with the prosecutor's office if they're making a case. What's the tag?"

"D period R-E-Z."

"One second." I can hear typing coming from his end of the phone.

"You want the good news or the bad news? Actually, it's all good news. Artice Isaacs is currently in county lockup awaiting trial for armed robbery. Now I feel good. This story had a happy ending."

"Can you give me a case number?"

"What? You're still not happy? This is his third felony. He'll probably actually do real time this go-around. Fine, have at him. Got a pen?"

CHAPTER TWENTY-TWO
CONFABULATION

A day later I'm sitting on a tiny metal stool bolted to the floor, designed for minimal comfort. Adjacent to me on the other side of the glass, a white guy—with an expletive neck tattoo that will probably make running for future public office difficult—is covering the mouthpiece of his phone as he yells at his girlfriend over some domestic issue while trying not to raise the ire of the guards. He seems like a real classy guy.

I have no idea what to expect with Artice. His rap sheet isn't exactly encouraging. Although his juvenile records are sealed, the fact that his first adult charge was at sixteen tells me that filing cabinet was full.

A foster kid whose mother was in and out of jail and apparently bouncing from pimp to pimp, Artice never had a real good go at life. He did his first county jail time as an adult for intent to sell. His latest endeavor was trying to rob an Uber driver after using a stolen phone to call him.

I take some solace that, according to his sheet, he never actually hurt anyone—but all that means is they never charged him for it. The cold, hard truth about career criminals is that they get charged for less than 10 percent of the crimes they commit. I keep that in mind whenever I read an "All this guy did was . . ." headline on a blog. On the other hand, our justice system is based on what we can prove and not what we suspect, and I'm not sure if there's a better alternative unless we want to be a police state.

I requested a meeting with Artice, telling him I was a reporter and making sure to put fifty bucks in his account at the jail so he can buy snacks and other things we take for granted on the outside.

When he's escorted in, the first thing I notice is a pair of gray, almost silver, eyes spotting me from the far side of the room. He lifts his chin slightly and flashes a grin.

A guard points him to the seat opposite me. Artice drops down and picks up the phone.

"My new favorite person! Your donation to the Artice Rehabilitation Fund is much appreciated."

"Happy to help," I reply. "Do I get to deduct that from my taxes along with the three hours I spent in the waiting room?"

"Sorry about that. I'll have my people get you through faster next time."

I wasn't sure what I was expecting, but I'm pretty sure it wasn't the happy-go-lucky young man sitting in front of me.

"Thanks." I'm not sure how much small talk to make. I'm bad at it even when I'm not talking to guys waiting to find out if they're going to be spending the next several Christmases behind bars.

"So are you here to find out my side of the story?"

He thinks I'm here about the Uber thing. "Nope."

Ready to launch into some rehearsed alibi, his expression changes as soon as he realizes I said I wasn't interested.

"Wait, aren't you the reporter that wanted to get my side on that?"

"That was a lie," I reply.

"Then what the fuck are you here for? If you're the prosecutor, I can have this case thrown out."

"I'm not a lawyer." I take the photo of his mural out of my folder. "I wanted to ask you about this."

He glances at it for a second, then turns his eyes on me. "I don't know who D. Rez is. He's obviously a very talented young man. If you're interested in an exhibition of his work, I might be able to put you in contact with him."

"Well, I'll put fifty bucks into D. Rez's canteen account if he can answer some questions for me."

Artice thinks this over. "You know what, D. Rez might be available. Hold on." He makes a motion of getting up and sitting back down. "How might I help you?"

Artice loves to play the clown. It's probably a skill he had to develop as he got bounced around from home to home and, later, facility to facility.

"Well, Mr. D. Rez, let's talk about the Toy Man."

His expression goes cold. The perpetual smile on his cheekbones fades away. For a moment I see a scared kid.

"I have no idea who you're talking about."

I point to the words *Toy Man* at the top of the mural. "It says it right here. And if I'm not mistaken, that's the same paint you used for the rest of the painting."

He's trying to figure me out, wondering why I'm really here.

"I want to know the story," I explain.

"I don't know anything about it. It's just something kids used to talk about. That's all." His reply is almost robotic.

"Did you ever meet him?"

He takes way too long to give me an answer to convince me otherwise.

"Meet him? He's not real. He's like Freddy Krueger. How do you meet him? Unless it's the actor or some shit like that."

"You hear about the killer in Montana? The one that might set the new record for kills?"

He nods slowly. "I may have seen something on the news. Big, scary redneck dude."

"That's the one. I met him."

"How did that go?"

"He almost killed me. I don't like talking about it."

"Did people believe you?"

Here we go . . . I think I understand his reticence. "Eventually. The problem at first was nobody believed he was real. I had to dig up bodies. Lots of bodies." I can still see the pale faces of the young women I found rotting in shallow graves. "I know what it's like when nobody believes you."

He shakes his head. "I don't know what you're talking about. I got sliced up by some gang kids."

Shit. There's something I wasn't expecting. "Is that what you remember? Or is that what you were told by the therapists?"

"Therapists. Fuck them. They get in your head and tell you what's real and what's not. They don't know shit."

I hold up the photo of his mural again. "Who is he? What did he do to you?"

"He's a fucking ghost."

"What's that mean?"

Artice looks into space as he thinks it over. I give him a moment. Clearly he's buried this deep inside.

He glances at the sheet again, his voice almost inaudible. "They told me I made it up. They called me a liar. I was just a kid. I wouldn't have known how to make up something as fucked-up as that."

"How fucked-up?"

CHAPTER TWENTY-THREE
WHITE CAR

Artice has his head cupped in his hand as he stares at the table and recounts his experience with the Toy Man. I keep my mouth shut and just let him talk. I get the feeling that this is the first time he's articulated what happened as an adult. While some details may fade, the passing of years can also bring on a deeper understanding of what actually happened.

The first thing I realize is that Artice's dates are fuzzy. Although I'll never know exactly when he first ran into the Toy Man, a quick bit of math reveals that it probably happened between six months and a year after Christopher Bostrom went missing.

Given the pained expressions on Artice's face, I can tell the memories remain vivid.

"Even before I saw him, I heard kids talking about the Toy Man all the time. He was supposed to be this dude who'd drive around in a big white Cadillac and roll down his window and ask if you'd been a good boy or not. If you said yes, he'd give you five bucks or maybe some action figure or something. Then he'd tell you it was a secret. He didn't want the other kids getting jealous.

"Of course kids being like they are, everyone talked. They'd whisper to you, 'Have you heard of the Toy Man?' They'd ask if you'd ever met him. Some kids would even lie because they didn't want to miss out.

"I never had shit. So you can imagine how excited I was about the idea of the Toy Man rolling up next to me. I swear I even stood on sidewalks, staring at every white car, hoping it was the Toy Man.

"Then one day, I'm walking down 120th, and along comes this big white Caddy. 'You there!' he yells out at me. Deep voice. Deep motherfucking voice. 'Have you been a good boy?'

"'Hell yes,' I tell him. And just like that, he waves five dollars at me. I walk up to the window, and he reaches out and grabs my hand. Gentle, but firm, and pulls me closer. He looks me in the eyes and asks again if I've been a good boy.

"I say, 'Yes, sir.' He asks my name, where I live, and then gives me five dollars. He says keep it a secret, then drives away.

"I'd never had five dollars in my life. You would have thought I'd won the lottery. I went straight to the ten-cent candy section in the store and bought me one of everything I could.

"I remember sitting on a bench eating all that candy, thinking that was the best day of my life. I was a dumb little fucker. For five bucks, he bought me.

"For days I kept hoping he'd show up again. Finally he pulled up again in that Caddy and asked if I'd been a good boy. I said, 'Yes, sir.' He then said he heard that I told some other kids he'd given me five dollars.

"I started bawling, saying at first that it wasn't true, those other kids were liars. Then I told him it was true and I promised I would never tell anyone again.

"Well, he started to drive away and, to me, it felt like Santa Claus flying right past your house. Then all of a sudden his brake lights come on, and it's like Santa changed his mind.

"The passenger door opens up and I hear his voice ask me, 'Do you want to go to Toy Land?'

"I had no motherfucking idea what that meant, but I knew I sure as hell wanted to go there. So I say, 'Yes, please, Mr. Toy Man.'

"And he says I have to get down on the bottom of the floor of his car because he's going to have to sneak me into Toy Land because kids ain't allowed.

"I was nine, man. That shit made sense. I wasn't thinking this was so he could keep me from knowing where the hell we were going.

"It could have been minutes. It could have been hours. I was so excited, I didn't care. Finally he says I can get out. We're in Toy Land. I open the door, and sure as hell, I'm in motherfucking Toy Land. I know it was a garage now, but back then, it might as well have been the North Pole. There was walls full of action figures, games, a whole fucking toy store. Plus there were balloons and music.

"He led me into another room where a big-screen TV was playing cartoons. Another one had video games. He let me play as much as I wanted.

"I remember he gave me some juice to drink, and I felt a bit weird. I was thinking it was just the way you felt in Toy Land."

Artice catches his breath. "So I play those games, and he does stuff. Grabbing me like it's a game. I was laughing and having fun. I didn't know what was going on." His face takes on a tortured look. "I was just a kid. Nobody ever gave me any attention."

My stomach is churning. "I'm sorry, man. Sorry for bringing it up."

He looks at me funny. "Shit. That ain't the real bad part. Fuck, I had counselors in juvie pull that kind of shit. It's where it went from there. After he'd grabbed my dick and all that, he had me get back in his car and hide down on the floor and he took me back to where I was picked up.

"Now, another kid, he'd mentioned the Toy Man grabbed him and all that. Some other kids called him a faggot, so I made sure that I kept my mouth shut.

"The Toy Man picked me up again a few days later. He asked if I told anyone. I said I hadn't. This time he believed me. He said he was going to take me to Toy Land again and had me crouch down on the floor of the Caddy like the last time.

"When we got to his place, he offered me some more red punch. But I remembered the last time I drank it I couldn't play Super Mario Kart worth shit, so I pretended to drink it but actually dumped it on the floor.

"I was sitting in a game chair, playing, when he comes in the room and tells me he wants to take me to a special room only the best boys get to go to.

"I remember asking him what was in there. He said a surprise just for me.

"So of course I followed him. We went into his backyard, and there was this garage. We went inside, but it was all dark. I was scared, but Mr. Toy Man told me it was okay. He turned on some music, and it was real loud.

"I could feel him shuffling around in there. We were standing on something like a gym mat, and every time he moved it slid a little.

"The light comes on and . . . Holy shit." Artice closes his eyes. "Mr. Toy Man is standing there buck-ass naked in front of me. The first thing I notice are all these scars on his body. Fucked-up shit. Then I see he's got a knife. A big-ass OJ knife. Worse thing, though, was the look on his face. Scariest thing I ever seen. He's always been this smiling, happy guy. This was like a demon took over.

"I didn't even notice the first cut." Artice makes a striking motion across his chest. "I had on some baggy, hand-me-down shit, so it didn't go in all that deep. But deep enough. I ran for the fucking door. Toy Man must have thought he locked it, or was too drunk to move fast. I don't know."

Artice pauses for a moment, his breath coming more quickly, his gaze far away. Then he smiles.

"Man, I was out that door and across his yard faster than a cat on fire. He had a fence, but I was a good climber. I remember the sound he made when he hit it like a rhino. Boom!

"He yelled, 'Come back! It's just a game!' Bull. Shit. I wasn't that dumb. I kept running and running until I came to a bus stop and some Mexican lady started screaming when she saw me.

"Next thing you know, I'm in an ambulance and some cop is asking me what happened. I told him I was in Toy Land and a monster took over Mr. Toy Man. So of course they thought I was nuts.

"A couple of days later, they had me drive around in an unmarked car and tell them which house it happened at. But I couldn't say. When I ran, I just ran. I never looked back.

"Counselors decided it was some gang-initiation thing and I was lying. Nine. There are some hard-core motherfuckers out there, but there wasn't no baby gang doing that kind of shit then. But they believed what they wanted to believe. Eventually, so did I."

I speak for the first time in several minutes. "I'm sorry to put you through that again. So, when you painted the picture of him . . . ?"

"That was me trying to warn kids, I guess. But the truth is, I didn't remember much. Little things would come back to me now and then, even years later . . . like the smell of that garage. Shit died in there. And other things—there were jars of shit on the walls. I don't know what, but it wasn't goddamn peanut butter." He lets out a long exhale. "And there you go. Artice versus the Toy Man."

"Jesus Christ." It's all I can say.

"Don't feel bad for me. Feel bad for all the little brothers who didn't want to cheat at Mario Kart."

"And you never found the house again?"

He shakes his head. "When I got older, I'd drive around, trying to find it, with a gun in my lap, looking for that white Caddy. I never found it. I don't know how far I ran that night. It couldn't have been that far. I was bleeding heavy. But far enough for the cops to not find him."

"Do you remember anything? Houses? Landmarks?"

"Sort of. But it's all jumbled."

"What if there was a way to retrace your steps?"

"What do you mean?"

"There can't be that many houses that match that description with the garage and the fence."

"If you got some photos, I'll look at them."

I think for a moment. "We may have something better."

CHAPTER TWENTY-FOUR
SIMULATION

An hour north of Barstow, California, there's a city that looks like something in Afghanistan. Complete with markets, mosques, and even a soccer stadium, it could be mistaken for a thousand places in the Middle East with its desert backdrop.

Located at Fort Irwin, it was built to train US soldiers before they're deployed overseas. There are similar training facilities at other bases, including a three-hundred-acre city in Virginia used for practicing urban counterterrorism tactics—it even has a partial subway.

Since the war on terror began, we've spent billions of dollars building simulations of the places where we might have to send troops. Some of these simulations are virtual.

When I went to work for OpenSkyAI, I was given access to an urban-threat assessment tool that's basically Google Earth from the future. Somewhere in the Northeast, there's a server farm with high-resolution images of every square foot of America (and other countries), complete with in-depth data that effectively creates a 3-D model of whatever you want to look at.

I can pull it up on my phone. As Artice relates certain details, I run a script that finds matches for what he said. We already know the bus stop where he was found. The next step is identifying the house.

I pull up the six closest candidates and create a 3-D run-through for him to watch. The first-person perspective is accurate even down to his height at the time.

I push my phone against the glass and play the locations through for him. The first four don't get much of a reaction. It's the fifth one that tells me we have a hit by the way his pupils dilate.

"That's the motherfucking house!" he yells, getting a stern look from a guard who's about to call our session to an end. He lowers his voice. "Goddamn it. If I wasn't in here . . ."

It's probably a good thing that he is. I'm not sure what he'd do to whoever opened that front door. In his shoes, I'm not sure what I would do, either.

"Artice," I say to get his attention. "It's possible this may not be the house."

He glares at me. "Don't be like them. Don't be like them."

"I'm just saying. Time changes things. The Toy Man may not even live there anymore." There's also the chance that Artice concocted all this. I can't fully rule that out.

Instead of getting angry, he just nods. "So now what? Call the cops? They'll believe you."

"You overestimate the credibility I have with them. I can't just call 911 and tell them I have the location of the Freddy Krueger of Compton based on the testimony of an inmate at county."

He lets out an exhausted sigh. "It's like when the Grim Sleeper was icing all those hookers. One of them even told the cops where it happened."

"She was wrong by one house," I point out.

"And that made all the difference in the world. So what are you going to do? Write an angry tweet? Tell all your white liberal friends how you helped out the poor black boy?"

"I was going to go knock on the front door."

Artice stares at me without blinking those penetrating gray eyes. "Are you fucking nuts?"

"It's not like I'm a nine-year-old kid. If he invites me inside, I'll decline. But I'm betting he's long gone."

"Why is that?"

"Because you got away. If he's smart, he stayed clear of the house for a while and then moved a few months later."

"To where?"

"I think he stayed in the general area, not too far away."

"So how do we find him?"

"Housing records. Utility bills. If this was his house, then he had to leave a trace."

"Yeah . . ." Artice thinks for a moment. "There's one other thing about him. I couldn't quite describe it when I was a kid, but it makes more sense now."

"What's that?"

"He talked funny. Kind of like a white guy, but not. Like he wasn't from here."

"New York?"

He shakes his head. "I didn't know accents back then. There was street talk and TV talk. I learned both. One to talk to my friends. The other to talk to any adult who could make my life difficult in a facility." He pauses again. "Man, I don't think you should be just rolling up there. Wait for me to get out, and we'll both go."

"When is that going to happen?"

"Maybe if you can say I helped get the Toy Man, sooner. Nobody got hurt. It was all a misunderstanding."

I'm not sure if I buy that, but that's not for me to decide. "I have to get something. Some kind of proof. Otherwise it won't mean anything."

"Yeah, well. Once you do, we can show them this." Artice lifts up his shirt and shows a huge scar that goes from his hip to his shoulder.

"Holy shit."

"You got that straight."

"How the fuck did you get away?"

"Fear, man. Fear. It's your best friend." He pauses for a moment. "But you know that. Don't you?"

"I'll show you mine another time."

Artice shakes his head and glances around furtively. "Don't say that in here."

"Oops, sorry."

"Let me know what happens. If you don't, I'll just assume the Toy Man got you. Whatever you do, don't drink the red punch." Artice has slipped back into his jovial persona, which I guess is a good thing for his sanity's sake. "You'll never beat Bowser in Mario Kart."

"Noted."

"Seriously. Watch yourself. Don't think just because you survived one monster you'll survive the next. I'm alive because I kept running *from* them. Not *to* them."

As he walks out of the visiting area, I take heed of his advice. The Toy Man went from a mathematical curiosity to a very real possibility in just a few days.

Artice could be messing with me like those kids back at Rico's house. He might just be a skillful liar who knows how to tell you what you want to hear. Although the only benefit in it for him that I can see is if he's telling the truth.

Finding the Toy Man might help his case and get him out. I don't know if that's overall a good thing for society, but I get the feeling if his life hadn't been such a shit show from the start, he wouldn't be in here.

CHAPTER TWENTY-FIVE
DEED

The title to 17658 Wimbledon has had four owners since it was built. From 1986 to 2005, it belonged to Kevin and Trudy Harrison. From 2005 to 2011, it belonged to a Jeffery L. Washington—this was the Toy Man period. Currently, it is owned by New Castle Property Management.

While normally I would have experienced a eureka moment at discovering the name of the homeowner, I'd already discovered in exploring South Central property records that the name on the deed may not be the real name of the person who purchased the home. There are lots of homes owned by shell companies or people of record who are either fictitious or have no idea their name is on the deed.

This house was paid for by Jeffery Washington in an all-cash transaction. Trying to find anything about Jeffery L. Washington turned out to be fruitless. I strongly suspect that he does not exist.

I couldn't find any example of another Jeffery L. Washington buying a home in the area after that time. Maybe he moved on, but it's more than likely an alias.

Still, it's not a dead end by a long shot. There are all kinds of records, from utility bills to phone calls, that may still be out there for the finding. While I don't have ready access to them, if I can get something strong to connect Artice and Christopher to the property, I might be able to convince even someone as cynical as Detective Corman. But I won't hold my breath.

My next best bet is to talk to the neighbors. The Toy Man had two of them that might have seen something. Of course, this still being South Central, there's a good chance nobody's going to tell me a thing.

After I've done my background search into the house, I give William a call. I don't want him to start kicking in doors, or worse, tell Mathis that we have a suspect, so I just tell him I've been running down some leads and will have more to tell him. Soon, I hope.

"What was that about the Toy Man?" he asks.

I figure I can at least tell him that much. "It's an urban legend some of the kids tell. He pops up every few years."

"And does he have anything to do with Christopher?"

"Maybe. I think he might be a real man." I don't want to tell William that this guy was a kid fiddler and a killer, but he can fill in the blanks.

"And you think he may have messed with Chris?" he says flatly.

"It's a possibility. Some of these guys like to groom kids. See which ones they can foster trust with."

He just sighs, then says after a long moment, "I wanted it to just be some random guy. You know, a drifter who just spotted him."

"I know. Maybe it was. It's just a story." I'm going to spare him Artice's harrowing tale until I know that there's more to it.

We hang up with a promise from me that I'll keep him up to date, which isn't exactly sincere—considering the fact that I'm just a block away from the house where I think his son may have been murdered.

I've driven around several times, watching the house until the scattered streetlights come on and bathe the neighborhood in a jaundiced glow.

I noticed that all the other houses had yard lights triggered by photo sensors, but 17658 did not. With the exception of a faint light coming through the front curtain of the tan, one-story house, the property remains completely dark.

That's not the only peculiar thing: the tallest fence I could find in the neighborhood is six feet. The one at 17658 measures eight, preventing anyone from looking over. There were also lines of shade trees in the backyard visible from the front of the house.

While being located in the middle of a suburb, it feels oddly remote and secure. The fence stretches from the sides of the house to the next property about ten feet away on either side.

On the aerial view, the house sits on a long lot, going all the way back to a service road. The garage, perhaps the one Artice described, sits at the far end. The other garage, the one built into the house, has a lock on the outside and doesn't look like it's opened often.

The biggest mystery to me is the identity of the owner. The house was sold in 2011 for about 20 percent under the going rate in the area, suggesting that it was a private sale—possibly from a homeowner in a hurry—or between two parties that knew each other. Maybe even the same individual.

This is what is making the hair on the back of my neck stand on end: Jeffery L. Washington could still own the home. He could even be in there right now.

Before I get out of my car, I consider my options, of which there aren't that many. The first is to drive to the airport and call Corman with what I know.

But unless the Toy Man answers the door buck naked and covered in blood with a knife in his hand, there's not a lot Corman can do beyond a more wide-reaching records search.

Chances are the Toy Man has erased anything that could connect him to the murders—if he's smart. After Artice got away, that would have been the prudent thing.

Of course, we're talking about a serial killer. He may have a very different idea about what *prudent* means.

I decide I just have to nut up and go knock on the door. I push my Glock and its holster into the back of my jeans under my jacket.

Even after my altercation with Joe Vik, I'm not a big gun guy, but thanks to some clever legal interpretation of our Department of Defense security agreements at OpenSkyAI, I'm allowed to carry anywhere in the US—although a local judge might discourage it.

The question is whether I'm willing to use the gun. Scratch that: it's whether I'll even be in a situation where I have to.

I give the yard another check, then walk up to the door at 17658 and knock.

From inside the house I hear a television being turned down and a dog barking.

Well, at least somebody is home . . .

CHAPTER TWENTY-SIX
BLOODHOUND

The door opens a crack, and a small gray ball of fur comes shuffling out of the house and plants itself at my heels, yapping a warning that I need to vacate the property immediately.

"Eddie!" shouts an old woman from inside. "Leave him alone!"

The dog darts back inside, satisfied that he's done his canine duty. When the door opens wider, I see a short, elderly black woman with large glasses looking up at me.

"Yes?" she asks.

I catch a glimpse inside the house to make sure that there's no naked serial killers ready to come lunging at me—other than Eddie.

"Hi, I'm Theo Cray." I show her my ID, which she grasps and holds on to for a closer look.

"That's not a very good picture, Mr. Cray," she says after letting go.

"I'm not very photogenic."

"Come in. Come in," she offers, holding the door open for me. "Would you like some tea?"

"Uh, okay." I step inside, suspiciously glancing at the space behind the door, wary that I might be walking into something.

The house looks like the furnishings haven't been changed since Clinton was in office. Wood paneling covers the walls of the living room. A large couch sits in front of a big-screen television that appears to be from the Toy Man's era.

As she shuts the door, I notice three rows of locks and one on the inside requiring a key. This sets off an alarm in my head. That's the kind of lock you use to keep somebody inside.

I watch as she goes into the kitchen and pours two cups of tea. The floor is scratched up and the carpet bare in spots.

"I was about to go sit on the back porch," she says, pushing past me with two mugs.

I follow her out to a small concrete pad overlooking a weedy lot of uneven dry earth. She sits and motions for me to take the rusty chair across from her.

"Are you the man from the church they said they'd send by?" she finally asks.

"Uh, no . . . Ms.?"

"Mrs. Green," she says, not at all bothered by the fact that I'm a complete and total stranger who just entered her house.

Eddie sniffs around my feet, then leaves the porch to inspect a patch of dry grass and growl at something. I nervously glance over my shoulder, afraid Mr. Green is about to garrote me.

"Is Mr. Green home, ma'am?"

"Mr. Green is in the Lord's arms now. Bless his heart."

"I'm sorry to hear that. Did you both live here?"

"Oh, no. Mr. Green and I lived in Lynwood. I moved here shortly after he passed."

She seems utterly uninterested in why I'm here, but I need some kind of in to ask questions. "I work for the government. I'm doing a background check on somebody who was applying for a job. I was wondering what you could tell me about the man who lived here before you."

Eddie finds something new to attack and scuffles around in the dirt before dragging his prey to her feet. She reaches down and scratches behind his ears, taking an eternity to answer my question.

"I didn't know the gentleman. I just spoke to a Realtor. He'd moved out when we bought the place."

"I see. Did he leave anything?"

"Just the television."

"Did your neighbors ever mention him? Say anything interesting about him?"

"Not that I recall. I think they said he was hardly ever here and were surprised when I moved in."

That's interesting. It could mean the Toy Man was using this as a kind of safe house—assuming this was ever his house. Maybe this was just where he took his victims.

Eddie jumps up and darts back into the yard to chase after something else he's decided is very important.

"Did the police ever stop by here?"

"What for?"

"To ask questions about the man who lived here before." I still don't know his name, unless it's Jeffery L. Washington.

"No. Not that I recall. Is the man in trouble?"

"They don't tell me much. Was there anything odd about the house? Maybe you found something unusual?"

She gives me a sideways look. "You certainly ask peculiar questions, Mr. Cray."

Eddie marches back to her feet with a stick to chew on.

"Sorry, Mrs. Green. They give me peculiar questions."

She waves it away. "It's no matter. People on the news are doing all sorts of peculiar things. Don't get me started about our president."

"Don't worry, I won't." I look across the yard to the shed. "What do you keep in there?"

"Just old things. Some of Mr. Green's belongings."

I'd love to have a look but can't think of way to ask that doesn't sound weird. "What did Mr. Green do?"

"Twenty years he was in the Marine Corps. Then he worked for the post office. A good man. A good provider."

"You have any children?"

She shakes her head. "No, sir. Just Mr. Green and I." She gives Eddie a pat. "And Eddie."

The dog drops his snack and rubs his jaw against her hand.

I lean over to get a better look at the object covered in saliva, and I'm struck by an observation a paleontologist once made to me: we have far more dinosaur species in the books than there probably actually were.

The problem stems from the era in which we thought of dinosaurs merely as giant reptiles. Lizards have pretty linear life cycles. A baby crocodile looks almost exactly like a full-grown one.

When paleontologists would come across two very different sets of bones, based on the reptile assumption, they'd deduce that this meant that there were two very different species of dinosaur—when in fact it may have just been one, an adult form and a juvenile form.

Although my specialty is computational biology, I know enough human anatomy to suspect that the bone Eddie is chewing on isn't from something that was on a kitchen table or wandered into the backyard after getting hit by a car.

It looks a lot like a child's rib.

I pull a glove from my pocket and reach for the bone. Eddie growls at me but gets pulled back by Mrs. Green.

I hold the dark-brown shard under the dim porch light for a better look as cold water rushes through my veins.

"I kept calling the city," says Mrs. Green. "I told them bones were coming up from my yard after every rainstorm."

I gaze back into the shadows of her yard and see jagged shapes poking out of the ground.

Everywhere.

CHAPTER TWENTY-SEVEN
CONCERNED CITIZEN

When I was on the hunt for Joe Vik—a man whose name I only discovered an hour before he nearly killed me—I learned that life was not like the movies. Law-enforcement investigations take a long time. You can spend hours or days waiting for someone to even talk to you. And even when you have all the pieces of the puzzle and have laid them out for everyone to see, it can take months for them even to acknowledge that they're there.

I had to break some laws to get Vik and do some things I'm not particularly proud about. At one point, Montana prosecutors, frustrated that their suspect was dead and they didn't have anyone to try, seriously considered building a case around me with the idea of making me a scapegoat, claiming I interfered with a nonexistent investigation. Thankfully, pressure from both the family members of the victims I discovered—who were all over television thanking me for bringing them closure—and the governor's office made it clear that I couldn't be painted as the bad guy. But even so, bad blood remained. I'd embarrassed agencies and made more than a few enemies among Joe Vik's friends—of which he had many. Some even in law enforcement, who couldn't reconcile the brutal serial killer with the man who sat at their dinner table.

All of this is going through my head as I dial Detective Corman's number. He's treated me like a nuisance, but not an antagonist. Heck, he even gave me all those other case files, in case I could find something he hadn't.

I've asked Mrs. Green to take Eddie inside in order to keep him from ruining any more evidence. God knows how many human bones he's already gnawed on.

Corman's voice mail picks up. "This is Corman—you know what to do."

I'd run the conversation through my head a half dozen times. I wasn't prepared for this.

I try dialing again. It still goes to voice mail.

Afraid he's shut his phone off for the night, I call 911.

"Nine-one-one, how may I assist you?" asks a woman.

"Hello, I'm at 17658 Wimbledon. There are bones coming out of the ground. Can you send a police car by?"

"Seventeen six fifty-eight Wimbledon?" I hear the sound of typing.

"Correct."

"Okay. It looks like you'll need to take that up with Animal Control. I can redirect your call."

"Wait? What?"

"If you're having a problem with an animal, you need to call Animal Control," she replies.

"Who said anything about an animal?"

"According to our files, there have been eight calls about a nuisance animal at 17658 Wimbledon dragging bones into the yard."

I look down at Eddie and his nose smushed against the glass. Mrs. Green is giving me a knowing look.

I lose my shit. "So you're not bothered that these are human remains? You're totally okay with the fact that I'm looking at enough material for at least three or four bodies?"

She changes her tone, but not in the way I hoped. "Sir, we've sent a squad car by before. Unless you're qualified to make a forensic analysis, I'd appreciate it if you didn't take that tone with me."

My shit loses *its* shit. "Does a fucking doctorate in biology from MIT qualify me? How about four goddamn papers published in *Human Origins*?" I shine my flashlight on a small jawbone sticking out of the earth. "Unless you take a very species-ist definition of what's a human and a tribe of goddamn Neanderthal children got really, really fucking lost, we're looking at human remains! Unless the LAPD wants to come down here and tell me otherwise."

Mrs. Green is nodding her head and giving me a thumbs-up.

Detective Corman is not going to be too happy with me when the press get ahold of this 911 call and the transcript is released. I sound like an asshole, but the emergency dispatch comes across as incompetent.

"Sir, we're sending a patrol car over now. In the meantime, I suggest you calm down."

It takes every bit of effort not to hurl my phone into the next yard.

I'm still standing in the backyard, taking photos of the bones, when blue and red lights splash over the house and onto the tops of the trees.

I've been careful not to step on anything that might break, but I want to be extra sure that I get as many pictures as I can before the crime lab takes over.

The shed is calling to me, but I don't even dare enter the structure until the police have had a chance to examine it thoroughly.

All I need is some trace DNA of mine to fall on the floor of the garage and the Toy Man's attorneys will squeal with glee when it shows up in a report.

I already went through hell with the attorneys representing Joe Vik's estate. The man had a lot of assets and people eager to protect them and his reputation. A friendly prosecutor told me that Joe and his pals might have actually been the center of a methamphetamine ring in the area. Which surprised me not in the least. There were so many weird things going on there.

The sliding glass door opens behind me while I'm squatting down, examining the edge of a pelvis jutting out of the earth. It looked like the last several weeks of rainstorms eroded away the yard—which had probably not been watered since California started curtailing water during the drought, which has me wondering how long it'll be before other secrets start unburying themselves.

"Are you the one who called?" asks a young officer.

White, short blond hair, he looks like he should be in a Boy Scout uniform and seems dangerously malnourished for a cop. Eddie might even give him a good fight.

"Yes, Officer," I reply as I stand up.

He flashes his powerful beam on the bone I was inspecting and stares at it for a moment. "Hmm. Looks like it might be a pig bone. We get those calls all the time."

Not. Again.

He can't see me close my eyes and count to ten. "Officer, with all due respect . . ." Fuck it. "Does that look like the extended ilium you'd find on a quadruped?"

I point to a round shape in the weeds. His flashlight drifts over and casts a blinding glare against the small, dull-yellow dome of a skull with one orbital socket visible.

"Holy shit," he mutters, then starts to walk forward.

I gently grab his forearm before he steps on evidence. "Officer, look down."

He spots the sharp rib bone stabbing out of the dirt. "Fuck . . ."

"No kidding."

He takes a large step back and calls into his radio, "This is 4421. I need Homicide and an ME down here ASAP."

"Affirmative," says a dispatcher.

A moment later a male voice squawks over his radio, "Long Beach, this better not be a *quinceañera* pig they buried in the backyard."

Officer Russell, according to his name tag, turns to me and shakes his head. "Have you ever seen anything like this?"

I have one hell of a story to tell him while we wait for everyone else to arrive.

CHAPTER TWENTY-EIGHT
ANONYMOUS

Who is the Toy Man? Three days after I snatched Eddie's gruesome snack from his mouth, I'm sitting at a conference table in LAPD headquarters as the lead detective, Cheryl Chen, explains the case to me as a courtesy, with an assist from Craig Sibel, an FBI agent out of their Los Angeles office. Corman is nowhere to be found because the discovery at Wimbledon is being treated as a new case.

Projected onto the screen at the end of the room is what I assume will be a horrifying slide show of what they've found so far.

Chen clicks a remote to the first image. Mrs. Green's backyard is sectioned off like an archaeological dig as forensic specialists in white suits stand and kneel on metal platforms, carefully extracting the remains.

"We've found seventeen bodies so far. Many of them are mixed together, so we'll need DNA forensics to confirm that, as well as to identify them.

"The suspect buried them under about a foot of dirt, which was then covered with sod. The problem, as you pointed out in your notes, was that over the last several years, Mrs. Green's not watering the grass and the fact that the house sits on a slight elevation led to gradual erosion as the grass died and seasonal rain fell. This exposed the upper layer, which then was exposed even further as her dog decided to investigate the decomposing bodies."

"How old are the children?" I ask.

"According to our medical examiner, all are between eight and thirteen. Sex is difficult to determine with certainty on the younger ones, but it appears they're all boys."

"How far along is the DNA work?"

"Our labs can answer some specific questions in days, but a broader analysis will take weeks."

"I have access to a certified lab that can do a lot more, a lot faster." Helping me solve the Joe Vik case was a laboratory that specialized in doing forensics for the CIA, identifying terrorists—before and after they were blown up.

"We're very happy with our lab," she says.

"If you want an outside report, they'd be happy to assist."

"Thank you. We'll let you know," Chen replies. In other words: *drop it.*

For the LAPD, this is a delicate matter. Not only do they have a yard full of bodies an old woman tried telling them about eight times— the fact that they only showed up when a white guy made the call makes it worse. But the really problematic aspect is that there are seventeen dead children in one backyard and neither the LAPD nor the FBI ever launched a formal investigation until they were found.

I drove by the house before this meeting. I counted twelve news trucks. I didn't even know there were that many channels to carry the news.

The question everyone is asking: Who was living in the house? Interviews with neighbors are conflicting. There are three different descriptions of a black man seen around, as well as one white man seen less often, but still on multiple occasions.

Chen takes me to the next series of slides. "We've found holes in the walls, possibly used for restraints. As well as the locks on the inside of the doors. Our forensics team has picked up some blood in the house, but that doesn't look like it was the primary killing area."

"The shed?" I reply.

"Yes. The floor and walls had been painted, but we picked up splatter underneath. We've only had enough time to go over a few square feet. Removing blood and tissue from under there takes longer."

She clicks to a rough-looking section of concrete. "The foundation is three feet thick. We found a crack where blood had been accumulating. This could give us a time line from the kills that we can match up with the decomposition of the bodies."

As blood trickled into the crack, it created a kind of sedimentary layer for each child that was murdered. In addition to additional blood samples, it'll give them a secondary time line.

"What about the ceiling?"

Chen clicks to the next slide. The roof of the shed is a collage of Day-Glo splatters. "He didn't bother to conceal that."

"He was in a hurry," I reply. Toy Man was only going to do the least amount of effort he had to so the next homeowners didn't ask any immediate questions, but not enough to fool a dedicated investigation.

This concerns me. Why was he so sloppy? Lonnie Franklin used an RV for a number of his murders and got less careful as he realized the cops didn't care about his victims.

The Toy Man was choosing his victims much more cautiously. Leaving this much forensic evidence around suggests he either suddenly became careless or felt he had little reason to worry.

Maybe the fact that we have no idea who he is, even though there are cops standing in his living room, suggests that there's more to the man.

"That's pretty much what we have so far, which isn't much. All we know is what he left behind."

"What about Artice?" I ask.

"He's been very cooperative. We're working on a sketch of what he recalled and trying to reach out to any other children who saw the suspect at the time. We'll see what the public comes forward and has to say. I suspect we might get another break sooner than later."

I'm not so sure. Even Lonnie Franklin's neighbors were hesitant to talk about him. His best friends suspected there was something going on, but they kept their mouths shut.

Part of the fear in this area is that you never know if a murder is just a random slaying or an ordered hit. Talking to the cops could put you on a list you don't want to be on.

Times have changed a lot in the community since the Grim Sleeper's heyday, but community-police relations are at an all-time worst.

"What is he?" I ask Agent Sibel. "Do you guys have a profile?"

He shakes his head. "Guys who kill in their own home usually don't go through all the trouble of making sure the property isn't in their own name. That's something a hit man would do. But he doesn't fit the profile of that. We've had zero leads from anyone to that effect." He shrugs. "We don't have a clue."

"What about the way the kids were murdered?" I ask both of them.

Chen replies, "We only have preliminary reports. But in a word: savage. These children were cut apart. But there's no evidence of sexual violation at the time of death. Perhaps before, but not after or during."

"Artice says the guy was a molester."

"Yes. But those may have been separate actions for the suspect. He might have molested them and then killed them later out of guilt or fear."

Sibel looks like he wants to say something, so I prompt him. "Your thoughts?"

"It's still unclear. Artice said he and none of the other kids recalled violence—other than when he tried to kill him, which suggests they were separate acts . . . ," he says hesitantly.

"And that's where we differ," says Chen. "I think he may have been grooming boys to be molested and then killing them to conceal the crime, whereas Sibel and his people think that the killing was the primary purpose."

"Molesting boys without violence but then murdering them as an afterthought?" I ask her.

"Correct."

I'm not sure if that jibes with the experience Artice described, but I keep my mouth shut. These are the experts.

Chen turns off the slide show. "We appreciate your help in this investigation."

She says this as if there had been an investigation and I called a tip line. But I let it slide. "Let me know if there's anything else I can do."

"Right," says Chen. "And if you have any other potential leads or ideas, please let me know directly."

Take it to her. Got it. A little territorial, but that's not my problem.

"I'll let you know if my computer models come up with anything else. Of course more data would be useful."

"Unfortunately I'm limited to what I can share with the public."

Ah. I'm public. Technically that's true, but there are also dispensations for bringing in outside experts. She's made it perfectly clear how she wants me to be viewed.

I should let it go. "Detective Chen, do you know how I came upon the bodies at Wimbledon?"

"I believe Artice reached out to you? Or a friend of his?"

Clearly she skimmed through that part of the notes I gave them. "Not quite. I was contacted by the father of a boy who still hasn't been accounted for." I hold my fingers a few millimeters apart. "When I came aboard, the case was this thin. There was zero to build on. But through some effort, I was able to find that house."

"Through the Toy Man story?" Sibel asks.

"Yes. A rumor."

"Mr. Cray," Chen interjects, "we're very grateful for your help. We'll make sure you get the credit you are due. In the meantime we're still trying to see if the killer is out there. Let's hold off on the awards ceremony until then?"

"For fuck's sake," I say. "That's not my point."

"What exactly is your point?"

"I have tools. I have resources. I can help."

"And we have a very capable lab."

"That's about twenty years behind the current state of the art. Ask your lab if they have anyone on staff who can do methylation-marker analysis or can build a biome map."

"We're first-rate in forensic investigation," she assures me.

"I believe you. But I'm talking about tools that will take decades before they're available to you. I can give you access to them now." What I really want to say is that I can give them access to me.

"We'll take that under consideration," she says, politely telling me to fuck off.

I resist the urge to shake my head. "Did you get any prints off Christopher Bostrom's bike?"

She shuffles through her notes. "I don't think we picked that up. But it's been ten years."

"And I promise you nobody has ridden it in that time. Please?"

"Fine," she replies, as if granting me a favor.

Sibel gives her a glance, then decides to speak up. "This hasn't been in the news, but we have gotten prints from the shed. Lots of them."

This is the first time I'm hearing it. "And?"

"Zero matches. We've checked every database. None. And these aren't partials. Full prints."

"So he doesn't have a record?"

"Not with those hands. Every utility bill. Phone record. Everything. It all leads nowhere. Fake names and fake companies. Bank records, zilch."

"How does someone manage that kind of footprint in this day and age?"

He shakes his head. "Usually it'll eventually point back to some law firm or something, but not even that. We know even less than when we started."

"Not quite," I reply.

"What makes you say that?" asks Chen.

"How many people know how to do that? That sounds like a pretty big clue, but you don't need me to tell you that. You got it covered."

I know I'm an arrogant prick. But I think I fucking earned the right.

Let them carry on. I'm not going to sit on the sidelines, because I know he's out there and he's much, much smarter than any of us really appreciates.

Like Joe Vik, he'd been invisible, even though he was killing right in front of everyone.

Now that bodies have begun to surface, his camouflage is showing its weaknesses.

CHAPTER TWENTY-NINE
OVERLOOK

I'm lying on my bed in my hotel room near the LA airport, talking to Jillian, whose face fills the screen of my laptop, backlit by the lights of Los Angeles visible through the window.

Looking at her has a calming effect on me. It's not just because her dark-blonde hair and small-town-hottie looks make my heart race, it's also because we've been through about the darkest thing you could imagine and have a bond I don't think any other couple could under-stand—although we're not technically a couple. We're both still trying to figure out what we are together.

I've spent the last hour explaining everything that happened so far, guilty that I've been out of touch for the past few days.

"So what do you think?" I ask.

"You're an arrogant asshole," she replies.

Got to love that woman. She doesn't mince words. "Other than that part . . ."

"What do you want me to say? You're full of yourself and you need to head back to Austin and let the real cops figure this one out? Because that's actually what I'm feeling you want me to say right now."

"No . . . no . . . I mean. Well? Am I full of myself?"

"Yes. There is no doubt about that. But how many of your smart-guy scientist friends aren't?"

"Fair point. But we also tend to be full of ourselves about areas we have no expertise in," I reply.

"Are you telling them how to lift fingerprints or interview a suspect?"

I don't mention the bicycle because I know what she means. "No. I'm just—"

"Worried that it'll be Joe Vik all over again? Don't be. There was only one of him. But be concerned this is some guy you know nothing about."

"Neither do they. That's what has me concerned."

"What are you afraid of?"

Leave it to her to get to the heart of the matter. "They're going to dig up the bodies, do their tests, and just leave it an open case until something else happens."

"As opposed to?"

"Being proactive."

"Like traipsing through the woods in Montana looking for dead hitchhikers?"

"Basically. I mean, I'm sure they're all competent."

"There's a backhanded compliment from the esteemed Dr. Theo Cray."

"You know what I mean." She's sometimes a little too insightful, knowing which of my buttons to push.

"Tell me what I mean."

"This Toy Man has operated for almost a decade, at the very least. They didn't even know he existed or that his victims were victims. We find his house, but not only is nobody home, his fingerprints—if they're his—don't lead anywhere."

"And you don't think they can catch him."

"I think," I start to explain, "that if he was catchable, they'd be onto him right now. They seriously have zero leads. Not even false ones. Of course that's going to change as people who have no clue call in and send them on wild-goose chases . . . About the only thing going for them is they haven't made public the Toy Man angle to the murders. I'm not sure if that's the best idea, but it'll help them separate who's full of crap from who's not."

"What if other witnesses come forward?" she asks.

"They had plenty over the years. And here's the other problem: this guy's last victim was a couple weeks ago, but the police aren't drawing a connection to that kid. It's like they want to believe that he had his spree, then died or went to prison somewhere else."

"So you think he's still in the area?"

I give her a small shrug. "Depends on the size of the area we're talking about. I've been comparing maps of possible incidents with some other data and discovered something interesting."

"Of course you have," she replies.

"Don't make me spank you."

"Don't tease. What did the brilliant Dr. Cray discover?—asks the breathless grad student in the tight sweater and short miniskirt." She sees how this distracts me and starts to laugh. "How did you ever teach?"

"For one, they didn't dress like that. They looked like homeless people. Second, never mind. Can I explain what I found interesting?"

"Yes, sir."

"When a predator overhunts an area and runs the risk of the population detecting his methods—like a herd of deer getting preyed upon by a wolf—the predator will ideally have a secondary population it can target . . . if there's an opportunity to do so. If the herd starts closing ranks, it'll move on but keep checking back and see if their pattern changes. If the prey situation returns to normal, or if their prey's reaction made it clear they didn't even know how to respond, the predator'll go back to hunting them. In some cases even more boldly, because they're not cognizant of him."

"So the Toy Man backed off but kept an eye on the area?"

"Exactly. Los Angeles was just too target rich to write off if he didn't have to. But I suspect he may have had a B site—an alternate location, either based upon some work or social pattern he had or because he got to pick and choose. The former might create a stronger signal I could find—I mean, he'd be easier to find because he's not in a place where his actions could be so easily masked."

"And they didn't jump all over this?" she asks sarcastically. "Theo, I barely know what you just said, and I was with you when you were searching for bodies and Joe Vik went ballistic."

"Cops aren't dumb. Glenn was smart. Way smarter than he let me believe."

"Yes, but even he didn't get you. And that may have cost him his life. A lot of lives."

We fall silent for a moment, thinking of Glenn.

She speaks first. "So are you asking me for my permission to go after him? It's not mine to grant. Selfishly, I don't want you to put yourself in harm's way again. But I know you. I don't think you'd be able to let it drop—especially if he's out there hurting kids. But . . . ," she says, "I get the feeling that there's something else you're trying to figure out. Another reason why you don't want to go home."

I take a deep breath. "Things at OpenSky are a little complicated. If I haven't screwed things up, there could be a really good opportunity. I don't know if I want it. But it's something that would be good for . . ." Here comes the word. "Us."

She recently spent a week with me, and we managed to do everything except talk about *us*. I think we were both too afraid to find out if the other still thought this was a fling and didn't want to bring it to a premature end with too many feelings, too soon.

"Us, Theo?" she repeats.

I feel myself redden. "I was just trying to say . . ." I stall out, attempting to backtrack.

"I like the way *us* sounds," she says, sending my heart into a flurry as if I'm fifteen.

"I do, too. It's just . . . fuck it. If I go after this asshole, I'm going to have to bend some rules. More than I already have."

"Worse than sneaking into an elementary school and breaking into a school-district office?"

"I neither snuck nor broke into anything. But, yes. I'm going to have to go outside the lines. Like . . ."

"Last time."

"Yes. And if I get caught, that nice little version of us I'd like to see happen may get complicated."

I watch her bite her lip as she thinks this over. "Theo, us is me and you. And you . . . well, I'm still trying to figure you out. And I may never fully understand. Sometimes you're the most thoughtful man. Sometimes it's like talking to a calculator, and I tell myself I need someone warmer. But then I step back and look at the whole picture, a man who risked his life to find out what happened to people nobody cared about, and I realize that your distance isn't because you're far away, it's because you're a thousand feet overhead, trying to look at all the little parts, seeing which ones need to be fixed. And even though it kills me when you're not looking at me, or it feels that way, I love the fact that you're still trying to put things together—to make them better. And I'd never sacrifice that, even if it meant your eyes were always on me."

"So what are you telling me?"

"Get the motherfucker. Stay the hell away from him, but go get him. It's what you do now. And if you get in trouble, I'll be there with either a shotgun or a lawyer."

I love this woman.

CHAPTER THIRTY
PARTICLES

I sit up in my chair in my hotel room and put on my most sincere face, pretending it will carry through the telephone line. Then I dial the number of the medical examiner's office and ask to be connected to Sanjay Shivpuri, the technician in charge of forensic evidence at the Wimbledon house.

"Shivpuri speaking," says an affable voice.

"Hello, Sanjay, this is Theo Cray. How are you doing?" I try to act as informal and friendly as possible.

"Very good. This is a surprise. I was just looking at the notes you sent over. Very helpful. I have to confess, I'm already a bit of a fanboy. I read your paper on extraction of DNA from follicles using detergents. That was great work."

"Guan and his team deserve the credit for that. All I did was clarify the lab work," I reply, trying to sound modest.

"Well, I appreciate it. Is there any other research I can look forward to?"

"Actually, I've been working on using iron nanoparticles to fix fragmentary DNA before doing a detergent bath. I've been able to extract much longer chains, and it may even have some applications in calcified specimens as well." It never hurts to dangle something tantalizing in front of someone you need a favor from.

"Very interesting . . . when will that paper come out?"

"I don't have a timetable yet. I'm still working on the process."

"At which facility?" he asks.

"My kitchen table." I haven't had a lab of my own since I skipped classes to hunt a serial killer.

"Your kitchen table? Well, if you want a collaborator, I have lab access at UCLA. Maybe I could help."

As a matter of fact, fanboy . . . "About that. Maybe we could field-test some new techniques on the forensics from the Wimbledon house?" *Me and you, pal, high-fiving like best buds do.*

"No," he replies flatly.

"Er, no? It would just be a comparison analysis. Not even a lab on record."

"I'm sorry, Dr. Cray, but Detective Chen was in my lab less than an hour ago and said that if I even said the word *DNA* to you, she'd not only have my balls, I'd lose my job. I'm partial to all three. But as a show of respect to you, I did say the word *DNA*, so understand that my heart is with you, if not the rest of me."

Well, this did not go the way I was hoping. It sounds like Detective Chen is determined to prevent the infamous Dr. Cray from having anything more to do with the case.

She's probably afraid of what happened in Montana. Even though I didn't run to the press and did as I was asked, my involvement was well known, which also complicated things for their forensics people, who had to clearly establish their own clear lines of research, separate from mine.

"I totally understand. The last thing I want to do is to interfere. But hypothetically, let's say if you had some gene sequences of the victims, and maybe, I don't know, extracted DNA from a semen sample of the suspect, and that information ended up in a file that was sent to an e-mail address that didn't belong to me . . ."

"Was that a question, Dr. Cray? Because the answer to that very circumstantial hypothetical is that Detective Chen knows about this thing we call e-mail and was very, very specific to me about what I was not supposed to do, as well as the means by which she would sever the most precious parts of my anatomy if I did so."

"So that's a no?"

"Emphatically."

"All right, last hypothetical: let's say you received some prepublication information from a cutting-edge research institute located in a certain Austin kitchen that described a few useful techniques that even the FBI labs were unaware existed?"

"I'd consider it my responsibility to investigate them," he replies. "And keep the results to myself."

Ugh. "Well, I guess that's better than nothing."

"It's all I can do. I wish it were otherwise, but you have to see it from Detective Chen's point of view. Should we catch this man, we can't have any confusion regarding forensic evidence—especially from someone as . . . controversial as you."

"I appreciate that," I reply half-heartedly.

"Also know that, between you and me, other than Detective Chen's threatening workplace attitude, she is very good. One of our best. They put her on this for a good reason. She's one of the few detectives we can tell actually understands the things we put in our reports. She's never lost a case because she gave the prosecutors bad forensic data."

Which is why she doesn't want crazy Doc Cray monkeying around with her evidence. I get it, but it frustrates me.

I bid Sanjay goodbye and hang up to go fill William in on what I can.

"But you're the best in the world at this kind of thing," he says as we stand in his kitchen, commiserating over the state of things.

"Actually, no. I'm not a forensic investigator. I don't know most of the techniques they use. My specialty has been looking at what others weren't doing and finding something interesting there."

"And last time you were able to collect all the evidence you wanted because you were on the scene way before them," William replies.

"Yes. If I took anything from Mrs. Green's backyard, that would have been tampering. One of the first questions Detective Chen asked me was if I took any samples. She even threatened to search my hotel room and offered me amnesty if I admitted it up front."

"But you didn't?"

"No. Maybe it would've been worth the risk. I don't know."

William picks up our empty bottles and throws them into the garbage, then takes the bag out of the wastebasket. "Let me take care of this."

I follow him through his house as he collects his trash. "I'm not sure if there's anything there to be found, but starting with DNA can be helpful for me. And if there's the odd chance the Toy Man left some of his own—maybe cut himself and got his blood on their clothing—that could give me enough information to make a 3-D model of what he looked like."

"Can they do that?" he asks, emptying his bathroom wastebasket.

"Sort of. The problem with police forensics is that most of what they do is geared toward what's admissible in a court of law. They don't want to walk in front of a judge with a procedure that has a fifty percent false-positive rate." I hold the front door open for him.

"Why would anyone?"

"Not in court. But if you pull one hundred random people off the street and fifty-one turn up positive, you can rule out forty-nine and focus on the others, using a more precise but complicated tool."

"You're a very clever man. Too bad we don't have any DNA or whatever for you to look at. Is there any chance of going back to her yard after they clear out?"

I shake my head, following William outside. "They'll be there for weeks. Even then, it'll be under a court seal. I'd be committing a felony."

"Get that for me?" He points to the trash can by the side of his house.

I lift the lid so he can drop the bag inside. "Too bad I didn't take a few souvenirs. Of course, the last time I took something out of coroner's truck—actually swabs from a dead girl—I ended up in the hospital with a fractured jaw."

"You're certainly a driven man."

"Sometimes." I drop the lid back down.

"Push that down tighter. I don't want anything getting in there and making a mess."

I pick the lid back up and stare at it for a while, my mind racing with what he just said.

"Theo?"

"Yeah?" I respond automatically. "Say, do you know where I could get some night-vision goggles?"

"Why? You plan on going night hunting?"

"Actually, close, very close. And we'll need a McDonald's for bait."

CHAPTER THIRTY-ONE
RAIDERS

Although the news trucks and police vans left, there's still a patrol car in front of the house at Wimbledon with an officer inside to make sure that the crime scene doesn't get contaminated while the technicians are off duty.

Barricades and tape make a perimeter all the way to the edge of the yard. In the field across the street, there are more barricades, cordoning off an area for the press to set up during the day.

I glance down at my map in the passenger seat of William's Chevy Malibu as he passes the patrol car, checking off a couple of circles I'd made.

"Want me to do another pass?" he asks.

"No. He's probably used to rubberneckers trying to get a look at the house, but we don't want to attract more attention than we need to. Slow down here."

As William turns the corner, I roll down my window and toss my french fries into the yard next to the Wimbledon house.

"You're killing me. Those smelled amazing."

"That's the point," I reply. "The cooking oil they use sets off our olfactory senses designed to seek out foods with high fat. We're programmed to be addicted. Add in salt and the fructose in ketchup, and it's the perfect food—if you're a Neolithic caveman getting all his other nutrients by eating gallbladders and animal intestines."

"Your girlfriend must love your pillow talk," William says, shaking his head.

"I'm not allowed to use any words with more than two syllables after midnight," I joke. "Park here."

William stops the car at the corner at the end of the street before the back alley that goes behind the house. Yellow tape and barricades have blocked off the back area as well, probably to prevent news crews from sticking their cameras over the fence.

"Now what?" asks William.

"You stay put. One of us will have to be able to pay the bail for the other." I climb over into the back seat and slide the night-vision goggles over my eyes.

"Somebody's gonna get shot tonight," he grumbles.

"You offered."

He turns the engine off to watch me.

"Actually, turn it back on and put your phone in the holder by the windshield. You'll look like an Uber driver waiting for someone."

It's barely audible, but I think I hear him mumble something under his breath about white people and their Uber obsession. I have noticed that a surprising number of complications people face in social situations end up with an Uber-related solution.

I keep my head low to the back of the seat so I can see over, but to any passing car it's not obvious that there's some night-vision-goggle-wearing weirdo watching a patch of grass.

"How long do you think it will take?" he asks, sounding curious, not impatient.

"I think I see a pair of glowing eyes scoping out the fries right now."

I spot them peering out from under some brush on the opposite side of the street from where I dropped the food. I knew one had to be around, most likely choosing the safest spot where he could watch the neighborhood but get away quickly.

"Here he goes . . ."

The raccoon does a low-to-the-ground crawl across the street, like a soldier trying to avoid a sniper.

He reaches the fries, sniffs, and looks around to make sure he's not being watched, then wolfs down a bunch.

After a few bites, he grabs onto more than he can eat and starts to walk through the grass opposite from where he came, making me realize it's a she.

"We have a mama raccoon. Looks like she's bringing some food to the babies."

Eyes peer in my direction as she hears me talking.

"She sees me," I whisper.

I don't move, waiting for her to decide there's no immediate threat. After a minute, she continues her path, straight toward us.

"She's coming this way," I say quietly.

"Are you afraid? Should I start the car?" William quips.

I have to bite the side of my cheek to keep from laughing. It's bizarre how humor works. Here we are, a hundred feet from a house of death, where William's son most probably met a horrific end, and we're joking about a raccoon.

I squint my eyes as a car passes us, blinding me for a moment.

"Damn it. She's gone." The raccoon vanished as the car approached.

"Try again? More fries? Or maybe we get her a Happy Meal for the kids?"

His voice goes soft at the last part of the sentence, probably at the resurfacing of a painful memory.

"No. She won't do that twice in one night. The difference between an animal like a raccoon and a fish is that a fish will come back to the same hook after a few minutes. Again and again, until it's caught. A raccoon is more cautious."

"You're like a walking Discovery Channel."

"They actually asked me if I wanted to host a show on biology and serial killers," I reply.

"What did you say?"

"I politely told them to go fuck themselves."

"Did they offer more money?"

"No . . ." I notice something at the edge of the sidewalk. "Wait here," I say as I hop out of the car.

I'd noticed a small gap in the curb where it appeared there was some kind of storm drain—something of a rarity in Los Angeles.

I squat and shine my light into the gap, and I'm greeted by three pairs of glowing eyes and a hissing mama raccoon.

The family is sitting on a pile of dead grass, twigs, and what looks like a femur.

I feel bad for evicting a single working mother, but circumstances demand it. I take the squirt gun from my pocket, give her room to escape, and spray her right in the face.

She darts out of her hovel with babies following behind and scurries across the street to another safe spot.

When I look back into the drain, there's another pair of little eyes staring back at me. I turn and see Mama peering from her new spot, having done a head count and realized she came up short.

Lucky for her, I bought a pair of welding gloves. I reach down, pick up the little cub, and carry her over to her mother. The baby darts into the bushes and they all scurry away, one happy family again.

Which is more than what I can say for the relatives of what's left in the dry storm drain.

I have William back the car up so that I'm not directly in the line of sight of the cop as I scoop the contents of the nest into the big white paint buckets I brought along for this purpose.

I have to stretch my arm all the way down in there to get as much as I can. Even a tiny fourth distal phalanx, aka a pinkie bone, could yield DNA of the victim, and if there's a fingernail still attached, it could reveal something about the killer if he managed to get scratched.

I don't examine everything as I scoop it up—I'm too focused on not having the police officer walk over and ask questions.

While I'm technically not violating the law, at least as far as I can tell, they might interpret that differently if they realized they missed some important forensic evidence.

It's their own damned fault and the reason why I don't have the highest confidence in their approach. While fences may mean something to people, to my raccoon pals and Mrs. Green's dog, they're illusory constructs.

Just because Toy Man killed his victims within his property line, that doesn't mean they all stayed there.

To an opportunistic scavenger that has to rely on a variety of food to feed her young, the bones and decaying flesh of a human child make no difference.

CHAPTER THIRTY-TWO
SAMPLE BIAS

Although William offered me the use of his house to do my lab work, the threat of DEA or IRS agents storming through his door loomed at the back of my mind. I didn't want to be sitting there with a magnifying glass in one hand and a child's decomposing skull in the other as they raided.

Instead, I opted to rent a suite at the LAX Marriott. While performing a forensic examination in a hotel room is less than ideal, I'd had some prior experience at making my own mini clean room in the field and felt I could extract what I needed with minimal contamination.

Just in case a hotel maid decided to ignore the **DO NOT DISTURB** sign I'd taped to the door, I put a sign on the inside of my room next to my samples that read, **MOVIE PROPS: DO NOT TOUCH.**

In the town that invented *CSI* and *NCIS* and has turned the decomposing flesh of murder victims sitting on lab counters into a dinnertime affair, I figured this would be a passable explanation.

My first order of business was to remove the contents of the buckets inside the tent I'd created over the desk and place each distinct item into a double-lined plastic bag, cataloging it.

In the event that I found more bones than the femur that had caught my eye, I wanted to be able to enable the medical examiner to have a clear idea of what came from where when I presented them with the materials—anonymously, of course.

As I pulled each item from the bucket, I gave it a bath in a washbasin using purified water and then sifted through the grime, looking for fingernails and tiny little ossicles from inside the ear.

William went home when he realized that this was going to be a very long and tedious process. Although he feigned interest as I explained how you could extrapolate sewer placements from a soil map, I lost him when I started in about locating old streams and lake beds, even in radically changed topography.

It was past three when I had identified all the distinct bones from the storm drain. There were eleven of them. Almost all fingers.

It appeared the mother raccoon had managed to steal away with a child's hand or two, or possibly a number of different fingers.

There was also the femur and several fragments that appeared to be from a tibia and an ulna, although I couldn't be entirely positive.

After taking photographs of everything using a digital camera that in theory wouldn't be traceable to me, I began the extraction phase.

Using a small jeweler's drill and a special polymer seal to avoid contamination with oxygen, I removed three samples from each fragment, leaving plenty of area for the medical examiner to get their own material from an uncontaminated section of each bone.

Part of me wanted to play a prank on Sanjay by fixing DNA samples from a Neanderthal sequence inside a gelatin and using it to replace the bone marrow of one sample.

Another part of me realized this is absolutely the worst idea of all ideas and decided I needed to call it a night.

I placed my control samples in a cooler with ice and packed the rest into a thermal bag and then dialed the number of a courier service used primarily for shuttling around bearer bonds, forensic information used by intelligence agencies, and memory drives full of information deemed too sensitive to send over the Internet or with a common carrier like FedEx or UPS.

A middle-aged man dressed in a suit and carrying a leather shoulder bag met me in the lobby and we did the handoff.

In seven hours, the sample would be in a lab in Virginia, and I would have results by the end of the day. Thankfully, I've done some favors for the lab owner and won't actually have to pay for it. I could probably clone a dinosaur for what that kind of lab work would cost. If the LAPD decides to prosecute me, I'll ask for an invoice and wave that in front of the judge.

While there's not much these DNA results can tell me that the LAPD won't uncover from their own, we do have some special tests that can see if certain genes are active and detect methylation and few other ways DNA is expressed—all in an effort to give us much more accurate data about what the victims looked like: this was one of the most critical reasons for the lab even existing.

While regular old DNA strands can put you in the ballpark for appearance, there are a half dozen other factors that determine how those genes are expressed. Put simply, most of the code is in the AGTC-style instructions, but some also clings to the surface.

I allow myself to get some sleep before my fatigued brain thinks up more hilarity that would send me to federal prison and get me forbidden from ever setting foot any place that has a microscope.

I'm so tired I don't even notice the smell of death as I drift off.

CHAPTER THIRTY-THREE
WAKE-UP CALL

Before the discovery of DNA—the molecule that serves as the primary carrier for genetic information, along with the origins of life itself—heritability was the biggest mystery in biology. From Darwin's finches to Mendel's peas, we could tell there was some unseen force controlling what was passed down from parents to children. And the closer we looked, rather than finding out the rules were governed by some mystical arbitrary force, the more we found that inheritance was mathematical and often very predictable.

When Watson and Crick were able to get enough usable information from X-ray crystallography to image the structure of DNA itself, we finally had the missing piece. But that puzzle piece was a mystery of its own. We expected to find simple bits of code that determined how smart or how tall you would be; instead we found genes that sometimes related to those factors and sometimes, infuriatingly, did not.

DNA wasn't a simple recipe book that could be readily understood. Great swaths of it were more akin to highly compressed instructions or spaghetti computer code thrown together in an ad hoc manner as evolution deemed necessary.

In our search for an explanation of life that didn't require a hands-on architect, we succeeded, but we also found out that when you take away the giver of order, you also lose the order.

Scanning through the bar graphs and readouts of the first DNA sequence e-mailed to me from the lab, I can see the messy, haphazard collection of instructions that make up a human life. While some would argue that the fact that this almost random pattern is proof of a miracle, I'd point out that by that logic, every living thing that manages to be born is a miracle—and if we're all miracles, then nobody is, because the word has lost its meaning. Life works or it doesn't.

This life met an untimely end, not through some fault of his own DNA—and I know that he was a male—but because there was some fault in either someone else's DNA or the environment from which he came.

Victim A was between seven and twelve years old, according to the length of the telomeres attached to the DNA strands. Assuming proper prenatal nutrition—which is not a given, considering the backgrounds of the children the Toy Man selected—he would have been about average height. He has the gene most commonly associated with longevity and male-pattern baldness. I have that gene, too. My hairline hasn't moved, and it remains to be seen whether my life meets an early end or not.

Ethnically, he has the mutations for various groups. While he's predominately African, he also has genes from the Middle East, Ireland, and central Italy. His skin would have been light compared to his ancestors who were pure African. He has the blue version of the HERC2 gene and the green version of the gey gene, giving him green eyes.

This is an unusual trait from someone from African ancestry, but given his Northern European roots, not that rare . . . Something is calling out for attention in the back of my mind.

I pull up the profile of Victim B and scan through his DNA. Very similar ethnic background to A, but he has Lebanese and Scandinavian genes. Most interesting: he also has blue HERC2 and green gey.

These two victims are not closely related, according to their genetics. The odds of shared eye-color genes are . . .

I pull up Christopher Bostrom's photo on my computer. Green eyes! What about Artice? His were gray, almost silver. That's an exceptionally rare gene—actually a gene combination involving OCA2, which we still haven't fully grasped, one more of those maddening details about genetics. Some eye-color genes play by strict rules; others are controlled by other factors we don't yet comprehend.

At least three of the Toy Man's victims had green or silver eyes. What about Victim C?

He doesn't have the genes for green eyes, but he does have an odd version of OCA2. Maybe he had some discoloration of his eyes, too?

It's too much of a coincidence to ignore. I call Sanjay at the LAPD lab.

"Sanjay," he replies.

"It's Theo. Quick question: Did you get your DNA sequences back?"

"I thought we had this conversation," he replies.

"I'm not asking you for them. I want you to check something. Or rather tell you to look for something . . ."

"All right. But this has to be one-way? Okay?" There's a pause as he clicks on his keyboard. "What am I looking for? I have the first file open."

"Check for HERC2 and green gey. You know where they're located?"

"I can find them. Okay . . . green eyes? Didn't Christopher Bostrom have green eyes?"

"Yes, he did."

"Huh. So does the first one I looked at. What are the odds?"

"That's what I'm trying to find out. Pull up another sequence."

"Okay. Huh . . . HERC2 and green gey. That's weird . . ."

I feel the adrenaline rushing. Either he pulled up the same first two samples I did, or up to four of the victims had green eyes.

"All right. Now pull up another."

"Just a second. I only have eight right now. Okay, here we go. Um, nope. Brown HERC2."

"Okay. Maybe it's not a hard-and-fast rule with him, but try the others."

"All right, looking at a fourth. No green eyes here. Checking five and six." A minute later. "Negative. It's still an interesting cluster. Two green-eyed kids."

"And Artice. He has silver eyes."

"Our man has a type. That's for sure. The problem for him is there are only so many of them to go around."

Something about what Sanjay said has me racing through my head. "Hold on a second." I type into my computer and research something, making sure I have the sequence right. "Do the others have less common variations on OCA2?"

"Let me look . . . just a minute. Huh . . . they do. That's really . . . really weird. The other six samples all have similar mutations."

"That's because green eyes aren't his number one preference," I reply as this puzzle piece comes into focus.

"Wait, OCA2 . . . that controls what?"

"Lots of things. But the mutated version you're looking at is found in one very distinct trait, probably the most standout visible mutation someone can have: albinism."

I hear an intake of breath on the other end of the line. "This is big," says Sanjay. "I have to call Chen. How did you come by this insight?"

"Sorry, can't tell you."

I hang up so he can tell his superiors that there may be a big break in the case and a way to identify which missing-children cases might be related to the Toy Man.

If our killer's been operating elsewhere, this could help pin it down.

Already Predox has indicated that there's probably a predator in Houston, Atlanta, Denver, and Chicago. I tell it to do a keyword search for albinism and a few other disorders that could cause a distinct appearance, like red hair on an African American.

An hour later, I'm scanning through the results when there's a loud knock at my door.

"Do not disturb, please," I shout over my shoulder. I still haven't boxed up the samples I collected. I need to get those anonymously to the LAPD forensics lab as soon as possible.

The knock is louder the second time.

"Hold on." I get up, barefoot and wearing just my jeans and T-shirt, and head to the door.

When I open it, Detective Chen is standing there with two uniformed LAPD officers, and none of them looks very happy.

She shoves a sheet of paper in my face. "I have a search warrant for these premises and a warrant to put you under arrest if I find proof of evidence tampering."

I glance backward at my mini lab and the specimens of dead children still inside their plastic bags, all lined up in nice little rows.

Fuck.

CHAPTER THIRTY-FOUR

Inquisition

I'm sitting at a table in an interrogation room. It's not a conference room, because the table is too small and the ring bolted into the side closest to me is clearly meant for handcuffs to go through.

Thankfully I'm not currently in a pair. Although, since the last time I found myself restrained I ended up in a vehicle that got knocked off the road by a man who wanted to kill me, I've spent a few hours learning the finer arts of handcuff escape from a guy in Austin who makes YouTube videos on the topic. I've also been taking after-hours self-defense lessons from a former MMA champion turned med student—in return, I'm helping him pass his boards—which I hope will remain theoretical knowledge only.

Chen and the detective next to her, Raul Avila, are, by my surroundings, making very clear their intentions—well, at least how seriously they want me to take them—but I'm still not clear on their actual motivations.

What I do know is that their ability to get a search warrant so quickly means that they have a prosecutor and a friendly judge available on call.

I also know the last time I found myself in a similar situation I couldn't keep my mouth shut and came precariously close to getting charged with homicide.

While the forces of light and goodness are on my side, Chen doesn't see it that way right now. She wants to know how I got my own DNA samples.

Even though I took them from a public street and have a ready explanation, I know to keep my mouth shut. Since the moment she shoved that search warrant in front of me, I haven't said a thing except, "Phone call."

"Dr. Cray, when did you collect those samples? Before you called 911 or after?"

"Phone call."

"You may not need a phone call if you can clear this up. Just answer that question."

"Phone call," I repeat, this time into the glass eye of the camera mounted at the other end of the room watching me.

"You've been very cooperative before; unfortunately, you were given strict instructions that you ignored."

I simply stare into the space between the detectives.

"You talk to him," she says to Avila.

"Dr. Cray, it's critical that we establish a clear chain of evidence. This kind of tampering can ruin our entire case," says Avila.

"Phone call." I want to tell them that my samples are outside their chain of evidence and were never even declared as such, but doing that would start me down a perilous path.

Chen is getting frustrated. "We can let you walk out that door in an hour. Or we can formally press charges and by the time a lawyer is able to get you an arraignment tomorrow—if then—your name is going to be in the papers with the words *evidence tampering*."

I say nothing, but this makes me smirk involuntarily. We both know that's the last headline she wants with this case. That would only help a defense attorney trying to throw out all the forensic evidence.

I think she catches my reason for my reaction and changes her pitch. "We can charge you with a number of things. Theft of body tissue. Health violations. Trespassing. There are several felonies. We're talking real time. Not fines." She turns to Avila. "Right?"

"Easily. But we can also help you out if you give us some explanations. What do you say?"

"Phone call."

Chen goes red. "You know, the more time we spend in here, the less time we're out there tracking this suspect down."

I break and mutter, "No shit."

Avila gives me an exasperated look. "Fuck this guy."

"Fine, Dr. Cray, have it your way. We're going to have you booked. You'll get to spend the night in jail with some real nice pieces of work. And tomorrow, maybe if you're lucky, you'll get an arraignment, and if you can find an attorney you trust more than our public defender, you might be out in a day or so. Meanwhile, we'll let the press make up whatever story they want about what we found in your hotel room that caused all this."

"Can we use a broad term on the booking, like *possession of contraband*?" Avila asks Chen, trying to intimidate me.

I sit there as stoically as possible. What they don't understand is that the only reputation I ever cared about died a while back.

Chen knocks on the door, and a deputy comes in and places me in handcuffs.

As I'm being walked toward the processing area, Chen calls out to me, "Don't even bother trying to reach me. I'm done with you."

I spend the next hour going through the humiliating procedures of being processed. Most of it involves sitting in plastic chairs next to a rogues' gallery of misfits, waiting for my name to be called and to be walked through various rooms, and getting fingerprinted, photographed, and subjected to a very thorough but not quite medical search for contraband.

Finally I'm led into a small cubicle with a telephone and allowed to make my phone call.

While I have an attorney in Montana who has helped me navigate some of the lingering aftermath of Joe Vik, he wouldn't be much help in Los Angeles.

So instead of calling a lawyer, I do one better: I call my friend Julian Stein. Julian is a venture capitalist, an ardent supporter of the sciences, and an iconoclast not afraid of holding unpopular opinions.

"Hey, Theo! What's up? Did that lab work help you out?"

"You could say that . . ."

"Uh-oh. What happened? Is this one after you, too?"

"No. Worse. The cops. Have a good lawyer?"

"Are you in jail now?"

"Yep. Just got booked."

He switches me onto speakerphone, and I can hear the sound of him tapping on the phone. "Los Angeles Police Department?"

"That's the one."

"What is it? Almost nine o'clock?"

"If I could have someone tomorrow for the arraignment, that would be great."

"Fuck that. You're going to sleep in your own bed tonight."

"That's in Austin . . ."

"Well, I could send a jet."

"I just need a lawyer."

"One second." More tapping. "She's on her way."

"Already?"

"Yes, sir. Mary Karlin. Heard of her?"

"Yeah. She's the trial lawyer you see on CNN and FOX. Kind of an attentionmonger?"

"Yep. That's why you want her. It's not for what she can do in the courtroom—it's more for what they'll do when they see her coming."

CHAPTER THIRTY-FIVE
JUSTICE

Two hours later, I'm in the passenger side of Mary Karlin's red Tesla Model X as she rapidly weaves through traffic, making me pray Elon Musk's engineers are as good as I've heard.

A petite fifty-year-old with bright-red hair and a mouth that doesn't stop, she barged through the police station with a US marshal and had me free before I even had a chance to take my shoes off. It was a whirlwind that still has me confused.

"You have Justice Davenport to thank. He was the one that ordered you released."

"Did he owe you a favor?"

"Ha!" She swerves past another Prius. "Hardly. He hates me. I just told him that if you had to spend the night in jail, I was going to have a press conference waiting for when you got out, during which I would explain how the LAPD booked you because they were embarrassed by how badly their investigation was going and wanted a ready scapegoat if they fucked up the prosecution."

"Huh. I didn't think about it that way."

"I have no clue if that's what they're up to. But it was enough to motivate them. So why *did* they arrest you?"

"You mean you got me out without even knowing?"

"I read the booking. It was rather vague. Which did them no favors. They stepped on their own dicks. You don't have to tell me, but I am your attorney and I'm as curious as hell."

"I took some material I found in a clogged storm drain near the Wimbledon house."

"Public street?"

"Yes."

"Oh, fuck, that's good. Clogged? That's an EPA violation the city committed. If it's a poor neighborhood, I have another federal recourse. Go on . . ."

"Well, I found some bones and extracted some DNA to do my own analysis."

"I love this!" she says as we speed down the HOV lane. "So it didn't come from their crime scene?"

"No. They didn't even know it was there."

"Do they know where it came from?"

"No. I kept my mouth shut. Detective Chen is under the impression I took it from the Wimbledon house either before or after I called the police."

"Did she ask you before if you had any other evidence?"

Chen asked me that several times, worried that I'd collected samples like I did in Montana. "Yes. Repeatedly. I told her no. That's the truth."

"I'm going to request the video of your questioning. She'll hate that. But the fact that you didn't even take anything from the scene of the crime—even before it was a crime scene—makes it a no-brainer. She'd never be able to hold you on that."

"Should I have told her? Maybe I could have saved us all some trouble."

"Fuck no! You never, *ever* know what they're going to try. You were a good boy in keeping your mouth shut. So these samples, what are they?"

"Bones."

"Gross. And they seized them from your hotel room?"

"Yep."

"Did she say where they were being impounded?"

"Actually, I think they sent them to the lab handling the Wimbledon case."

"Ooh! They fucked up," Mary says excitedly. She punches a button on her car's screen.

"What's up?" asks a young woman.

"Get me Davenport," she says.

"One second."

Mary turns to me before deciding to focus on driving, "That's your property. They can't enter it into evidence or even look at it in context with the Wimbledon case under the warrant they served you with."

"I want them to have it."

"So do I, but not if it means using it as a threat against you."

"Now what, Karlin?" says a gruff older man's voice.

"It seems your LAPD detectives seized some property with a sham warrant and have already sent it over to the Wimbledon lab."

"So?"

"So? Well . . . if you don't want anything that could be of value thrown out, I suggest you call Judge Lau and tell him he needs to have his detectives unfuck this, ASAP. They've already threatened to throw the book at my client—who, by the way, found his DNA thingies in a drain on public property nowhere near the house. I'm already talking to Kleiner about a wrongful-arrest lawsuit."

"No, you're not. He's sitting here with me."

"Well, I have him on speed dial. Same thing." She asks me, "Did they take anything else?"

"My computer and my gun."

"Clown show. Hear that? If Lau is there, I suggest you advise him on how to fix this."

"Go fuck yourself, Karlin."

"I have to. There's no one man enough in this town to do it right." She presses the "End Call" button.

I just stare at her, confused. I have no idea what just transpired.

She sees my expression. "You know the expression 'if you pull a gun, you better be prepared to use it'?"

"Yes . . ."

"They bluffed big-time. Chen and whoever decided to intimidate you. If I had to bet, it was actually Grassley, the prosecutor who's lining up for this, that told them to get you in line. The problem is, they treated you like a perp, not a concerned citizen. Which was not only disrespectful, it backfired."

"But is this going to affect the case?"

"There's no effect. You'll probably have your stuff delivered tonight by LAPD."

"I meant the Wimbledon case. Is it going to affect that? Because that's what matters."

"Oh, that. Right. I forgot you're an honest-to-goodness do-gooder. No. They were up in your business because they think they have somebody and wanted to shut you up."

"Wait? They *have* somebody?"

"You didn't hear it from me, but they've filed for extradition orders from Brazil. I think they found a fingerprint and a blood match with someone already in jail down there."

"Holy shit."

"They got lucky. Some contract killer the gangs used. He got caught by the Brazilians a few months back."

"Wait, a few months? That doesn't make sense. The last victim we know about went missing only a month ago."

She shakes her head. "I don't know about any of that. But they think they have the guy."

"I think they're wrong."

Mary pulls in to the driveway of my hotel and puts the car in park. "I'm not sure what to tell you, other than they aren't going to want to listen to you. Let them bring this guy in. If not all the evidence fits, hopefully it'll shake out."

"But that could be months . . ."

"Easily. You've done what you can."

"I don't know about that. The real guy's still out there."

"Maybe. But what I do know is that the next time Chen knocks on your door, she's going to be very, very thorough—possibly going as far as entrapping you. My professional advice is to stay clear. I can only pull my magic tricks so many times."

I open my door. "Thank you. Um . . . how does billing work?"

"This one is on me because you're fighting the good fight. Next time I send Julian a fat invoice. Have a good night. And if they don't bring your computer by breakfast, call me. Oh, and I'll figure out a way to tell them to keep the DNA-thingie stuff."

As she drives off, I try to figure out how I need to proceed. This Brazilian connection may or may not change things, but I can't wait to find out.

Before the knock on my door, Predox was flagging something, a potential pattern I hadn't been aware of before, which could make matters even more urgent than they already are.

CHAPTER THIRTY-SIX
NEW REALITY

As I sit in front of my rapidly returned laptop, looking at the whirling bands of colors and trying to decide what questions to ask Predox, I'm reminded of one of the gifts of science: when you discover a new truth, you also gain a new way of looking at things that can change your perspective.

Newton's new math made it possible to discover the orbital cycles of heretofore unknown worlds. Einstein's more refined science of relativity, which took into account how space could be warped, allowed us to understand why Newtonian mathematics couldn't accurately predict the orbit of Mercury so close to the sun.

More recently, when astronomers looked at a three-dimensional map of the icy bodies that make up the distant Oort Cloud of the outer solar system, they noticed a peculiar pattern: objects appeared to be clustering toward one side, like water in a tilting bowl, acting as if something were pulling them.

This lead to the theorization of a previously undiscovered planet in our solar system—which would have been called Planet X had astronomers not decided that Pluto, the original planet nine, didn't quite qualify as a planet.

This new Planet Nine, while still hypothetical, has a growing amount of data supporting its existence. The astronomers who made this observation and fully accepted its reality made yet another discovery: for years, scientists had observed that the sun had a particular tilt of almost three degrees compared to the plane of the solar system.

There was no accepted explanation, other than maybe that's just the way the solar system settled—like a house on a slight incline. However, the Planet Nine astronomers realized that, if there were a massive object in the far reaches of the solar system, its effect on the inner system wouldn't be negligible. Like an immensely long lever, it would create a slight tilt on the inner planets, making it look like the sun was tilted, when it was actually us . . . At least that's what the scientists theorized.

When I accepted the reality that the Toy Man was choosing his victims primarily because they had unusual features—and not solely because of their availability—this gave me a new lens to look at the overall question. If this is true, what else is true?

If the Toy Man selected his victims because of peculiar aesthetics, what other factors affected his choices?

Every murder has at least five important factors: a victim, a means of death, a location, a time, and a murderer. Solving for one or more of them can lead you to a solution, much like an equation, assuming they're not all random.

The Toy Man's victim selection is even far less random than I first realized. His means—murder by knife—might tell me something if I had more forensic data, but I don't. The location, at least for the bodies at the Wimbledon address, appears to be one and the same, but I don't want to say that's an absolute certainty. Latroy was almost surely killed somewhere else, years after the Toy Man left the Wimbledon residence. And while the murderer's identity is an unknown, we have approximate times for three victims: Artice and his near-death experience, as well as when Christopher and Latroy vanished.

One question to ask is whether the dates of their deaths were a matter of convenience or had some intentionality to them. Convenience would be if the Toy Man had a work or travel schedule and he happened upon the victims on that day. Intention would imply he killed them on that day for a reason.

Christopher's abduction took place on March 22, 2009. Latroy vanished sometime around February 15 of this year. According to police reports, Artice's encounter took place on June 19 of the same year that Christopher disappeared.

None of those dates has any religious significance at first glance. If they have a personal significance, it will be nearly impossible to discover without talking to the Toy Man.

I ask Predox if those dates fall on a full moon and the answer is negative, ruling out that the Toy Man is a werewolf.

I ask if there's any number correlation based upon the time between the murders, and Predox spits back out 354 hours.

Three hundred and fifty-four hours is not a strong signal to me on first glance, but then I remember that Predox is giving me the most accurate result, not the one that has the most context.

Three hundred and fifty-four divided by twenty-four equals 29.5 days: the same length of the lunar cycle.

Okay, so my first instinct about a full moon was in the right direction, but I was asking about the wrong phase.

I look up their dates again and feel that little jolt when my brain is rewarded for doing something right.

They weren't murdered during the full moon: they were killed (or nearly killed, in the case of Artice) on moonless nights.

While I can't immediately imagine what the significance of this would be, other than allowing the Toy Man to wander around his backyard in the nude and bury the bodies without worrying about a neighbor seeing something, it does help me in one other major way . . .

Statistically speaking, of the approximately one thousand children currently missing in California, thirty-five of them—on average—should have gone missing on a new moon.

This allows me to narrow down my search to children with green eyes or some other feature similar to the DNA findings I've made so far who were abducted around those dates.

Unfortunately, Toy Man has a habit of choosing children who don't always make it onto the missing-persons lists, so my data may be limited.

I ask Predox for any disappearances that match this, and the answer chills me.

Eighteen days ago. One lunar cycle after Latroy went missing. Just ten days before I picked up this hunt.

Vincent Lamont, age thirteen, was reported missing in Snellville, Georgia, fifteen miles outside Atlanta.

He was an albino.

I perform a search for the past decade in California, using the new-moon timing and the Toy Man's preferred physical characteristics, and find that there are at least twelve more children who fit these criteria that are still not accounted for.

The Toy Man must have one or more kill sites in Los Angeles.

The question is do I try to find them and whatever clues may be there? Or do I go to Georgia and try to see if I can't find him there . . .

One is safer and could lead to more forensic data.

The other may put me on a path I've already gone down and that nearly killed me.

My fingers are already booking the ticket before my brain catches up.

While Detective Chen pursues her tenuous connection, I'll be following my own lead. I don't really care who's right, as long as we catch him before he kills again.

CHAPTER THIRTY-SEVEN
STAKEOUT

I've built myself my own operations center in my hotel room at the Atlanta Sheraton just north of Georgia State University. I've got print-outs of all the known victims. Maps of where he struck in South Central and color-coded note cards with possible facts and assumptions stuck to the wall.

I also have a large wall calendar marking off the days until the new moon: less than two weeks.

I have no direct reason to believe that the Toy Man will strike again on the next moon, but if there's some kind of ritual importance to the killing, it might be highly likely.

He's seen the news. He knows police are crawling all over his old house and are trying to find him. If he's the superstitious kind, he might decide he needs to keep killing to protect himself.

Or not. I have no idea how his mind works.

There's also the chance that at any moment Chen and company are going to announce their Brazilian break in the case. If that happens, Toy Man—assuming the Brazilian suspect is not the break they think they have—will believe that he's once again slipped away and is free to continue killing.

I can't let that happen.

It's interesting that I've found myself in Atlanta, in the area where serial-killer profiling got its first, major real-world test.

Between 1979 and 1981, the murders of twenty-eight children and adults were linked together in what were called the Atlanta Child Murders because most of the victims were under eighteen.

It took half a dozen bodies before the authorities realized there was a serial killer on the loose. Because they were so-called black crimes, police were hesitant to draw the same conclusions as they would had the victims been white—for a variety of reasons, most racial and not racist, but with the same unfortunate consequences.

Once the community was aware there was a predator on the loose, playgrounds emptied, people were on the watch, and rumors began to spread.

This was an area where, a generation before, the KKK had operated openly and was responsible for dozens of murders. Some KKK members still worked in law enforcement and held public office.

While some insisted they were a vestige of the past, it was hard to fully accept that notion at a time when a former West Virginia KKK recruiter, Robert Byrd, held office as a Democratic senator in Washington, DC.

Horrific statements caught on tape by a local Klan leader only exacerbated the issue as he praised the murders and helped fuel conspiracy theories for years to come.

However, when FBI profiler Roy Hazelwood took a tour through black neighborhoods in a police car driven by black police officers, he noticed that the sight of his white face made people retreat into their homes and off the streets.

This was a major break in creating a profile of the killer. Profilers surmised that a white man going into these communities would have attracted a considerable amount of attention—especially after the murders became well publicized.

Flying in the face of community beliefs and media speculation, Hazelwood and his FBI team suggested that a black man was responsible. Based upon prior experiences with serial killers, they made a number of assumptions: the killer was young. He was a police buff. He probably lived alone or with his parents.

Unfortunately, while that profile narrowed potential suspects down by some degree, it still described hundreds of thousands of young men.

What investigators needed was a pattern in his killings. While his victims were poor and thus likely to go off with a stranger for a few bucks or a convincing story, the suspect's means of disposing of their bodies changed once the press started covering the case.

He stopped putting bodies in out-of-the-way places and began to leave them where they could be more easily found—that was, until a forensic specialist casually mentioned to the press the killer might change up his method by dropping bodies in the water to erase any evidence.

This media blunder actually ended up being used to the investigators' advantage. FBI profiler John Douglas surmised that, because of the public announcement, the killer would now look for bridges and other areas overlooking the Chattahoochee River to dump bodies.

In a massive effort, police officers and even trainees were stationed near every bridge in the area to watch for the killer.

After a month of staking out twelve bridges with zero suspects, investigators decided to shut down that operation on the following day.

Unfortunately for Wayne Bertram Williams, he chose that night to drop a body from the James Jackson Parkway Bridge while a police-academy trainee remained on watch underneath.

When the young officer heard the splash, he radioed to the cops staking out the road and Williams was stopped.

It took several days for a body to be recovered, but one was finally found 120 yards from where another victim had washed ashore.

Williams was released but put under constant surveillance. As he held impromptu press conferences in his front yard, belittling the police and even bragging about failing a lie-detector test, investigators methodically built their case against him.

He would eventually be tried for the murders of two men and implicated in the deaths of twenty-nine others.

Reading the FBI archives of the case on their public website is an interesting study of the gradual process by which a case is built. It's difficult in the beginning to know what's important and what's not.

While profiling went on to become a powerful tool, it's led more than one investigation astray as overconfident profilers paid more attention to their gut and intuition than to the facts.

As my hero Richard Feynman would say, "It doesn't matter how beautiful your theory is; it doesn't matter how smart you are. If it doesn't agree with experiment, it's wrong."

I'm not an expert on the human mind or even the procedures that a detective follows to catch criminals. I'm a scientist with flexible boundaries, but still a scientist, accustomed to the samples in front of me telling me the truth. Sure, I might encounter an ant that disguises itself to look like a spider or even a leaf, but the ant isn't trying to fool me personally.

The Toy Man, on the other hand, is an intelligent free agent who can modify his behavior beyond his genetics and adjust to his environment in ways that I can't predict.

While the profilers at the FBI have thousands of cases to draw upon and make inferences from—for example, a correlation between one kind of stab wound and an obsession with women's shoes—so far, my research has been based on what I can fit into a Euler diagram and chart in a spreadsheet.

The sad truth about most serial-killer investigations is that they're not even initiated until after the killer's peak period; or worse, once they're in place, investigators have to wait for more bodies to pile up.

I'd rather not have that happen.

Sitting on the edge of my bed, looking at the limited facts I have at my disposal and the desire to catch the Toy Man before he kills again, I'm going to have to go outside my logical comfort zone.

Beyond Artice's physical description and the mention of an accent he couldn't place, I already have a hazy idea of a profile for this man, but I'm not very comfortable with what it tells me. His is a mind alien to my own.

Whereas I live in the world of science and testable predictions, he resides in the realm of magic.

And the rules of magic are utterly unpredictable.

CHAPTER THIRTY-EIGHT
BELIEVERS

Sitting at the back of the lecture hall, I listen to Professor Miriam, a small black woman with short gray hair and a powerful voice that fills the room, while her students dutifully take notes and casually ask questions during her presentation on the spread of Pentecostalism.

I find myself enraptured as she talks about her field experiences visiting churches in Finland, Brazil, and other places. She's my kind of academic: someone who steps outside the campus.

As the class ends, her piercing eyes spot me, and she beckons me to the table at the front. "Theo? Come on down here."

I wait for her to answer the questions of some straggling students, admiring how she invites them to stop by the house for what I assume is a weekly picnic in her backyard, where she answers their queries and creates another opportunity for them to engage with one another.

When we're alone, she invites me to take a stool opposite her at the table. "First up, I keep telling them I don't know anything about serial killers, but your e-mail was very polite."

"Thank you, Professor," I say. "I don't know much about them, either."

"Miriam, or Auntie if you have a passing grade in my class," she says with a smile that tells me that privilege alone is probably its own incentive.

I came across her work when I was trying to find an expert on rituals and magic. She's written a considerable amount about that kind of belief in America and been routinely cited by other scholars—a sign of the quality of her work.

"I had some questions about magic. I'm doing some research into the serial killer responsible for the murders in Los Angeles."

"Research?" she says skeptically. "Like the kind you did in Montana?"

"Ideally, this outcome will be different."

"And you came all the way out here to talk to me? I'd think there are plenty of people in California that could give you better answers."

"Not exactly. I happened to be in the area and wanted to ask you some questions about rituals."

"Well, as I said in my e-mail, I get asked from time to time to look at cases where the police think there might be some kind of magic or ritual connection, but the problem is that we tend to see those connections when they're not really there. Sure, sometimes serial killers like to draw some pentagrams, send letters to the newspapers saying they see demons and such, but more often than not, they're just sick people looking for any excuse to justify their behavior."

I nod.

"And after they're caught, they like to build up their own narrative, creating even more elaborate stories than the little girl with the red hair gave them a hard-on." She laughs. "Pardon me—sometimes I talk like that because it keeps my students' attention."

"You seemed to have them in the palm of your hand. You're an exceptional lecturer. I envy you," I say sincerely.

"I'll tell you the secret." She leans in over the table. "I love my students. Especially the challenging ones. I see them as my children. I recognize that even at that age, we're still a kind of a parent to them. I embrace that. When people ask me if I have any children, I say about a thousand of them. Anyway, what led you to think this killer has some kind of unusual belief system?"

"There's a couple patterns. His victims all have green eyes or some other unusual feature, like albinism."

"That's interesting. How is he able to select them?" asks Miriam.

"For one, they're all poor and come from broken families. But as far as finding them, it could be that he's in a role where he encounters lots of children or he has access to records that makes searching for them easier."

"Like child services?" she replies.

"Yes. That's what scares me. He might have a dangerous amount of information available to him. Although, if he's operating in multiple states, that would mean that he might not work for one particular municipality."

"Is there one company that handles those records nationwide?"

That's a brilliant question. Predox had listed a state software consultant as a potential vector. "Possibly a contractor that works in multiple states. Maybe even a subcontractor that fulfills the work for a local bidder. It's one line of investigation I'm pursuing. But the reason I came to see you was that, besides the victims having unique characteristics, all of the killings appear to have taken place on a new moon."

Miriam's posture stiffens. "That's not in the news."

"No. I realized this when I started looking for factors the killer might be controlling for."

"Do the police know?" she asks.

"I've e-mailed them . . ." Chen won't even take my call. I keep getting pushed to voice mail any time I try to reach someone on the investigative team.

Miriam taps her gold-painted fingernails on the table. "That's peculiar. That's actually a very strong magic connection."

"That's why I wanted to talk to you. I was reading up about voodoo."

She chuckles. "Voodoo? Dr. Cray, that's often about as accurate as calling Judaism paganism, or the Romans calling Christianity 'that new Jewish thing.' It's a word that's been spread so thin, it's lost its meaning."

"Well, that's why I came to see you. I'm just an ignorant biologist in search of enlightenment."

"You're forgiven. The voodoo that you're familiar with is probably the variety where African slaves mixed their folklore with Catholicism. But a great deal of what we call voodoo is actual African belief systems in places other than Africa.

"Most belief systems that don't have a central text like the Koran or the Old Testament become extremely pragmatic, adopting whatever else is around if it fits. New Orleans voodoo has a lot of French Catholicism embedded in it, while Brazilian forms have incorporated some of the indigenous beliefs from there.

"As I'm sure you know, green eyes and albinism are considered supernatural in about every culture because these people were clearly marked by god. The problem is that in some cultures, this can be a mark of evil and an indication that these people are to be scorned. In Africa they call them 'witch children,' and every year a thousand or more are murdered in remote villages. Which is not unlike how having a particular birthmark could get you accused of being a witch in America not too long ago."

"Would this man be killing these children because he thinks they're witches?"

Miriam considers this for a while. "Possibly. But in communities where they do those kinds of ritual killings, it's almost always someone they know and have attributed misfortune to. I assume these children are unknown to him beforehand. Right?"

"Probably," I reply.

"In what condition have the bodies been found?"

"All I've seen are bones and bits of ligament. I don't know what they found below the ground. The police have said absolutely nothing about that."

"And the bones that you've seen, were they physically connected?"

"No. Almost all of them were loose and separate."

"Very interesting . . . ," she says. "Very interesting."

"What?"

"It sounds like the bodies were chopped up."

"Yes. I understand it makes them easier to dispose of."

"But unnecessary if you have a big backyard to bury them. These children may have been butchered."

My stomach begins to churn. "To what purpose?"

"He's not just killing witches—he's taking certain body parts for magical purposes."

I feel like I want to throw up. "So it is ritual? Like a cult?"

"Ritual, yes. Probably not a cult. And it's even worse than you realize."

"What on earth can be worse than someone chopping up little boys for magic spells?"

Her answer leaves me speechless.

"He's eating them, too."

We both sit in silence. Everything she said makes sense, but the facts were too separated and too behaviorally rooted for me to come to the same conclusions that she did.

"Let's just hope they're going to catch him. Didn't they arrest a person of interest in Brazil?"

I slowly shake my head. "Yes, and there may be a connection, but I don't think it's him. The last missing child disappeared while that man was in jail."

"I didn't hear about that on the news," she replies.

"It's not. They think all the murders happened in Los Angeles."

Her eyes pierce right into mine. "Oh, Lord, not here . . . Not again . . ."

CHAPTER THIRTY-NINE
BOTANICA

I've been around magical belief in one form or another all my life, from the Texas churches distant family members tried to draw me toward to the shamans and medicine men I encountered doing research in South American jungles. I once even imbibed a potion to make the locals happy and had a surreal experience resulting in me waking up in a tree making monkey noises. Ten years later, my colleagues doing field research in Honduras tell me the locals still ask when the Monkey Man from America will return.

Yet, as I walk through Yewe's Botanica—a metaphysical store of sorts—in a poorer section of Atlanta, I realize that I've frequently been around belief in magic, even involved in token ceremonies, but have never really been immersed in it.

The small store is filled with special prayer candles, powders, and oils with names like Dove's Blood and Mr. Guyer's Luck Powder, as well as a variety of totems ranging from feathers to rocks with shells glued to them like eyes.

I have no idea what any of this means. Are they based on some kind of preexisting magical history? Or is Mr. Guyer an entrepreneur concocting new product lines?

I notice that a number of the items have Los Angeles–area addresses on them, which tells me I overlooked a very important vector while I was there.

The proprietor of the botanica is a wiry, mahogany-skinned older man who looks like he has West Indian ancestry. When I entered, he was on the phone explaining to a customer that they had been out of something called Snake Bite for several weeks, but were expecting a shipment from the distributor in a few days. Thank goodness for that.

My purpose in the shop is to get an understanding of what this world is like and to try to learn what kind of network the Toy Man may be a part of.

One of the things that's become clear to me, when it comes to serial killers who are centralized in one or two areas, is that they're usually connected to some kind of social grouping that relates to their victims.

For John Wayne Gacy, many of his victims were the young men he hired to work on his construction projects. In addition, he mingled with male hustlers while also spending time with cops. More than one parent of a missing teen pointed to the man who spent a lot of time around the young people he'd hired.

Lonnie Franklin liked to party with hookers who had crack cocaine addictions. His friends were aware of this part of his life, and some even suspected his intentions were darker. Long before the police were on to him, prostitutes were warning one another about a john with violent tendencies.

Atlanta serial killer Wayne Williams fancied himself a music producer and even had his own amateur radio transmitter. It would come out later that he promised many of his victims the opportunity to become a music star. When police first stopped him, he said he was on his way to audition a female singer who didn't actually exist.

All three of these men traveled in circles in which they could meet victims, but they also intermingled with people they aspired to be.

Gacy hung out with cops. Franklin liked to be around other "players." Williams tried to roll with music producers.

If the Toy Man really believes he's in the realm of the occult, then it seems likely that in both Los Angeles and Atlanta, he's at least familiar with the people in that scene.

At the front of the shop, there's a bulletin board filled with flyers for prayer groups, psychic readers, healers, and a variety of other supernatural cottage industries.

"Anything I can help you with?" asks the owner.

I try to phrase my words so I don't sound completely ignorant. "I . . . was wondering . . . I don't know much about this . . ."

"Neither do I after fifty years. What kind of problem do you have?"

I turn away from the flyers. "Someone has been troubling me . . ." Better to keep it vague than make up a lie I'll lose track of.

"The purple one. Some say that helps." He points to a shelf filled with different-colored candles.

I take a purple one off the rack and set it on his counter. "Anything else?"

"A talisman?" He realizes he's got a sucker on the line. "Let's see." He makes a gesture of surveying his shop before settling on the shelf of high-priced items behind him. "Some say a crystal like this might work. It's onyx, I believe."

He sets a faceted schorl on the counter. It's not even remotely related to onyx, but I don't quibble. "How much?"

He studies me for a moment, trying to decide what high price to settle on after telling me an even more ridiculous amount. "It's one hundred. But I can let you have it for seventy-five dollars."

I pick it up, pretending to assess the value. "Okay . . . if you say it will work."

He shrugs. "I only know from my own experience."

Not a great sales pitch, but I'm not here to play the skeptic. I pull out a wad of hundred-dollar bills and set one on the counter.

He sees the bills, which is what I wanted.

"I don't know the right way to ask this," I start to say, "but I was wondering if you might be able to tell me where I could find someone. Somebody who knows about, what's the right word? Hexes?"

He points to a flyer on the board. "You want Ms. Violet. People say she's the best. What's your name, by the way?"

I'm sure he's asking me this so he can tell Ms. Violet that he sent a mark with a fat wad of bills over to her establishment.

"Craig," I reply.

He hands me my change and a bag containing my purchases. "Go ahead and take the flyer. I think she's who you want to talk to."

I'm sure she is. If she's the one he sends the richest clients to, then very probably she's also one of the most important people in this network, and quite possibly someone that the Toy Man has encountered.

CHAPTER FORTY
BLESSED

When I pull up to Ms. Violet's practice, there's a group of people sitting on plastic chairs outside the house, apparently waiting to be seen.

Her home is in an older neighborhood of mid-twentieth-century houses with gravel easements and slightly overrun lawns.

My rental car is the most expensive one parked in front of the house, with the exception of the Mercedes in the open garage.

When I walk up the sidewalk, a tall black man who appears to be in his forties, wearing a button-down shirt and khakis, greets me with a firm handshake.

"Mr. Craig, Ms. Violet is so glad you could pay her a visit."

This must be the man I spoke to on the phone, Robert. He explained to me that Ms. Violet was a woman of God and provides her services for free. If I try to offer her money, she'll take it as an insult.

When I asked when I could visit her, he told me that there were a great number of people waiting to see the wonderful woman. After a long pause, I inquired about making a donation and was told that I could see her the next day as a thanks for my generosity.

"How much is appropriate?"

Andrew Mayne

"We had a man yesterday who tried to give her one thousand dollars, and that was too inappropriate," Robert informed me. "If he had been a rich man, that would have been acceptable. But he was poor, and it hurt Ms. Violet to think that his children might go hungry."

What a sweet woman. "Would five hundred dollars be acceptable?"

Of course it would. Robert already knew how much money I dropped on a worthless rock and what was in my billfold.

"That is very generous of you. If you must, just put it into an envelope and give it to me, so Ms. Violet doesn't have to know who did this kindness for her."

But of course. I give him the envelope after shaking hands. "I hope this is appropriate."

He pockets it without looking. "You're a kind man. A very generous man."

Before showing up I took the time to do a little research on how some psychics operate and discovered that many of them have secret networks through which they share information about clients. The goal is to figure out who the big fish are and bleed them for as much as possible.

Worried that while I was talking to Ms. Violet they might run the plate on my rental car and get my real name, I took the slightly illegal step of stealing a plate from another rental car in the airport parking lot while I loaded my luggage.

This would confuse anyone doing a search on the plate but would likely be attributed to a clerical error and not the intent of "Craig" to deceive anyone.

Robert points to a plastic chair for me to sit in, next to an elderly woman knitting a long scarf.

Next to her sits a much younger woman, bouncing one child on her knee while another plays at her feet with a toy car.

I suspect that the saintly Ms. Violet has a progressive rate structure and my visit is offsetting the others'.

Predictably, Robert has me wait long enough to know that Ms. Violet is a very busy woman, but not too long to test my patience and rethink my patronage.

After about fifteen minutes, I am ushered inside the house, which is decorated with more votive candles and religious paraphernalia than a wing of the Vatican, and into a room in the back of the home where the curtains are drawn so that only a flicker of the setting sun is visible.

Ms. Violet is a heavyset black woman with large glasses and a sincere smile.

When I enter the room, she gets up, bounds around the table, and embraces me in a hug that nearly off-balances me.

"Mr. Craig! I've been so looking forward to our visit!" She gestures to a statue of a saint sitting on a side table. "He told me I'd be meeting someone special who traveled quite a distance."

I can see that she's already aware of the rental car. Just for giggles, I had put a copy of the *Chicago Tribune* in the back seat. I'm curious to see how long it takes before that gets put to use.

"Please, have a seat, child," she says, ushering me to sit down in the chair across the table from hers. "Now, let's see those hands of yours."

She takes my wrists and turns them palm up and spends what has to be at least three minutes staring at them while making mmm-hmm sounds, as if she's reading the paper and seeing news she already knew about.

Finally she lets them go and sits back with her arms crossed. "What can I do to help you with this problem?"

Right now I surmise that she's able to cold-read a little about me, plus use some of the information the botanica owner told her and whatever Robert has gleaned from my rental car.

But she's smart enough to not use it unless she has to. I suspect that she knows from my body language I'm skeptical, even though I'm trying to hide it. She wants to know what she has to do to convince me, possibly to keep me coming back.

I make it easier on her. "There's a man who has been giving me problems." In my head I think of Park back at OpenSkyAI. My best lie will be one based on truth.

"Is he jealous of you?"

"Yes." She's good.

"Mmm-hmm. I can see a little bit of his aura around you. He's thinking about you right now. But this ain't about a woman, is it? This is about your business."

"Yes. I think he's trying to make my life difficult."

"Take my hands," she tells me. As she clasps mine, she kneels, her head down in prayer. "Lord, please help this man. Don't let this other man wish his evil on him. Protect this child of yours. Look after him and all his friends and family up north. And when he gets home, see to it that he no longer be troubled."

She lets go of my hand. "I'm going to give you something special." She reaches up and unclasps a crucifix from around her neck. "When I was a little girl and the bullies used to make me cry, my grandmother gave this to me and said that when I wear this, Jesus walk side by side with me. And the bullies would see that and leave me alone."

"I can't accept this," I reply, pretending that she doesn't have a drawer full of these for every rich idiot that visits her home.

"No. Grandmother told me to give it to you. And I always do what she says."

"Thank you," I say. "I don't know what to say."

"If he still bothers you, come back and let me know." She gives me her warm smile again. "I'll get Grandma after him."

So far I've been presented with a perfectly Christian prayer session with only a little psychic showmanship. It's not what I came for.

"Ms. Violet . . . this man. He's an evil man." I hold my hands in prayer. "I thank you for bringing this blessing onto me. But . . . there's something about him. I don't know if it's enough that he stays clear of me." I put my hand to my heart. "I would never wish harm on another man, so help me god. I was wondering if there was some other kind of . . . blessing."

She sizes me up for a moment, then shakes her head. "Mr. Craig, what you're asking me to do, I will not do. I'm a Christian woman and only use my blessings for light. You're talking about something that I've promised the Lord I would never allow myself to be drawn in to." She angrily points to the door. "If you're wanting that kind of magic, then you have to leave and take Satan with you. He's not welcome here."

"I . . . I was only . . . Never mind." I drop the matter, not sure where else to take it. Although there was something odd about her refusal. Was I supposed to offer more money? I make a dramatic gesture toward my wallet. "I could pay for the inconvenience . . ."

She stands abruptly, almost pushing the table into me. "Mr. Craig, leave my house! That kind of darkness can't be undone! You don't know what you're asking for!"

I get up. "I'm sorry. I'm so sorry."

"I'll pray for you, Mr. Craig. I'll pray for you."

Robert is waiting for me in the hallway.

"Please tell her I'm sorry," I say to him, not quite sure what the hell just happened.

He pulls me into the foyer and speaks to me in a low voice, "It's all right. She'll forgive you. Ms. Violet is a sweet woman."

"I didn't mean to offend."

"She knows that. It's just the thing you asked for . . ." He shakes his head. "It comes at a heavy cost on the soul."

"But it can be done?" I ask.

He glances over my shoulder back at her room. "We don't talk about that in this house."

His hands reach down, clasp mine, and press a slip of paper into them.

I open it in my car.

It's a phone number.

The person you call when you want a darker kind of magic.

CHAPTER FORTY-ONE
STONES

"Don't be so nervous," Robert says to me from the passenger side of my rental car. "The Moss Man is nothing to be afraid of."

The number was Robert's personal cell number. The Moss Man was the person he said he could put me in touch with for something a little more powerful, as he put it.

My instructions from Robert, who I realize is some kind of middleman for the various psychics and charlatans in the Atlanta area, were to put $900 in fifty-dollar bills between the pages of a Bible and sleep with it under my pillow, then pick him up the next evening in a parking lot south of Atlanta. From there he'd take me to meet the Moss Man. I was also supposed to bring a picture or some item that belonged to my enemy.

I settled on a pen I could say I'd swiped from the desk of my nemesis.

When I picked him up, he told me to take I-75 South until further notice.

I got the impression this wasn't going to be a trip to the suburbs. Eventually he had me take a turn through a small town whose two major sources of commerce were a water park and a dollar store.

My anxiety set in as he had me turn down a dark, unpaved road.

Along the way he regaled me with stories about the Moss Man, how he healed people, even raising an infant from the dead, and how, back in the day, the state governor would pay visits to the Moss Man for his help.

I didn't ask if the money came from the state budget or his reelection campaign.

Next, Robert tells me that I shouldn't be worried, even though the sight of Moss Man has caused some people to become paralyzed with fear.

In addition, apparently the Moss Man speaks a language that nobody but Robert and a few others can understand, because the devil took his tongue.

As all of this is being explained to me, the song "The Devil Went Down to Georgia" plays through my head. If Moss Man breaks out a fiddle and starts playing, I'm pretty sure I'll lose it.

All told, assuming the $900 was the final tally, it's been a pretty good show so far. I'm sure my venture-cap friend Julian and his crowd would pay much more for this kind of entertainment. When all this blows over, I might talk to Robert about being a booking manager.

"Some good old boys decided they had enough of Moss Man and went out after him with their dogs and their shotguns," Robert says, continuing to build the man's legend. "Three days go by and nobody heard from them. A few more and the sheriff sends his deputies. All they find is some piles of ash and the guns. Someone said they saw the Moss Man later on with a couple of mutts at his heels. When they asked him where he got the dogs, Moss Man said the devil bring them to him." Robert watches my reaction. "Crazy talk. I know. But everyone has Moss Man stories down here. But hardly anyone ever seen him. You lucky he said to bring the white boy from Chicago to him. He don't tend to no strangers normally."

I wonder whether he called the Moss Man directly or their exchange took place over their Slack channel?

"Turn here," Robert tells me as we approach what appears to be just another line of trees.

"I don't think there's a road."

"There is." He points to a small white stone near the edge of the path.

I make the turn and branches brush against the car, making me thankful I sprang for the scam of full protection. Normally I don't, but I didn't want to be charged extra if I brought the vehicle back with bullet holes or the smell of dead bodies. Both of which happen to my cars more than I care to think about.

The headlights cut through the darkness and illuminate insects big enough to qualify as birds and more low-hanging branches that drag across the roof like a jungle car wash.

"Okay, right here," Robert instructs me. "Grab the Bible."

I pick up the brown paper bag from the back seat after he gets out, not wanting him to see the gun tucked into the waistband of my jeans. Or maybe it would be a good thing?

I tell myself there's not much point to robbing me out here, as I've already agreed to give them the money.

"This way," says Robert, pointing to a thin trail barely illuminated by the light of the moon through the canopy. It's in a waning phase, reminding me that there's not much time to find the Toy Man.

I reach for a small flashlight, but Robert nearly swats it out of my hand. "Didn't I tell you no flashlights? That's how the devil finds you. We want to stay in God's light," he says, pointing to the moon.

So when there's a new moon—or rather, no moon—God isn't watching . . . *Interesting.*

Robert leads me down the path, which is barely visible, but he has a certainty about him. I check landmarks, making sure he's not doubling back so he can pull some kind of ruse, but the shadows stay consistent and I don't get the sense we've gone in a circle. I've got a pretty good knack for that. Whenever I hike, I tend to make a mental hydrological map in my mind and pay attention to the kind of rocks and flora. Trails usually follow erosion patterns created by flowing water or the paths carved by animals in search of streams.

"Here we are," Robert says as we come to a small clearing.

White stones like the one marking the road form a perfect circle about twenty feet across.

He takes a seat on a log inside the circle and motions for me to do the same. "This is a safe spot. The devil won't find us in here until we call him."

Until? I've found that I'm feeling a little less sarcastic as the croaking frogs and chirping crickets create an eerie backdrop to the foggy woods.

Moonlight breaking through the trees creates small pools of light that fade into the distance. It feels like we're a thousand miles away from civilization. Or a thousand years. I can't even hear the omnipresent sound of cars on a highway.

"Now we wait for the Moss Man and see if he shows."

After about twenty minutes, Robert points to some moving bushes in the distance. "That's him," he whispers.

I get a small chill when I see the leaves sway like a rolling wave passing around us.

"What's he doing?" I ask.

"Making sure the devil didn't follow us."

In a flash I have a realization that chills me even further. While Robert and Ms. Violet knowingly engage in theatrics, that's just for business. It doesn't mean they don't actually believe this.

The moving wave of leaves fades away before me, and I'm suddenly aware that the frogs have stopped their croaking.

I get the feeling that I'm being watched.

When I glance down at the shadows of Robert and me at our feet, a third figure now stands between us.

CHAPTER FORTY-TWO
SEER

Turning around takes an eternity. In that expanded moment, my brain fires at high speed, trying to make as many neural connections as possible, assessing whatever threat I may be about to face.

The number one danger is that when I turn around, I won't be looking at one more play actor in Robert's elaborate occult dinner theater, but rather the man I came to Atlanta to find.

I now realize the stupidity of going this far. If the Toy Man is the Moss Man, he may not know who Craig from Chicago is, but he'll more than likely know Theo Cray, the man who uncovered his house of horrors.

When I see who is standing there, I feel a wave of relief, not because this man isn't unsettling, but because, on first glance, he looks nonthreatening.

The Moss Man is blind. I can tell from the opaque white corneas of his eyes, even though his face remains in shadow. He's barely over five feet tall and dressed in torn brown pants with a rope belt and a loose white button-up shirt. The wooden cane he's holding is almost as tall as I am.

He hands Robert his cane and motions for me to stand and move to the center of the circle, where he begins to pace around me and stare at me, examining my every square inch. Without asking, he grabs my left wrist and pries open each finger, then scrutinizes my palm and says something that sounds vaguely Creole to Robert.

"Moss Man says you're holding something in your left hand."

I stare at the empty hand, trying to ascertain what he means.

"A secret. He says you're holding a dark secret."

Moss Man walks over to a burlap sack he dropped by the log and riffles through it, finally coming back with a bottle.

It's the size of a whiskey bottle but has a clear liquid inside. The label is black with a coiled cobra and the words *Snake Bite*.

Moss Man takes a knife from his waist, grabs the tip of my thumb, and makes a small nick. He then squeezes it over the mouth of the bottle.

My blood trickles into the alcohol, creating dark clouds.

Moss Man then yanks a handkerchief from his back pocket and ties it around my thumb in a knot that hurts more than the incision.

He screws the cap back on the bottle, gives it a shake and holds it up to the moonlight, checking for something.

I can't figure out how he even knows where the moon is, unless he's not totally blind or he has some other means.

Satisfied at what he sees, he unscrews the cap and takes a swig, grabs my hand again and sprays the mixture of blood and booze on my left palm.

I guess that takes care of that problem.

I glance toward Robert, curious as to what happens next, but Moss Man grips my chin with a surprising strength and gazes into my eyes, my nostrils, and then my mouth.

"He's looking for the devil," Robert offers.

Satisfied, Moss Man reaches out with the bottle and touches it to my lips, inviting me to drink.

The liquid tastes like grain alcohol and vinegar. My cheeks flush, and I feel a migraine made up of ice crystals jabbing into my brain. A moment later I feel a little bit woozy as my inner ear decides to do a backflip.

I have no idea what's in Snake Bite, but its effect is neurological as well as alcoholic.

"You're in luck," says Robert. "Snake Bite is very hard to find."

Yeah, I definitely get the impression you can't buy it at Costco.

Moss Man pushes me to sit down and then says something to Robert.

"Do you have the item that belongs to the man you want to hex?"

"Yes."

I reach into my pocket, but Moss Man almost slaps at my hand.

"Wait," says Robert. "He needs to build a fire first."

Moss Man gets up and reaches into the brush around the white stones and grabs various sticks and logs, a pretty impressive feat for a blind guy.

He heaps them into a pile in front of me, some of them hitting my crossed legs.

When he's satisfied that he has enough kindling, Moss Man sits across from me and uses a book of matches to set the pile ablaze.

It's not a large fire, more like the kind you make to boil a kettle of coffee.

Moss Man says something to Robert again.

"Do you have the Bible?"

"Yes." I point to the paper bag by the log. "Do I pay him now?"

"The money is not for him," Robert replies as he picks up the bag and hands it to me.

Moss Man lays his hands out flat. I take the Bible out of the bag and lay it on his palms. He holds it over the fire and starts to rip its spine. Bills fall into the flames, followed by the pages of the Bible.

It may have been the moonlight, or my cynicism, but at least one of the bills I watched catch on fire looked like a Xerox copy. Either way, the real trick is how Robert switched them on me.

Moss Man stirs the flames with a stick until it's a healthy blaze. He holds out his hand again.

"Hand him the item from your enemy," says Robert.

I give Moss Man the pen. His fingers feel the shape of the object before he snaps it in two and drops it in.

What would he have done if I'd brought him a solid piece of metal like a house key?

The smell of burning plastic reaches my nose, and Moss Man takes another swig from the Snake Bite. He sprays it into the flames, creating a fireball that singes my face. He does this six more times.

The fire burns hotter, then finally reaches its peak. There's only a little Snake Bite left.

After the last ember is gone, Moss Man grabs a pinch of the ash and drops it into the bottle. He gives it a shake, then stares at it in the moonlight.

Uncapping the bottle, he pushes it toward me, instructing me to drink it.

"All of it," says Robert.

There's at least three shots in there.

Against my better judgment, I take it all down in one gulp. This time my scalp burns and my throat feels like it was ripped out by a yeti.

My head suddenly becomes too heavy for my neck, and I go sideways. The ground feels really nice, and I decide to stay there for a little while. Moss Man gets up, and I watch as his bare feet retreat back into the woods from which he came as the fog and the trees envelop him.

I lie there awhile, trying to process why I came and what I hoped to get out of it. At some point, Robert comes over and helps me to my feet, slinging my arm over his shoulder.

"Let's walk it off," he tells me as we head back down the path we came.

"That wasn't so evil," I tell him as I try to keep my feet from dragging.

"Wait until the hangover," he replies.

"Are there other kinds of magic?" I ask between stumbles.

"What do you mean?"

"Darker. Even more powerful."

Robert carries me in silence for a while. "I know of another man. A man Moss Man and Ms. Violet will have nothing to do with."

"And you?"

He shakes his head. "No, this I won't do."

"What if I pay? A lot."

There's a long silence as he thinks this over. "No. This man is an evil man. While Moss Man knows how to trick demons and get them to do him favors, this other man, he is the devil himself."

CHAPTER FORTY-THREE
DUE PROCESS

I'm awoken by the sound of my phone buzzing on the nightstand. Even after I answer it, my head is still vibrating from the lingering effect of Snake Bite, ash, and my own blood.

"Cray," I say, stifling a yawn.

"This call didn't come from me," says a voice on the other end.

I check the display. It's a 323 number I don't recognize. "Well, you're in luck, because I have no idea who you are," I reply before moving to hit the "End Call" button.

"It's Sanjay."

"Oh, great to hear from you. What happened? Did Chen get you fired?"

"Not yet. It hasn't hit the news, but we found a suspect."

"The guy in Brazil? The hit man?"

"Yeah . . . I won't ask how you knew that. Anyway, we found some prints that matched him in the house. Plus, the bicycle that belonged to Christopher Bostrom. We got a print from under the seat."

"That's great," I say again.

"I'm not finished. The suspect, Ordavo Sims, was murdered last night in his jail cell in Rio before we could have him extradited."

"I wish I could say I was sorry."

"Well, here's the thing: he was actually wanted as a material witness, because most of the prints in the house aren't his. He may have been an accomplice."

"I was afraid of that."

"Yeah, but Chen and company are kind of eager to declare this case closed. Ordavo was implicated in some gang-related killings. There are even witnesses that have him using a knife to kill someone."

"But he was in jail when Latroy went missing," I point out.

"For Chen, that doesn't matter. All they care about are the bodies at the Wimbledon house. If they have someone to pin that on, then the matter is finished."

"But not for you," I reply.

"Professionally it is. I'm being told to wrap up my work on the case since there's not going to be a trial. Chen is going to hold a press conference tomorrow and announce the hunt is over."

I can tell this is bothering Sanjay. "So why are you calling me?"

"Because it's bullshit. There's things we found . . . and Chen would shoot me if she found out I leaked this . . ."

"Cannibalism?"

A moment of shocked silence. "Yes. We've found some small indentations. Also, some of the better-preserved corpses are missing parts. Penises, eyes, hearts, and other organs. We think he ate them."

"Or bottled them," I suggest, recalling what Artice said he saw in a follow-up report.

"What?" asks Sanjay.

"This guy believes in magic. For him, those body parts have supernatural properties. Is she going to announce any of that?"

"No. We've been told to not pursue the cannibal angle. They have a strong story if it's just a hit man who liked to molest and murder little boys in his spare time. They're not saying how he afforded the house. I guess he got some really good rent control? It's all bullshit. Anyway, I'm going to send you everything."

"I can't ask you to do that," I reply—partially afraid it might be a trick.

"And I can't live with myself if I don't. There's nothing I haven't already told you except some more forensics about what they dug up in the backyard."

"Bodies?"

"Yeah, and some trash. You can take a look. Anyway, I'm sending you a link to a Dropbox account. If Chen asks where you got it, lie."

"No worries. I won't rat you out."

"Uh . . . sorry about what happened," he says, acknowledging my arrest. "I didn't say anything to her. She pulled my call logs and saw that I was talking to you when I accessed the DNA profiles."

"It's okay. I wasn't trying to call you a rat. Your situation is different than mine."

"Oh, okay. Thanks. Where are you, by the way?"

I have to look at the hotel room to remind myself that I'm not home. "Georgia."

"Decided to get away from this bullshit? I don't blame you."

"Not quite," I reply.

"Are you still on this?"

"Yep."

"And you think he's in Georgia?" Sanjay asks.

"I guess Chen didn't share my messages to her about some Atlanta-area kidnappings." This does not surprise me.

"No. All she cares about is the Wimbledon house. Have you contacted the Atlanta FBI office? They'd have jurisdiction now."

"Not yet. All I have is a hunch and a hangover."

"You're an odd man. Well, if there's anything else I can do, and I don't know what that is, just let me know."

"Thanks. And Sanjay . . ."

"Yeah?"

"You're doing the right thing. You know it because the easy thing is to not care and keep your life uncomplicated."

We hang up, and I get a glass of water to try to clear my system.

After I feel reasonably sentient, I climb back into my bed with my laptop and pull up Sanjay's folder.

There are hundreds of pages of forensic data I want to go over later about the bodies. But right now I'm mainly curious about what else they found in the backyard.

I find a document that reads like an archaeological dig, describing what they found in every stratum of soil.

Aside from the bodies, there were ash pits containing charred paper and broken bottles.

There's no bloody knife or weapons, only the kind of garbage you'd find in a lot of backyards.

I'm about to close my laptop and try to get some more sleep when I decide to click on the report again. And I get rewarded: something important was right in front of me.

When I turn to the page describing the debris, there's an image of a shard from a broken bottle. I recognize the shape immediately. It's why my head is still splitting.

The Toy Man was also a fan of Snake Bite. Lots of it. The report makes it seem like every kill was also accompanied by a bottle of the vile stuff.

This doesn't prove a connection to Moss Man or Robert, any more than *The Catcher in the Rye* links serial killers. It does mean that my instincts were right.

I put my jeans on to go back to the botanica. When I reach into my pockets, I notice something odd: my wallet has been moved.

When I check the contents, the cash is still there, but my driver's license is in the wrong spot.

It seems Robert was not only adept at switching real money for counterfeit in a Bible, but also an accomplished pickpocket.

He knows who I am. Now the question is, who else has he told?

CHAPTER FORTY-FOUR

JACKLIGHTING

In 1889, George Shiras, an attorney from Pennsylvania, developed a new technique that would go on to change the biological sciences and the way we view wildlife to this day.

Shiras, who had grown up near the Ojibwa First Nation people, learned a particular style of nighttime hunting called jacklighting, in which one puts a fire in a pan at one end of a canoe while the hunter sits in the back in the shadows with a rifle.

When animals on the shore saw the light, they'd freeze. The hunter would then aim his rifle between the two glowing dots of their eyes and kill them from afar.

Shiras's application of the technique was far more humane. Instead of using a pan of burning coals, he used a bright kerosene lamp. And instead of a rifle, he used a camera.

When Shiras started setting his cameras on shore and using trip wires to ignite magnesium-powder flashes, he created an entirely new kind of remote photography in which the photographer didn't even have to be there.

His photographs, published in *National Geographic* in the early 1900s, showed a stunning view of wildlife rarely seen before. From raccoons on riverbanks to blurs of grizzly bears leaping past the lens, Shiras showed us what animals did when no human was around.

This method of photography continues to be used to this day. Recently it's been used to discover clouded leopards in Borneo and new species of deer in Vietnam.

For scientists, this tool allows you to be in many places at once. Rather than staking out one water hole or location and hoping to find your subject, you can place multiple cameras and see which ones hit pay dirt.

I have no idea where the Toy Man is, where he's going, or what he plans to do next. Like a photographer seeking some elusive animal, I have to set as many camera traps as possible to try to capture my prey on film—technically SD cards.

My hunch is that his rituals involve Snake Bite, the Sriracha sauce of occult magic in this area.

Research into the company revealed that Snake Bite is manufactured by a Vietnamese distillery and sold around the world. The US distributor is in Los Angeles.

A call to them revealed that a truckload was leaving a Tennessee warehouse and was on its way to Atlanta. They kindly gave me the name of the four locations that sell Snake Bite.

Because it's not listed as an alcoholic beverage, but instead as a "homeopathic topical salve," they've been able to avoid running afoul of local liquor laws. To their point, I would readily testify that no human being should consider this a beverage.

Now that Robert—along with potentially anyone else in his small community of occult practitioners—knows who I am, visiting the other three botanicas and asking the shopkeepers to tell me if a tall black man who looks like he might be a child killer comes to purchase some Snake Bite is probably not a practical idea.

I don't want the Toy Man even aware that I think there's a connection between him and what I've learned so far. Doing so might cause him to change his behavior.

I've got five small cameras the size of key-chain fobs sitting on my hotel room table. Purchased online and delivered next day, each one takes a photo any time it detects motion. Otherwise, it shoots a picture once per minute.

My plan is to place one near the entrance of each of the botanicas and swap them out every twenty-four hours as their SD-card memories fill.

The risk, besides the Toy Man never showing up, is getting caught in the act of placing or switching them out. My plan is do this while they're closed.

But getting a photo of the Toy Man is only the start. Of the hundreds of people I expect to capture in photographs, I have no way to tell who is my quarry. And once he leaves the store, without subpoena powers, I have no way to compel the store owner to give me any information about a suspect, assuming they even know anything.

What I need is a way to track them down.

Unlike Shiras's animals, which leave paw prints in the mud and dirt, creating a trail that can be followed, the clientele of the botanicas won't make it that easy.

What I need is a way to tell if someone who has been there to purchase Snake Bite has been in another location the Toy Man has visited—hopefully allowing me to track him back to where he lives.

Ideally, this would be some other vector I can locate before the new moon. Worst-case scenario—and this is the absolute worst case—if the Toy Man chooses another victim and we're able to find the body, I need a way to tie him to one of the botanicas.

How do you track someone you've never come in contact with?

My answer is somewhat sinister and potentially illegal, depending on how one wants to interpret certain federal laws.

It's also somewhat amusing to me that I'm doing this within throwing distance of the Centers for Disease Control and Prevention.

When I placed my order yesterday for the surveillance fobs, I also placed an order for another item—four, to be precise.

Instead of Amazon, these items come from a laboratory in North Carolina. They sell medical supplies to the defense industry—at least that's their cover story. What they actually provide are custom-designed bacteria used for very specific purposes.

The Toy Man's advantages over me are numerous. I'm not a law-enforcement investigator, a forensic pathologist, or even skillful enough to spot when someone is lying to my face. I am, however, a rather unorthodox scientist who has a particular set of tools at my disposal. One of them is the ability to engage in biological warfare.

CHAPTER FORTY-FIVE
THREAT ASSESSMENT

When you sit around a hotel bar with a bunch of advanced-warfare strategists, the kind of men and women who spend half their time on campuses and the rest in closed-door sessions at the Pentagon, and ask them what scares them the most, it's not a suitcase nuclear bomb—more people will die on our highways this year than one briefcase-size nuke would likely kill in a densely packed city—it's the threat of some biologist working for a rogue power or a poorly monitored superpower making something in a petri dish that could wipe out a high percentage of humanity.

This isn't a new threat. As far back as the 1940s, the US government was pouring millions of dollars into understanding the threat of biological warfare, even going as far as spreading our own bacterial agents in the wild to see how they spread.

In 1950 a naval ship in San Francisco Bay sprayed *Bacillus globigii* and *Serratia marcescens*, two theoretically benign bacteria, into the morning mist to see how they spread.

The results, not to mention the aftereffects when a number of people became ill from what may have been these presumed benign strains, were frightening. In addition, it reinforced the idea that a foreign power could launch an even more lethal agent at the United States. For that reason, secret biological-warfare testing continued, including spreading presumably harmless bacteria in subways and other public spaces to see how quickly they could be dispersed.

Sixty years after that first test, we have a billion-dollar germ warfare program designed to mitigate that threat, as well as a *trillion*-dollar biotechnology industry that keeps coming up with new ways to scare us.

Today I can sit at my computer and play with a program that mixes and matches genes like LEGO blocks, click "Send," and have a laboratory custom make a bacteria with that gene sequence.

This technology has already saved lives and theoretically will save far more than it kills with its bad applications—at least we hope so. The genie was let out of the bottle when a nineteenth-century monk started playing with pea pods; trying to limit the tools or the flow of information is only going to make the good guys less capable and informed.

Probably.

But along with all this interest in the military applications for engineered bacteria has come a number of nonlethal ways to use germs. One of them is in a project I was tangentially involved with as a consultant.

Suppose you think Terrorist A is part of a terror network, but you have no idea if he knows Terrorist C in another country. If they're smart enough to not use electronic communication that links them and always use an intermediary—Terrorist B—how do you connect A to C without waterboarding Terrorist B or even letting him know you're onto him?

You could follow everyone who meets with A, then follow everyone who meets with them and hopefully find a short connection to Terrorist C, but the problem is you quickly run out of agents to follow all the possible intermediaries. As the human-connection tree branches out again and again, you soon find that there aren't enough people on the planet to manage the job.

This was one of the problems the intelligence community was dealing with: the sheer cost, and ultimately the impossibility, of employing enough people to follow other people.

One solution, and the project I was brought in to consult on, was to use not people but bacteria.

A wealthy superpower with a first-rate science program could modify a benign bacteria—the kind that's already in your glass of water—with a special tag that would allow you to differentiate it from its brothers and sisters.

You could then spray this on Terrorist A as he passes you in the street. As the bacteria multiply in his mouth and nasal passages, he'll spread it for several days before his immune system kills it off.

It sounds like a potential nightmare scenario in the making.

Well, it isn't and it is.

The problem with the San Francisco experiment—beyond the ethical ones—was that they didn't have access to designer bacteria. They had to use strains that were presumed harmless but still rare enough that they could attribute their spread to their testing.

Using a common benign bacteria wouldn't have worked, because it would already be crawling all over everyone in San Francisco.

Whereas now we can take a friendly strain like *Neisseria lactamica*—and not a turncoat germ like *Streptococcus pneumoniae*, which can too readily mutate into something harmful—add some markers to the genome, and wait to see if our special strain shows up on Terrorist C by stealing his Starbucks coffee cups and swabbing anything else he touches.

Through the miracle of adaptation, we can even get a rough estimate of how many people our bacterial spy had to go through to reach Terrorist C, telling us the "distance" between them. And then using some software I helped create, we can estimate the size of the network by looking for the number of mutations we find on Terrorists D and E.

This sounds scary to some people. To me, it's not. The statistical likelihood of a mutated dangerous strain of *Neisseria lactamica* being unleashed in a project like this is about one-trillionth the likelihood that you'll launch a civilization-destroying superflu the next time you sneeze *Streptococcus pneumoniae* in a crowded McDonald's.

What is scary to me is that a friend of mine told me that, while the hunt for Osama bin Laden was still ongoing, there were serious talks about engineering a particular strain of flu virus that would target only him. Researchers were about 50 percent certain they could do this with a several-billion-dollar budget. But they had to explain to officials the other 50 percent probability, which was that a slight mutation could wipe out the entire bin Laden family—including the benevolent ones. And an even bigger mutation, actually just a defect in the part that looked for his specific gene markers, would stand a high probability of wiping out 90 percent of all primates on the planet—including *Homo sapiens*.

The project was abandoned. Or so I'm told.

Fast-forward to today: the intelligence community now has access to specifically engineered bacteria and viruses that can perform a number of nonlethal tasks, if you know what to ask for. They don't name these germs for their true intent. Instead they're given boring number sequences and categorized for uses that are supposed to be limited to the petri dish.

I special ordered five separate strains of *Neisseria lactamica* with a couple of modifications not in the books. Since I don't have access to high-end laboratory equipment or even a nifty scanner with custom assaying chips, I have to be able to spot my strains in the field. That's why they have a special gene that will make them glow pink under an ultraviolet light when sprayed with a protein compound.

So after I go place my spy cams at each botanica, I'm going to enter each store and douse every bottle of Snake Bite I can find, covering them with my microbial bloodhounds.

Call it revenge for the headache I still have a day later.

CHAPTER FORTY-SIX
BIAS

The hard part wasn't putting the little spy cams near the aluminum door frames of the botanicas or even spraying their inventory of Snake Bite as I followed the delivery truck while it made its rounds from shop to shop. The challenging part was sorting through the thousands of images gathered by the cameras and narrowing them down to the 323 people that all walked through their doors over a two-day period.

My camera placement on the second day at Blessed Angel Spiritual Wonders was a little off, and the only usable images were the ones captured in the reflection of the door as people entered and left.

Out of all of them, I have a feeling one could be the Toy Man, which is encouraging and frustrating because the image is so poor. Compounding that is the awareness of my own bias. I've already cast someone in the role of the Toy Man in my head, and this man meets that description. Is it because I think he matches what Artice told me? Or because he's my idea of a scary black man?

I could second-guess my innate prejudices all day long, but in the end, it's never a substitute for an expert opinion. In this case, the opinion of Artice himself.

I'd scheduled to have Artice use the jail's video-calling service to speak with me in case he remembered anything else that might be important—also to let him know I was actively pursuing this and I hadn't forgotten him.

As I wait for the conference software to tell me he's calling, the waning moon is visible through my hotel window, reminding me there are only four days until the Toy Man kills again, if he's keeping with his schedule.

While another killer might hold off while there's an investigation under way, I suspect that the Toy Man won't . . . for several reasons. The first is that police are looking for him on the wrong side of the country and searching a house he abandoned years ago. They haven't even found his other Los Angeles killing field. The second is that he's arrogant. Like other highly intelligent killers, he wants to believe that his actions are invisible and that he can't get caught. Were he to stop, that would be an admission to himself that the cops could be at least as smart as him. The last reason I think he's going to kill again on the new moon is because he believes in magic. This is the most powerful time of the lunar cycle for him to conduct his blood ritual.

My computer chimes, and Artice's somber face appears. He's not the unflappable young man I saw before.

"Artice?"

"Yo, Theo." He glances off to the side. Usually there's a guard in the room when they do these sessions, so he's probably just reminding me.

"Are you okay?" I ask.

"Yeah . . . um . . . I had a visit earlier from a Detective Chang . . ."

"Chen?"

"Yeah, her and some dude prosecutor I hadn't spoke to before. They showed me a photo and asked if it was the Toy Man."

"Was it?"

Artice lowers his head and cups the phone. "Between you and me? No. I never saw that guy before. But they really, really wanted me to say yes."

"Did they say a name?"

"Yeah, something Sims."

Clearly they're putting pressure on their only witness to name the late Brazilian hit man Ordavo Sims. But how far are they willing to go?

"They pressured me hard, man. All I had to do was go before a grand jury and say that was the guy. No trial or anything."

That's so wrong, dangling something like that in front of Artice. I try to keep my anger to myself.

"But I said I wasn't sure. Then they told me that I was just a kid back then and everything is different when you're young and memories can get all messed up."

"How did that go over?"

"I told them to go fuck themselves. I already went through that shit before with people telling me I made up the Toy Man. Now they think he's real, but they're going to tell me who he is and who he isn't? Fuck them. I don't care what they put in front of me or what promise they make. If that ain't the Toy Man, then it ain't him, you know? I'm not gonna let them go easy on me knowing he's out there hurting some other kid. How can a decent person live with that?"

Indeed. Even a guy like Artice, who's caused his share of mayhem, sees that. "So now what?"

"They said they were going to let me think about it and come back tomorrow."

"Did they offer you anything specific as far as a deal?"

"No. But I got the feeling the prosecutor guy was willing to talk to the judge on my case and maybe do something. Who knows. I don't trust them. Anyway, what you got?"

"I have some photos, too. Unfortunately, I can't do much to help your case."

Artice nods his head. "I know that. But if it goes down like the last time you went after one of these motherfuckers, then that's cool with me."

I cough. "Uh, I'm hoping for a less physical resolution."

I take the photos from my folder with the backs to me. I've gone to the extra effort shuffling them so I don't know which one is which. I want Artice to give me his own opinion and not one influenced by my body language. We all think we're good at hiding that, but chances are, the better you think you are, the worse you actually are.

"Okay, I'm going to go through these one by one. When you see one that may be him, let me know and I'll set it aside. I'll warn you, some of these are pretty sketchy images."

"Got it." He moves closer to the screen.

"Nope. Nope. Nope. Nope." He's not even hesitating.

"Do you need more time?" I ask.

"Are your hands getting tired?"

"Sorry. How about this one?"

"Nope. Nope. Nope. Nope. Nope . . ." Artice pauses.

I'd been unconsciously looking away from the screen, trying to avoid seeing a reflection of the image.

"Artice?" I lower the photograph.

He's almost hypnotized. His eyes are wide and his mouth half-open.

"Artice?"

"That's him."

"Let me set this aside, just in case, and go through the rest," I reply.

"You don't need to." He's shaking his head slowly. "That's him."

"Just to be sure?"

He gives me a dutiful nod. "Fine, but that's the motherfucker right there."

I show him the rest of the photos, getting a series of impatient noes from him. Finally we reach the last one.

"Nope. It was that first one."

I turn the photo over.

It's the same one I'd pulled from the stack myself. I show the image to him again. "Are you sure it's him?"

Artist stares directly into the camera, bypassing my image on his screen so his eyes are looking into mine. There's a coldness and a hurt in his expression. He's been doubted for so long and now I'm questioning him.

"The asshole even has his same white Cadillac," Artice replies.

"Cadillac?" I reply, flipping the image over.

This was one of the photos caught in the reflection of the door. Sure enough, when I look at the upper corner of the image, there's the unmistakable grille and front windshield of a white Cadillac.

The nagging question in my mind is whether I was drawn to the photo because of the expression on the man's face and Artice's graffiti, or was it the fact that my animal brain, my early warning system that listens for noises and looks for the signs of predators, saw the Cadillac but never communicated it to me consciously.

"Hey, Dr. Cray?"

I look to the webcam. "Yeah?"

"You got a name for him?"

I shake my head. "It's tricky. I don't want him knowing I'm after him. If the store owner knows him, I don't want him being tipped off."

"Okay . . . so what's your plan? Send an anonymous tip to the police?" Artice says sarcastically.

"No. Not that." I'm searching the image for more details. Unfortunately the license plate is blocked by a bush. However, in the upper portion of the image, I can see something on the dashboard. It's a parking receipt of some kind.

"I'm going to try to find out what that is." I hold the photo up for Artice to see.

"You better have some *Blade Runner*–level shit if you're going to see that. From here, it's just a blur."

I glance over at the SD card the image came from and start thinking about the algorithm used to create the video file of the image and the one I'll have to create to produce a clear photograph.

"Wavelets, Artice. Wavelets."

CHAPTER FORTY-SEVEN
FOURIER

In the early nineteenth century, French mathematician and physicist Jean-Baptiste-Joseph Fourier, who had previously accompanied Napoleon on his expedition to Egypt, became fascinated by the concept of heat transfer and how two objects exchanged energy. Why didn't one give up all of its heat to the other or vice versa? This led to a great number of other questions.

One was trying to solve the riddle of why the earth wasn't a giant snowball. When Fourier calculated the distance from the sun to the earth's surface, he realized there just wasn't enough energy hitting the ground to keep us warm. This led to the discovery of the role of the planet's atmosphere and water vapor in moderating Earth's temperature, and ultimately to the discovery of the greenhouse effect.

But it was Fourier's work describing the mathematical functions of energy transfer that gave way to the Fourier transform. Roughly summarized, it meant using arithmetic to reconstruct a larger signal by looking at only a smaller portion of it.

Fourier transforms became the basis for computer compression, and they are the reason I can fit all of those surveillance images and videos on a tiny SD card. The processor doesn't have to write everything to the memory chip—just enough that I can get a usable image.

The problem with this kind of compression is that it loses information. Assuming even the tiny lens on my spy cam was able to refract a clear image of the Cadillac dashboard to the even smaller photo-sensor array, and that they in turn had the resolution to resolve what was on that slip of paper, by the time the processor squeezed that image down, any helpful data might have been lost.

However, it was because of the lossy nature of Fourier transforms that mathematicians started looking at other compression and reconstruction techniques. Wavelet compression was based on the idea of using the whole wave of a signal and creating a lossless version of it by getting the precise function that created it. Although it's much more processor intensive than a Fourier transform, it uses memory much more effectively.

Sadly, my spy cams use the same Fourier-based algorithms behind lossy compression, and there's only so much data I can pull from the photo.

But on the other hand, the same math behind wavelet theory can also be used to reconstruct a signal across time.

Photo software that can pull a clear image from a blurry photograph caused by camera shake works by calculating how long the shutter was open and measuring the amount of movement. By treating the blurs like paint strokes, it can essentially roll back time and figure out what the top of the brush looked like—or the shape of your eye.

When our suspect walked through the door and triggered the motion detector on the spy cam, it recorded about four seconds of footage. Because I was using the motion JPEG compression method for video at fifteen frames per second, this means my little camera caught sixty photographs of his face and the front of his car.

Because the door was moving, it caught his face from several angles, like a scanner used to make a 3-D image of his head.

I've already got a 3-D model from those images using off-the-shelf software.

While getting shape data was easy because his head was close enough to the glass, trying to get a clearer image of what's on the Caddy's dashboard is more challenging, because it's a two-dimensional object photographed from sixty slightly different angles.

But all is not lost. Part of the magic of wavelet transformation magic is that I can input certain known factors that give the software more information than is apparent in the image.

While the grille of a Cadillac is just a rectangle to the algorithm, I know precisely how many centimeters across it is and can accurately estimate how far away from the door and the lens it was as the image was taken.

By stabilizing the little paper square in 3-D space, I can overlay all the other images, adjust for specular changes, make estimates of refractivity of the paper, and even use a little artificial intelligence to build a best guess of what certain shapes are in the image.

After five hours I have a copy in my hand of what's on the dashboard—well, almost. I can make out what is supposed to be a bar code and might even be able to reconstruct that if I had other sample bar codes and could figure out what the blurry streaks might be, but the important part is the logo, which is quite clear and unambiguous.

I spent twenty minutes looking online for an Atlanta parking garage that used a double *E* as its logo and was about to extend my search statewide until I realized that in all of my mathematical pat-myself-on-the-back wizardry, I forgot to flip the image over—because it was a *reflection*.

I also adjusted our Toy Man image accordingly and put a scar over his left eye above his right, where it belonged.

Thirty-three Peachtree is the location of the parking garage and where his car was before he parked on the street in front of the botanica. The garage is part of a forty-story office building. If he went back there after visiting the shop, my little microbial bloodhounds could still be there . . .

CHAPTER FORTY-EIGHT
Photo Booth

Cooped up in my hotel room, concocting my elaborate scheme to observe my little tracker bacteria in the wild, I overlooked the difficulty of tracking them in the wild—or rather, at 7:00 p.m. in a still-occupied office building.

My goal is to see if the microbes show up on elevator buttons and any door handles on the floors the bacteria-covered buttons lead to. The problem is, my little guys only glow when they've been sprayed with a special threonine-and-glucose mixture and exposed to ultraviolet light. Since the glow is far too faint to see in a normally illuminated indoor space, the samples have to be placed in a virtual dark room and observed with either the eye or my iPhone camera.

While in some fantasy world I have the time to flood their entire fire-suppression system with my glow catalyst and then engineer a superhack to cause a city-wide blackout, I have to think of a plan that's a little more pedestrian.

The answer to my problem comes to me as I glance at one of the many Amazon Prime shipping boxes threatening to displace me from my hotel room like Tribbles.

I cut the bottom off a medium-size box and then tape it back on like a door, mounting my UV light inside the box.

This way I can open the flap and press it flat against any suspect surface and have a peek.

Also, I realize, given Amazon's use of independent delivery contractors, I could probably pass myself off as one by carrying the box. I hastily make a label addressed to Thompson Consulting on the twentieth floor of the building.

I give myself one last look in the mirror to make sure nothing screams *computational biologist masquerading as delivery man who is secretly releasing an untested genetically modified microbe into the general populace.*

When I pull up at 33 Peachtree, cars still pass in and out of the underground garage, but it's mostly empty.

The entry gate spits out a ticket, and I feel a little pride over the fact that it looks a lot like the one I made—except you can read the bar code on this one without having to resort to cryptographic measures.

I find a spot close enough to the lobby elevators, which I have to resist testing. If security's watching, I don't want to get kicked out or arrested before I get to check the main elevators.

My anxiety starts to grow as I step inside and press the button for the lobby. I didn't scope the place out and have no idea if the entrance is being watched or if I'll need to sign in.

When the doors open, I find myself staring down the hall and right into the eyes of a security guard sitting at a desk.

There are two elevators to the left and two to the right, but presently his attention is on me. I wave the box in the air like it's some kind of universal multipass.

"Do you know what floor you're going to?" he asks.

I stutter for a second, then remember to read the label, which adds a degree of authenticity to my bumbling. "Uh, twenty."

"Take either one on your left," he tells me.

"Uh, thanks," I reply with all the suaveness of a thirteen-year-old about to sneak into an R-rated movie.

I stand in front of the brass-colored doors, waiting for them to open. The floor numbers go from eleven to twenty—which means that after I've looked in both upper-floor elevators, I'll have to take a trip down a flight of stairs to catch the ones that service the first ten floors of the building.

"You need to press the button," the security guard shouts across the foyer to me.

"Um, right." I press the button and, a moment later, the doors open.

I step inside, press "20," and breathe a sigh of relief. As the elevator ascends, I remember that I have something I'm supposed to be doing here. I already wiped and bleached my hands in the car to make sure I didn't carry any of the strains into the building, so at the very least, I don't need to worry about contaminating the buttons myself. I take the bottle of activator from my pocket, spray the buttons, then step out into the hallway. In case the helpful guard is watching me on a security camera, I make a show of walking all the way down to Thompson Consulting, then turn back around.

I try not to glance around for security cameras. One of the tricks of urban camouflage is that if you look sufficiently boring, people will soon get tired of looking at you.

I go to the other elevator bank, press the "Down" button, and, when the doors open, reach my arm inside and spray its buttons as well.

I have a thought as I do this: What if the guard is watching through a camera inside the elevator? Could I pass the odd behavior off as being the actions of an eccentric germophobe?

Better not to find out.

I press the button for the eleventh floor, step back out, and call my original elevator.

By the time it arrives, I already have my UV light on and the box's bottom flap open. I have to be quick if I'm going to check all four elevators.

As soon as I enter, I kneel, press the box against the buttons, and congratulate myself for not impulsively touching a button, causing it to illuminate, and ruining my little darkroom.

When I peer inside my box, I see only the purple light of my UV lamp. No telltale smudges.

Of course, one problem looming in the back of my mind is that my suspect may have stepped into the elevator and told someone else what floor to press, leaving no trace.

I send the elevator to the eleventh and step back outside.

While I wait for the other lift, I try to figure out how much time I have before the guard notices I haven't come back down. Will he call the cops or come get me himself?

Either scenario is acceptable if I get my data. I'm not really doing anything illegal—assuming they're not too brushed up on microbiology or the Nuremberg Charter.

Stepping back into the second elevator I sprayed, I kneel and place my box over the buttons.

I'm greeted by a glowing smudge.

Hello, my little friends.

Miss me?

All . . . two colonies?

He pressed two buttons—"14" and "17." Perhaps he was kind enough to press the floor for another person. What a guy.

That also means I have two floors to check—each with ten to fifteen office doors.

The thrill of the hunt sends my adrenaline spiking, and the fear of discovery twists my guts as I press the button for floor seventeen.

CHAPTER FORTY-NINE
Speed Round

Here's the plan, I tell myself in the five-second trip from the twentieth floor to the seventeenth: I'm going to speed walk through the hallway and spray every door handle as I pass, then double back and use my camera obscura to peer at each door handle as quickly as possible. If there are thirty knobs total and moving from each one to the next takes ten seconds, that means a maximum time spent on this floor of just under five minutes.

If I'm lucky, I'll see my microbes on the first few attempts—but I understand mathematics well enough to know I'm just as likely to spot them in the last group, long after somebody has reported the kook on the seventeenth floor trying to break into offices with an Amazon box.

This idea sounded so much better in my hotel room.

The elevator doors open, and I zigzag through the hallway, watching over my shoulder, spraying doorknobs, and not paying attention to what the plaques by the offices say.

I can always look that up in the directory later. Speed is what I need right now.

I make it to the end of the left side with my spray bottle and realize that, instead of wandering back and forth across the hallway like a drunken sailor, I could simply pass close as I head to the end of the hall and then hug the other wall on my way back.

There's a reason the DIA recruited me for an office job and not fieldwork.

As I pass the elevator bank and start spraying the other knobs, I hear the ding of an elevator arriving on this floor and freeze.

A woman carrying a large pizza box emerges, sees me, smiles, and heads down the hall. I watch her stop at a door and realize she needs to grab her keys.

"Let me help you," I call to her as I jog toward her office.

I place my faux box under one arm and take her pizza in the other.

As she searches her purse for keys, she points to my box. "What's that?"

I'm about to point out that they don't tell me what's in the deliveries. Then I look down and realize the flap is open and my box is glowing purple on the inside like a gay disco for mice.

"A . . . science experiment," I reply.

From the look she gives me, I'd have been better off with the mice explanation.

She puts a foot in her door, takes her food, and all but calls me a weirdo nerd with her facial expression. "Have fun."

As soon as the door closes, I kneel and box the knob to see if she's in league with the Toy Man.

It's clean, but I hope she enjoys the threonine on her pepperoni—it'll taste, well, not that special.

I move to the next door, shadow the knob, and peek in at it: nothing. Same with the next eight.

My pulse is starting to race at the thought that she's going to call security, but I keep going. I'm not calling the game until they throw me out or arrest me.

As I reach the end of the hallway, I try to figure out the traveling salesman problem of hitting all the doors on fourteen as quickly as possible. I then wonder what I'll do if his fingerprints don't show up anywhere, because someone opened the door for him. *Damn you, southern hospitality.*

One step at a time, Theo. I can always park near the garage elevators and wait to see if he shows up.

I could even plant a camera in the main elevators and aim it at the keypad.

I have options, is what I tell myself. No glowing smudge isn't the end of the world—well, not for me.

What's killing me is the likelihood that the Toy Man has already selected his victim and is creating an opportunity to snatch him off the street.

The emergence of Ordavo Sims has made me suspect that he may have been some kind of accomplice to the Toy Man. Possibly he used bolt cutters to steal Christopher Bostrom's bicycle so it would be easier to give the boy a ride home—not just as a matter of convenience. I could see how a distraught boy upset that his bicycle had been stolen would be emotionally vulnerable and easy prey for a man who offered him a new one if he got into his car.

The thought of this has me so worked up that I check a door, dismiss it, and start back down the hallway before realizing that I just looked at a glowing smudge.

I rush back to the door, kneel again, and squint into my box.

There's glowing bacteria smeared all over the door.

The Toy Man walked through this door.

I snap a photo with my iPhone. And thanks to the resiliency of the suspension agent the bacteria are coated in, I get a partial fingerprint.

He was here just a few hours ago . . .

My blood turns to ice water.

Right here . . .

He touched *this* door.

Suddenly, the Toy Man is more than a phantom image. He's a real man who walks the same plane of existence as I do.

I step back to see what office he stepped into. Was it his? Did he just visit here? What was the story?

When I read the letters on the door, I'm almost equally startled by the sound of someone answering a phone on the inside. Never have a few simple words made my heart skip like these.

I feel fucking numb.

The plaque on the door says: DEPARTMENT OF HOMELAND SECURITY.

CHAPTER FIFTY
SAFE SPACE

There could be a thousand reasons why he entered this office. None puts me at ease. The mere thought that this evil man could comfortably walk through this doorway, while, on the other side of the country, law-enforcement agents are trying to piece together his crimes, is a frightening notion.

Compounding my confusion is this is a satellite office, not the main DHS center in Atlanta. This is the kind of place where they put divisions when they run out of space or need to keep operations separate. The question is: *What operations?*

My hand presses the button next to the door before my brain can decide if that's a prudent move or not.

What if he answers?

"May I help you?" says a man's voice over an intercom.

I look up and see a small camera facing down on me. Was someone watching when I examined the doorknob with my box? Will I have to answer some awkward questions if they allow me to step inside?

I pull my DIA contractor ID from my pocket and flash it at the camera. "Hello . . . I had a question about someone who may work here."

There's a buzz, and the door unlocks. "Come right in, Dr. Cray."

Their camera has an image recognition system that read my badge in a fraction of a second. Now they not only have my name—they also know everything about me.

I grasp the doorknob—the same doorknob he touched—and step inside.

The office is small. The reception counter nearly spans the room in front of glass doors. To the right of it stands an ordinary, closed door, which I'm guessing connects to another office suite. That would suggest that the DHS office has another, unmarked hallway entrance next door.

Behind the counter, a young white man in a white shirt and tie is sitting at a computer. There's a half-eaten Subway sandwich by his keyboard.

"How might I assist you?" he asks cordially. "Most everyone has gone home for the night."

I stare at the glass doors behind him and read the titles.

Jack Miller: Assistant Deputy—Global Affairs
Kim Dunn: Global Affairs Liaison
Carter Valchek: Global Communications

These are spooks, and the repetition of the word *global* tells me that they're not focused internally. Instead, they are intelligence-agency workers who talk to other government spooks in foreign countries. They're covert counterterrorism. Covert, because there's no mention of terrorism or narcotics.

The only reason the door was opened for me was because of my DIA card. Otherwise, I would have been told to go to the main office. I'm certain of it.

I try to think up a convincing lie that won't get me ensnared in my own blundering. "I was at the other office . . . they sent me here." I pull a print of the spy-cam image from my pocket, not the better, 3-D–reconstructed one. "One of my coworkers was injured in a hit-and-run. We're trying to find witnesses. She said she spoke to this man right before and he might be able to back up her testimony."

The receptionist stares at the photograph, glances at me for a fleeting instant, then returns to the picture. He shakes his head weakly—an unconscious tic when you're lying.

"He doesn't work here?"

He shakes his head more emphatically—what you do when you have something truthful to agree upon. "No. He doesn't work here."

I could ask him to check the camera logs, but that would be a security violation, and there's no way he's going to contradict himself on his lie.

The Toy Man was here. He might not work here, but he had important enough reasons for this man to lie to me.

"So this isn't a DIA matter?" he asks, realizing that he shouldn't have let me inside.

"I can't really say," I reply, leaving him to his own suspicions.

"Well, I can ask around. Is there a number where I can have somebody reach you? And would you like to leave the photograph?"

While I'm 99 percent certain this man knows the Toy Man, I'm fairly positive he has no idea what he truly is. If by leaving the photo and my burner's number I can place more suspicion on the suspect, then all the better.

I write the number down and slide it over to the receptionist. "Any help would make a difference." Then I add, trying to sound ominous, "We need to ask him some questions about Los Angeles."

The receptionist takes the photograph and sets it on the counter, not bothering to read the number or look at the image again. "I'll look into it," he says.

I thank him and head back into the hallway. If there weren't a camera above the entrance, I'd stoop to putting my ear against the door to try to hear whom he calls to tell about my visit.

The walk back to my car is filled with questions and hypothetical scenarios.

Why does the Toy Man have business with DHS?

Is he an informant of some kind? Informing on whom? About what?

There's a slim chance I can find out at least part of who he is. I'd avoided using it because the number of false positives is immense, but now that I have another data point, I might be able to filter through a lot of them and get some usable answers.

CHAPTER FIFTY-ONE

INSECURITY

The intelligence world includes many different categories of information, ranging from public information, such as phone directories, to top-secret gathered intelligence, like the conversations people in those phone directories are having.

As a contractor to the DIA via OpenSkyAI, I'm extremely limited in what I have access to. I'm given briefings that are relevant to the operation I'm asked to function in as an observer, and sometimes I even get answers to questions that they deem relevant.

Actual DIA agents like Birkett have access to a wider amount of information through an intelligence portal, but even that comes with restrictions and safeguards. Anything she looks up is logged. If she decided to see if an ex-boyfriend had been using another cell phone—information that is probably stored on some server in a basement in Virginia—it would raise red flags and possibly tag her with a felony, assuming anyone wanted to make the case.

But even work-related research can be challenging. I've asked her multiple times to get a piece of intel, only to be told that higher-ups deemed it nonessential, or worse, to discover that the info's flat-out wrong or outdated.

While I'm convinced that we need to be vigilant to protect our secrets, there's some solace in realizing that most of what the government knows about you is buried under miles of bureaucracy. There's a reason that, so many times after something bad happens, we learn that some other intelligence agency had been sitting on a report and did nothing about it. They never even knew what they had.

Increasingly, one of the most reliable sources of intelligence for the DIA—and one I have no trouble getting access to—is private intelligence sold to corporations and investment firms.

If I contacted the CIA and asked if the Chengdu Aircraft Industry Group was building a new J-20 fighter in a defunct industrial park five hundred miles west of Sichuan, I'd get a terse rebuke about classified intelligence.

However, if I log on to the Strategic Developments Awareness portal—a private company in Albany, New York—and type in a query about fighter-aircraft production, I'll get a satellite map showing how much energy is being consumed in an "abandoned industrial zone" and images that show a recently built highway that is unusually long and would make a great runway.

If you're Boeing or Lockheed, this information is extremely helpful in preparing your bids to the Indian and Saudi governments for an upcoming contract—if you've suddenly been made aware that generals in the People's Liberation Army Air Force might be whispering in their ears.

While the SDA portal won't tell me if the Russian attaché in New Zealand is actually a Putin inner-circle spy, a related portal called Global Connect serves as a kind of LinkedIn for rating the degrees of connection between various business and government figures. I can type in the attaché's name and find out that sending requests through him that have a net positive outcome on Putin's personal assets tends to have a higher degree of success than a Russian attaché to Australia.

It's not hard to work your way through the system and figure out who the "inside sources" are that talk to the *Washington Post* and which Mexican politicians have more business connections than political ones to Bolivians involved in cocaine export.

This information is almost all gathered through perfectly legal means. And it's actually encouraged by the US government, because while it would be a trade violation for the CIA to tell Boeing what their spies have discovered inside Chinese factories, it's presumably beneficial to the United States' trade deficit if Boeing had the same kind of information that Beijing is actively stealing from American computers and briefing their businesses about on a regular basis.

So, while it would be wonderful for me to put the image I have of the Toy Man into one of the DIA, CIA, or NSA portals and get back possible matches complete with life histories and dental records, I don't have that kind of access. Technically, my security clearance is on par with the person who answers the telephone at the front desk in DIA headquarters. But I can use the private portals like Global Connect or Face Tracer to track down possible leads.

Like the other portals, Face Tracer data is most accurate when money is on the line. If the Toy Man is a card counter who has been kicked out of casinos or spotted in Antwerp selling conflict diamonds, there's a good chance I'll get a reliable match. If not, he's just one of seven billion other people who have a few thousand other folks who kind of, sort of look like them.

I once found six guys in Indiana alone who looked like me. So Face Tracer isn't the most promising place to start. Plus, there's the somewhat controversial problem that most facial-detection algorithms are tested on white or Asian faces, due to a combination of how skin reflects light and inherent researcher bias. This means that Face Tracer will probably produce quite a number of false positives, but I'm prepared for that now.

I upload the images, including the original ones from the reflection and my reconstructed shots, and let the system start sorting through them.

First it tries to create its own data points: distance between pupils and nostrils, eyebrow shape and others, especially ears—your ears are almost like a fingerprint.

Next the system sorts through a database of billions of images. Some of them are taken from social-media websites, others from newspaper accounts and a thousand other sources.

And boom, Face Tracker has given me seven results. Fewer than I was expecting, which makes me concerned he might not be in there.

I discount three immediately because their profile doesn't fit. Two others are only images with partial data.

The last two, one with a 96 percent probability and the other with 98 percent, appear to be the same man.

But according to Face Tracker, they're not. And when I put their names into Global Connect, I'm given two different biographies.

One is named Oyo Diallo, who served as an aide to a Nigerian warlord before going missing after a conflict with Boko Haram.

The other is a Pentecostal preacher named John Christian.

I flip between the images. It's uncanny that two men could look so much alike yet be so different.

Then I read the biographies and everything starts to make sense.

Fuck.

They're the same man.

How does the leader of an African death squad become a Christian minister in the South? It's a chilling question, and one I'll need to have some solid answers to before I take my claim to the FBI or whatever authority I need to get involved.

On the surface, it sounds outrageous, but after checking a few news items and clarifying some historical precedents lingering in the back of my mind, the connection becomes even more plausible.

In 2016, a disturbing story began making the rounds on the news. A security guard working at Dulles International Airport was exposed as a former Somali strongman accused of being a war criminal. He had allegedly committed such atrocities as dragging people to death behind jeeps, burning villages, and ordering mass executions.

While these allegations were only being addressed in civil courts—the United States had no jurisdiction over those actions—people were still stunned to find out that he had passed FBI and TSA background checks. This was despite the fact that his wife's own visa status came into question after it was found out she claimed to be a refugee of the conflict her husband had helped create.

Some quick research reveals that human-rights groups claim there are at least one thousand accused war criminals living in the United States, a number of them alleged to have committed crimes as bad as John Christian / Oyo Diallo's.

While our own natural-born citizenry isn't lacking in individuals who have gone off to other countries and committed wartime atrocities—and despite the fact that our government has historically made more than a few exemptions for persons of value, such as the German rocket scientists we brought over at the end of World War II—the idea that a man like Oyo could be walking around freely makes my skin crawl. What poor refugee didn't get asylum here because Oyo knew how to play the system or some government official was asleep at the switch?

It takes me a few minutes to find an exact image match. While that's not admissible by itself, the time line syncs up perfectly: a year after Oyo goes missing, John Christian shows up. Both have Pentecostal backgrounds—a faith not uncommon in West Africa. Both have the same scar over the eye.

Even more convincing—at least to my newly cynical world-view, having spent the last year in antiterrorism efforts—is that John Christian's missionary work would be the ideal front for a gunrunner sending arms to war-torn regions.

On paper it's a strong case, but I need to get more evidence so I don't look like a conspiracy-theory crackpot when I try to point out that not only was the real Toy Man *not* killed a few days ago in a Brazilian prison before he could be extradited, he's actually a war criminal living as a minister in Georgia.

CHAPTER FIFTY-TWO

TRACKER

A day later, I have three addresses I can tie to John Christian.

The first is a small home on the outskirts of Atlanta. When I drove by, it seemed obvious that, unless it has an expansive basement, this is not his killing ground.

For starters, it's in a tightly packed neighborhood with almost no fences. His home is a two-bedroom, single-story house with a small backyard that's visible from the street, and his living room has a wide window revealing a spartan interior with a rather large cross mounted to the wall.

It's where you'd expect to find a simple man of God, not a dangerous predator who likes his privacy. The home is the complete opposite of the one at Wimbledon—which reinforces my suspicion that he has multiple homes for different parts of his life. There's John Christian's home, and then there are the Toy Man's lairs.

I saw no car when I drove by, so I got out, took a few pictures, and kept going.

The second piece of property attached to him is his church. About ten miles away from his house, the church is a distressed, white-painted metal structure sitting on a half acre of land with a few other buildings.

There, in the middle of the parking lot next to five other cars, is the white Cadillac from Artice's nightmare.

It's like seeing the cresting waters around a shark's fin in the ocean. It's something you've known exists—but until now it's been lurking deep beneath the waves.

Now it's in my world.

My plan is simple: I think Oyo has other property that I can't find through records: a place he doesn't want anyone to know about. When the new moon comes three days from now, that's where he'll commit his act. In order to stop him, I have to know where that place is.

I'm not a skilled surveillance operator—and even they work in teams. In order to catch him, I'll have to resort to something a little more straightforward and risky. It involves me pulling up next to his car for about a minute and praying that he doesn't come walking out and see me.

It's also illegal, but I'm far beyond caring about that. Somewhere there's a young boy whose life depends on me.

Turning the wheel into the parking lot feels like trying to push the rudder of a massive sailing vessel. Ignoring the looming Oyo storm would be so much easier.

I drive down the small asphalt road and take the spot next to Oyo's Cadillac, which appears to be only a few years old and still has California plates. I suspect that he leases them or buys a new one every few years, not for the sake of vanity, but because it makes finding hair and fibers from previous crimes impossible.

At the height of their suspicion, police literally sat across the street from Ted Bundy, waiting for a search warrant while he washed his Volkswagen Beetle, scrubbing away the forensic evidence they were desperately seeking.

I take a breath and then pull out the map I'm using as a cover for my actions. It's a bit of an anachronism, but still plausible. I've already prepared a touristy question I can ask the first person who spots me, if necessary.

With the map on the steering wheel, I take out my little device and make sure everything is working.

Because I don't have access to the wafer-thin devices the DIA uses in its operations, I have to improvise with the hope that Oyo isn't paranoid enough to sweep his car for trackers. My gadget is a simple, off-the-shelf cell phone I bought at a Walmart, plugged into a USB battery brick, and packed into a small black hobby box I got at RadioShack. Glued to the box is the largest neodymium magnet I could find on short notice.

I check to make sure nobody is coming, open my door, and lower my body to the ground.

If I'm spotted in this awkward position, I've already got my own phone in my other hand so I can stand up with that, pretending to have dropped it.

As I squat and nervously try to stick my tracker on the undercarriage of his car, repeatedly popping my head up over the door like a nervous gopher, I'm keenly aware that I'm not cut out for fieldwork.

It takes me an eternity to find a spot for the magnet, and once I do, it makes such a loud metallic clang I'm afraid folks will hear it all the way in the church. But nobody comes running out. I give the jury-rigged tracker box a firm tug. *Good.* At least it won't be coming off by itself.

I pull myself back into my driver's seat, adrenaline still pumping. I give one more check to make sure I'm not being watched and start to back out of my parking spot.

I pull away from the church and turn in to a gas station across the street and down half a block.

As I fill my rental car's tank, I keep an eye on Oyo's car, waiting to see if he comes running out to see what the mysterious man was doing to his vehicle. He doesn't.

After topping up, I debate if I should wait to see what he does next, but decide that my skills aren't quite up to that task. I need to stick to data points and not this hands-on shit. As I've proven repeatedly, it's not my best talent.

Next up is for me to check the third piece of property I found linked to the Toy Man and his church. It's raised a number of red flags in my mind, but it seems a little too brazen. I can't imagine that Oyo would do his crimes somewhere that it would be easy for the police to get a search warrant—but who knows? Maybe he's perfectly at home in his John Christian persona.

CHAPTER FIFTY-THREE
Retreat

In my research into John Christian / Oyo Diallo's ministry, I found out that they have a small parcel of property west of Atlanta near Sweetwater Creek State Park. Called Children's Christian Camp, it's two acres of land with three buildings, a small pool, a rather uneven soccer field, and a fire pit—according to Google Earth.

The website says it's a Christian retreat for poor and underprivileged children. While this sounds like a child-killer's delight, the camp itself isn't exactly what you'd find in a *Friday the 13th* movie. There are no fences and the buildings lie largely in the open, with plenty of neighbors. Like Oyo's house in the suburbs, this isn't where a murderer would feel comfortable chasing buck naked after children.

However, the camp itself seems like the ideal place to spot and groom potential victims.

While Oyo is away, I decide to drive over to the currently empty camp—according to the schedule, at least—and look around.

I park my car and walk around the buildings. They're all older wooden structures painted white with dusty windows.

Peering through them, I spot a cafeteria and an activity room where the shelves are filled with board games. The other buildings include four stand-alone bunkhouses with ten bunk beds in each, as well as a free-standing shower and bathroom structure like you see at campgrounds.

In the pictures on the camp's website, the kids spend a lot of time in tents and doing activities in the field. There's no lake and none of the amenities of a regular summer camp, but for a kid from a poor family, it doesn't seem like the worst place in the world . . . other than the fact that it's run by child killer . . .

At the far end of the property is a state forest. To the west side lies a compound with a high fence—to keep the children's noise out, I suspect. On the Internet, the neighboring property was listed as McGentry Nursery, but there's no signage visible from the camp side of the property. What growth I can see over the fence looks a little overrun.

I walk around the camp again, making sure I didn't miss anything like a fallout shelter or some kind of underground bunker. While I'm not sure that I would know it if I stood over one, I'm reasonably sure the Toy Man's lair isn't buried beneath his Children's Christian Camp.

Although this could be a killing ground, and while the kill house at Wimbledon was also where he buried some of his victims, it seem fairly unlikely someone as intelligent as Oyo would be willing to risk a bunch of hyperactive kids playing a game of dodgeball over a trove of poorly concealed bodies. He has better hygiene than that. Most serial killers don't.

There have been numerous instances when police have shown up on a serial killer's doorstep while victims were screaming for their lives just a few feet away in muffled crawl spaces or locked inside hidden rooms. They found twenty-six of John Wayne Gacy's victims buried under his home. What was left of Jeffrey Dahmer's was in his refrigerator and in almost every part of his home.

I walk over to a ring of logs surrounding a fire pit. Using the toe of my shoe, I kick around the ashes, just in case there's something that shouldn't be there.

Despite containing some melted plastic and foil, it doesn't appear to be a cremation pit. Everything about the camp is what you would expect. Whereas simply glancing at the house on Wimbledon gave me anxiety.

I return to my car to head back to my hotel so I can take a look at Oyo's location data and build a map of the places he's driven to in the last few hours. I hope at least one of them is his secret place. Finding that now could literally be a matter of life and death.

As I reach for my rental-car key fob, my phone rings, startling me.

"Hello?" I reply as I take a seat.

"WHAT THE FUCK, THEO? WHAT THE FUCK?"

"Birkett?" It sounds like the angriest version of her I've ever heard. "What did you do?"

"What do you mean?" I nervously glance around, expecting police sirens and helicopters. "Los Angeles? That thing?"

"That thing? Jesus. No. I'm not talking about your weirdo hobby. I'm talking about how I'm trying to smooth things over with Park so he doesn't make your life difficult, and how I'm talking to a friend who handles contractor internal affairs for the DIA. I ask to see what Park may have said after your, uh, *disagreement* with him, and she mentions someone pulled your RA jacket."

"My what?"

"Risk-assessment jacket. It's the file where they list all of your potential security liabilities. It's how we keep track of all you assholes and make sure you're not about to go all Snowden on us and spill your guts to the Russians. Someone was very interested in you."

"Park?" I reply.

"No! How can someone this smart be this stupid?"

"It's a daily struggle," I reply.

"It's from another agency."

"Which one?"

"I can't tell you that shit. But let's imagine the DIA with one different letter in our acronym."

The CIA. "Why the hell are *they* asking about me?"

"Why the hell . . . wait . . ." She stops as she realizes she was about to repeat my question. "Why the hell *are* they?"

"If I told you I didn't have a clue, would you believe me? And should you even be asking me this?"

"If they'd filed a proper gag request, then no. But they didn't, so it's office gossip, but seriously, Theo. If I find out you've been burning classified docs onto Lady Gaga CDs, I'll have your balls."

"That was Manning, not Snowden."

"I FUCKING KNOW THE DIFFERENCE!" She takes a deep breath and manages to sound slightly less combustive. Slightly. "This isn't just you—it's me. I pulled so many strings to get you this job. I made a lot of promises. Your back-and-forth with Cavenaugh doesn't help—but at least he respects someone with the conviction to air his grievances. If you're up to some shit, my ass is done. And I like what I do. I will personally hunt you down, cut your dick off, or make sure that when you're in federal prison some motherfuckers do that to you. Understand?"

"Yeah . . ."

"UNDERSTAND?"

"Jesus, yes! Whatever my convictions, they don't involve me spending time in federal prison or the rest of my life in Russia depending on a bunch of former KGB spooks looking after my well-being."

"Good. I'm glad we're on the same page."

"Yeah. Trust me. I wouldn't do anything like that to fuck you over."

"Fine." She takes another long breath. "I believe you. But I wonder if you could be a sociopath."

"I ask myself the same question."

"You're not helping me feel better. Just tell me, is there anything you could have done that raised a red flag somewhere?"

Well, shit. "Um . . ."

"Theo?"

I'm not going to tell her about my little germ experiment or what that uncovered—especially because it involves putting genetically modified microbes on the literal doorstep of the DHS.

There are absolutely no good optics on that.

Plus, she'd be duty bound to tell her superiors, and right now, someone pulling strings doesn't like me. It could be Park using an intermediary to fuck with me, but I don't want to push it in case it's not.

"You saw my name in the news?" I ask rhetorically. "Maybe somebody in some other agency was just curious? In the coverage I'm just listed as a consultant for OpenSkyAI. Maybe someone at some other agency was curious about what I was doing there?"

"Mmm-hmm," she says, not buying my explanation. "What else you got?"

"I can't say . . ."

"You're so goddamn transparent. What?"

"I can't tell you anything other than this: The house of horror in Los Angeles? The suspect that died in Brazil? He ain't the main guy."

"So this is why you're in Atlanta?"

"How did you know that?"

"I work for an intelligence agency, dumb ass. Also, I had to make sure you weren't off to the welcoming arms of the Chinese. Never defect there. Jesus Christ."

"Got it. So . . . what I can tell . . . well, the guy who I think did this . . . um . . . he might . . . he might be an informant."

"Okay," she says patiently. "For who?"

"Possibly the Department of Homeland Security."

"Muslim?"

"No. It's more complicated. And not a domestic informant."

"Shit, Theo. You went sniffing around a protected informant?"

"I don't know that's the case. But this guy is bad. Real bad."

"That's why we use them as informants. The good guys don't know anything."

"Yes," I reply. "But this is the guy that murdered at least seventeen kids in Los Angeles."

"If you got proof, send it to me and we'll get it to the FBI."

"I'm working on it."

"What does that mean?"

"It means that I need to make sure they follow through right away. This guy may be about to kill a kid. And if I screw this up, he'll cover his ass and go do it again and again while I'm answering awkward questions."

She sighs loudly. "You better know what the hell you're doing."

"No shit."

"And watch your back. Not everyone on our team is playing by the same rule book."

CHAPTER FIFTY-FOUR

PACKAGE

Birkett's ominous warning is in the back of my mind as I walk down the hallway of my hotel to my room. I was already paranoid, but now I'm even worried about people who are supposed to be on my side.

I put my key in the door, flip the light on, and see a distinguished older man in a three-piece suit lying on top of my bed, reading a Clive Cussler novel.

I back up and check the door number.

"You have the right room, Dr. Cray," the man says as he sets down the book. "Please, have a seat. My back has been acting up, so I took advantage of the firm mattress."

I look for a gun or some kind of weapon. His hands are folded across his stomach in the least threatening way possible. He looks like a totally relaxed lawyer or businessman.

I drop into a chair across from him, trying to get some read on who the hell he is and why he's here. I should call the police, but he's engaged my curiosity—plus, my gun is within reach.

"Comfortable?" asks the man.

"Yes . . . Are you?"

"Much better. It was a long drive."

"And what was the purpose of the drive?"

"To assist you, Dr. Cray. You're a man with lots of questions, and I'm here to provide what answers that I can."

"Well," I reply, not sure if this man is insane or just creepy. "Who are you?"

"You can call me Bill."

"Just Bill?"

He nods. "Just Bill."

"Well, Bill, I can already tell you're not going to be very helpful. It's been pleasant." I stand up and motion toward the door.

He doesn't move. "Dr. Cray, do you know the preferred treatment for trigeminal neuralgia?"

"No. I'm not that kind of doctor."

"Precisely. I'm not that kind of question replier. You need to ask relevant questions. Please have a seat. What you should be asking me is how I'm going to help you."

"With John Christian?"

"With not going to jail, Dr. Cray. May I call you Theo? That should be your most pressing question at this moment. How are you going to avoid spending the rest of your life in prison?"

I get it now. This guy is some holdover Cold War spook they pulled out of retirement to scare me.

"Funny," I reply. "That's not really a major issue for me right now. I'm wondering how you live with the idea that you're protecting a murderous piece of shit that's about to kill again."

"I have no idea who you are talking about," he replies.

"You have no idea about the seventeen dead kids they pulled out of the backyard of a Los Angeles home that one of your assets used to live in?"

From Bill's stare, I can tell he really does have no idea what I'm talking about.

"Seriously?" I groan. "You're just some guy they call up when they want to scare the shit out of someone, but they don't tell you why?"

"They tell me. I've seen some security footage of a man acting very peculiar in the hallway in front of a Department of Homeland Security office, possibly spraying some kind of chemical agent, before foolishly stepping inside and presenting his identification."

I get up from my chair and walk to the door. "For a solid minute, you had me worried."

Bill doesn't move. "I'm doing you a courtesy."

"Right. You're all heart. When DHS or the CDC comes knocking on my door, I'll start to panic. But when some CIA fossil sends some other fossil to scare me because they can't even imagine the size of their fuckup, I'll just have to take a pass on a freak-out." I open the door. "Time to go back to your suburb in Alexandria or wherever and tell your pal he should take a closer look at who the hell he's getting his information from."

Bill gets to his feet. He has a slightly amused look on his face. He stops at the door. "You're not going to like what happens next." He shoves his hand into his pocket.

I grab his forearm. "You're not going to like where I put that, Bill."

He slowly withdraws his hand and pulls out my little black box. "It wasn't hard to find the first time; I'm sure it won't be the next."

He drops the box into my hands and then starts walking down the hallway. He's almost at the elevator when I decide to run up to him.

"Wait!" I call after him.

Bill turns around. "Yes?"

"What do you know about him?"

"I've been given a very simple task, Dr. Cray. I'm the messenger. Message delivered." He turns away.

I grab him by the elbow. "Stop that spy-novel shit. Forget all the message delivering. Let me talk to the idealist in there that signed up when Khrushchev was banging his shoe and threatening to bury us.

The guy who knows right from wrong . . . Do you know who the fuck John Christian really is?"

His face is a blank expression. I see a man who has been so beaten down by the system that he just doesn't care anymore. When the phone rings, he delivers a pizza. He doesn't care what's in it or whom it's really feeding. All he knows is that when the order comes, he'd better deliver the fucking pizza.

I let go of his arm. He turns back to the elevator and presses the "Down" button. In the polished metal of the elevator doors, his cold eyes watch me. The blank expression is gone for a moment.

I walk back to my room, trying to figure out if I'm going to wake up in the middle of the night with Bill strangling me with piano wire or if I'm going to get a harsh letter from Human Resources about my treatment of the elderly.

I stare down at my tracker. The old fossil didn't even bother turning the phone off before giving it back to me. Did he even realize that it kept a complete log of everywhere Oyo went and where Bill was after?

Sheesh.

CHAPTER FIFTY-FIVE
HUNTING GROUND

When I went after Joe Vik, the only deadline in my head was getting back to school before the semester began—which I failed at. While he'd murdered someone I knew and his other victims left me unsettled, I still thought of Joe Vik in the past tense. Uncovering his crimes was like brushing away the dirt on an archaeological site and realizing that the Neolithic tribe practiced ritualistic murder—it could be shocking, but it was a thing of the past. You didn't worry about the skeletons leaping out of the ground and continuing their murderous ways. You didn't worry about the safety of some contemporary person. With Vik, even though I knew he was still an active killer, I had no time frame to motivate me. Taking two days or two weeks didn't seem like it would cost anything except my own professional career.

With Oyo it's different. The sun is up, and by the time it sets, he'll probably have his next victim. By the time it rises again, a young boy will be dead.

I'm tearing myself apart, because I could have done more over the last few days. If I'd run to the news, someone would have covered the story. I could have brought some temporary attention to Oyo and saved a life. Maybe.

But then what? He'd slip away and show up somewhere else, wiser to the fact that I was able to find him. He could leave the United States and pop up in some other country where his murders would be even harder to find. Which makes me wonder, what was his friend Ordavo Sims doing in Brazil? Was he more than a lackey? Is Oyo part of something bigger than I understand?

I don't even understand *him*, let alone what else he could be a part of. The man isn't merely a sociopath manufactured by a conflict. Like Joe Vik, he's someone with a particular talent for concealment and murder. He's a natural-born predator in a world of prey.

His concealment is so strong that I've lost him already. The tracking data from my phone shows that he left the church and went to his house and then another house in a nice Atlanta suburb that belongs to a wealthy attorney. After that, he returned home and the tracking device came straight back here—courtesy of Cold War Bill. There's no mysterious trip to a suspicious warehouse on the outskirts of town.

The attorney he visited in the suburb, Greyson Hunt, represents a variety of international corporate clients and is exactly the kind of person someone like Oyo would want to cultivate. Beyond that, there's not much of a connection.

I'm out of options. As a last resort, I've parked down the street from Oyo's house and have been watching his Cadillac in his driveway. It hasn't moved. I don't even think he's home.

He's slipped me.

I wait until 9:00 a.m. and call the church. I'm that desperate.

"Friends of Salvation Church," says a cheery woman.

"Hello, I was wondering if Minister Christian was in?"

"I'm sorry, but he's at a religious conference in Denver," she replies.

"Oh? When did he leave?"

"Last night, I believe. He should be back in a week. Is this a spiritual matter?"

"Of sorts. Thank you."

A religious conference. It's a good cover. Tell everyone you're leaving a day early, go do your killing, and then head straight there.

If anyone asks questions, their memories will be so hazy it would be hard to pin down where exactly you were at that point. It would be up to investigators to make the case otherwise.

It also explains why his Cadillac is sitting in his driveway. Oyo can't be spotted around town in that when he's supposed to be elsewhere. Atlanta is a big city, but it still acts like a small one. Word travels.

Oyo probably has another car and another identity—one tied to his hidden lair—the one I can't find.

It's the thing right in front of you that's the most important.

The family calling the cops over a hundred times about John Wayne Gacy.

The Laotian boy who ran from Jeffrey Dahmer's apartment, screaming, only to be returned there by the cops because they thought it was a lover's quarrel.

One of Lonnie Franklin's victims brought the cops almost to his doorstep, only to be off by one house.

The warning signs for Ted Bundy were everywhere. Each time the police got close, he moved on to another jurisdiction. At the height of his murder spree, there were cops that knew exactly what he was, but they were limited in what they could do.

Somebody knows something, and the one person who seems to know more than anyone else around here is Robert.

There's a remote chance he may be an accomplice of Oyo—but there's also the possibility he's another bystander simply trying to keep clear of the man.

With no other viable plan, I call his cell phone.

It goes straight to voice mail.

I try again a few minutes later. Voice mail.

These are desperate times, so I drive to Ms. Violet's home.

Robert is on the porch, talking to an old white woman with a black poodle sitting in her lap. There's a BMW parked in front of Violet's house, which I assume is the old woman's.

As soon as I pull up, he glances at me and his expression changes. He'd been making the woman laugh, keeping her company while she waits her turn to go inside and have her fortune fabricated.

Robert strides across the lawn and meets me as I get out of my car.

"Mr. Theo, you don't have an appointment for today."

I'm no longer Mr. Craig. Apparently he did have a look inside my wallet.

"I'm not here to talk to Ms. Violet. I want to know about this man that you and the Moss Man stay clear of."

Robert glances over my shoulder at the woman sitting on the porch, making sure she's not paying attention to our contentious discussion. This tells me she's a valuable client.

"I don't know what you're talking about."

"Someone who practices a very bad kind of magic. The kind involving human sacrifice."

Robert searches for a response. "I don't have anything to do with that."

"But you know about someone who does."

His face is a mask.

"Oyo, or John Christian, as he's known around here."

Robert blinks at the mention of the name, then shakes his head. "I don't know who you're talking about." He reaches for my door handle. "Please come again some other time."

I nod to the woman. "Is she important? Maybe a widow or has some dead kid? What's she worth to you?"

"Mrs. . . ." He stops before saying her name. "She's an old, dear friend of Ms. Violet. Now please, let's talk some other time."

"Why don't I talk to her? What would she and her rich friends think about a story involving someone you know who murders little children? How will that go over?"

He grabs my arm. "Mr. Theo, don't do that."

"Then tell me something. Because this man you're protecting is about to kill another child."

He shakes his head. "This man is very powerful. You don't know who you are dealing with."

"Tell me something, Robert. Tell me something so that when you look your god in the eye, you can convince yourself you're a good man."

He's struggling with this.

"Let me put it to you this way: soon the whole world is going to know about Mr. Christian. What do you want your part of the story to be?"

He scratches the back of his neck, wrestling with what to do. "All right. All I can say is that there's a place we know not to send our children."

"The summer camp? I was there. There's nothing there."

"That's all I can say," Robert replies. "Maybe you didn't look close enough. Now if you don't leave, I'll call the police."

"Well, that's ironic."

He waves his hand in the air and walks away with his shoulders slumped. Clearly this got to him.

I decide not to chase after him. He's at the point now where he doesn't care how much I harass his clients. He's more concerned with his own safety.

CHAPTER FIFTY-SIX
INSIDER

I peer across the dark field from my hiding spot in the trees, waiting for Oyo to show up. Both the sun and the moon have already set, and the only illumination in my night-vision goggles comes from the light of the stars.

His children's camp is deserted with the exception of the occasional possum that takes a stroll across the grounds, looking to see if the humans have returned and brought with them their offerings.

I parked my car a quarter mile away and walked the distance here, clinging to the tree line so Oyo couldn't spot me from the road. I've only seen four cars pass in the last hour. None of them pulled into the retreat.

I don't know if Robert's clue was intentionally misleading or if I misinterpreted it. Right now I'm at my wit's end, trying to figure out what to do next. I'm not sure what I expected to see: Oyo pulling up and opening the door to a secret cellar? Dragging a child into one of the camp buildings?

I took a walk through the woods behind the camp. The trees are fairly spread apart and the trails well marked.

It's not some sinister forest from a dark fairy tale. It would be hard to hide anything in there. I can imagine a few moonshine stills and some squatter shacks years ago, when the area was less developed. Now it's the kind of place day hikers walk through on a regular basis.

It also doesn't feel like the kind of place a predator would feel comfortable. Much as humans have an aesthetic sense of a safe space—small bodies of water surrounded by trees, long, open vistas—predators have environments in which they feel comfortable.

For serial killers it's usually their home or their car. Gacy had his crawl spaces. Bundy had his mobility.

What does Oyo have? His double lives, living side by side? The ability to be a man of God to the public and a servant of evil in private?

There's something masterful about how he intertwined the two worlds. His past atrocities put him in a position of power that was useful to intelligence agents looking at what they thought was a bigger problem.

After my encounter with Cold War Bill, I suspect that Oyo isn't simply an informer: his ministry may be one of those mysterious enterprises that clandestine parts of our government use to funnel guns and money to parts of the world where we're fighting secret wars.

That means the people calling the shots are literally on the front lines. They look at my interference as an act of treason—maybe not in law, but in spirit.

While I find it hard to believe they really know what Oyo is up to, I suspect that nobody wants to dig all that deeply. It's collateral damage in a greater conflict, from their point of view.

I check my watch. It's getting late. Not quite witching hour, but Oyo probably has given his victim his sleep juice by now.

Wherever they are.

I could be back at his house in an hour, but I am certain he's not there.

I'm also kicking myself for not inspecting his church. While I seriously doubt he'd bring a victim back there, it still could have some clue to his whereabouts.

I decide he's not showing up and crawl from my hiding spot. This was a bust. Best-case scenario: Oyo got worried and decided not to pull anything tonight, and I'm just working myself into a frenzy.

I don't *know* that he was going to kill tonight. It just seemed right—but how things seem isn't the proper way to do science.

I have to work on logic and facts.

Fact: Oyo hasn't shown up at the retreat.

I walk through the camp, peering into the windows with my night-vision goggles. Empty buildings waiting for children to return and fill them with their voices.

Right now the only sounds are crickets and frogs . . .

I close my eyes and listen more closely. There's another sound. Almost like dripping water.

I move closer to the source, trying to understand what it is.

There's something random about it.

It's a kind of "ploink" noise.

There's also something familiar.

It's not a natural sound—it's an imitation of one.

I cock my head to the side and place the sound somewhere in front of me.

My eyes still closed, I walk toward the source.

Something metal rattles as I bump into a barrier.

When I open my eyes, I'm looking at a foliage-covered chain-link fence—the one standing between the camp and the old, overrun nursery.

Carefully, trying not to rattle the fence any more than I already have, I pull myself up and peer over the edge.

There's an overgrown wilderness of plants and small trees. At one end there's a small house with an open glass door in the back. The inside is lit by the glow of a large television.

A cartoon frog is jumping from one lily pad to another.

A child's laugh pierces through the night air, and chills run through my body.

Before I climb the fence into the wooded lot, I have a realization: I should have looked more closely at the other homes on Wimbledon . . .

CHAPTER FIFTY-SEVEN
LAIR

My feet touch the wet soil, and I'm in a different world. The dark leaves of the wild ferns and saplings are black cutouts against a dark-gray sky. It's a mini jungle that reeks of a thousand scents. Rotting vegetation, blooming flowers left unattended, and, underneath it all, the sickly sweet smell of decaying flesh. I'm reminded of *Amorphophallus titanum*, the so-called corpse flower, which resembles a giant loaf of french bread emerging from an inverted bell. But that's not the source of these scents.

The flora are too densely packed for me to gauge the size of the nursery, other than what I recall from the Google Earth view. The lot is at least as deep as the retreat's, although it's nowhere near as wide; with the thickly spaced plants and trees, it might as well be the Amazon.

I can barely spot the glow of the television in the house from my new vantage point, but my feet find small flagstones, which I presume meander their way to the front of the property. Even though my curiosity is calling me toward the back, I have to go check and make sure the child playing the game is still unharmed.

I thread my way through branches and thick ferns, trying not to make scraping sounds or upset any of the dozen cracked statues and fountains that lie on either side of the path.

As I draw closer, the "ploink ploink" sound of the game grows louder. I hope this means the child is still conscious.

The foliage begins to thin out, and I find myself on a concrete patio. The house is directly before me. To my right is a passageway lined with trellises. This may have been the customer entrance back when this was a functioning business.

Through the open sliding glass doors, I see the back of a small brown head sitting on a couch facing the television. Occasionally he bounds up or down as his frog reaches some level.

I remain motionless, looking for my prey.

The game pauses, and the boy's head moves forward. I take another step and see him reach for a glass of grape-colored liquid.

I'm about to run into the living room and slap it out of his hand when I hear the basso of a voice. I can't make out the words, but from somewhere else in the house, an adult is speaking.

I have my gun. I could go in there now . . .

What if it's not him?

What if it is?

Unless my plan is to shoot him in cold blood, I need more. I need something I can point to if I call the cops. I can't just tell them my gut says they should dig up the backyard.

I'm a trespasser.

Suddenly I understand how those detectives felt as they watched Ted Bundy wash away the evidence in his car. Powerless within the law.

I tell myself that this child's fate will be similar to Artice's—he's safe until Oyo brings him to the killing room.

The killing room is somewhere behind me. Somewhere in this twisted garden.

I retreat back into the overgrowth and follow the path the other way, deeper into the dark. My night-vision goggles give me a narrow field of view—so claustrophobic that I'm tempted to simply feel my way by touch.

I use the goggles to keep an eye on the small flagstones and watch for anything that could trip me. One clumsy move and I could let him know I'm here.

The path winds left and right but never backtracks. I assume it was set by the gardeners who previously owned this property, and was meant to give visitors a leisurely view of all they had to offer—and not some demented labyrinth meant to deceive a person trying to escape.

Oyo is a clever opportunist, not a landscaper, I tell myself.

The trees and shrubs give way to another open space. It's a small clearing with a broken fountain in the middle. Tilted at an angle, the peak rises to a sharp point. Dead leaves and brush fill the basin, while vines wrap around the cement, strangling the spire.

A shed stands on the other side, its wooden walls even darker than the sky. A window on the side is covered with newspapers, concealing what's inside.

The only source of light is the reflection on the gleaming padlock mounted to the sliding door.

It's unlocked.

I walk around the fountain and listen for a moment. I can still hear the distant sounds of the game.

Artice's account of the shed at Wimbledon is forefront in my mind, along with the forensic details the LAPD was able to pull from it after the fact.

The stench of decay is even stronger here, plus there's some acidic smell I can't quite place. A cleanser? I can't see the point of that. Toy Man's murder scenes can't be cleansed.

I grab the door handle and pull as gently as possible. The wood makes a small squeak as it slides from the ill-fitted frame.

I hesitate, waiting for an immediate reaction, but none comes.

I pull the door open wider, and it begins to slide open on its own accord.

The first thing I notice is a black tarp on the ground. As my gaze drifts upward, I see row after row of wooden shelves on the back wall.

Filled with glass bottles and metal cans, the shed's interior doesn't seem that out of place for a nursery. This would be where you'd keep your seeds, fertilizers, and pesticides.

I step forward for a better view. My grainy night vision begins to resolve details in the darkness.

These aren't seeds. The bottles are filled with murky liquids. Most are impossible to interpret, but the ones with human ears and eyeballs are unmistakable. Other jars contain parts I don't even want to acknowledge.

The urge to throw up is so sudden and visceral, I can barely control it.

I've smelled dozens of corpses and even participated in human dissections, but I feel a different response now. This is the body's reaction to evil.

I take my phone from my pocket and take a photo. The flash goes off and I panic, afraid that the light will somehow be visible from the house.

It's unlikely, but still sends a shudder down my spine.

I slowly back out of the shed and push the door into place. I almost lock it, then remember this was how I found it.

When I let go of the lock, I realize that the video game has stopped playing.

I pull my gun free and step away from the door. The wind is blowing, stirring the leaves.

I walk around the fountain and take a side path leading to another side of the nursery.

One careful step at a time, I try to find my way back to the house. Occasionally I catch the glow of the television through the branches, giving some indication of direction. Thorns claw at my clothes, and vines threaten to trip me. I stoop to remove one from my ankle. When I stand again, the television is no longer visible.

Did he just turn it off? I squint, trying to make out any detail in the dark. I can see a faint glow thirty yards in front of me, but it appears that it's being blocked . . .

The television flickers back into view as the eclipse passes.

Someone else is out here in the undergrowth.

CHAPTER FIFTY-EIGHT
MAZE

I move even more cautiously than before, trying to discern the difference between the breeze rattling leaves around me and the sound of another man moving through the brush.

Attempting to keep as low a profile as possible, I put my gun at hip level and sweep it back and forth as I move to the next stone.

There's a crack beneath my feet. I glance down and see the image of a child's jaw through my night-vision goggles.

A jointed skeleton of a finger sticks out of the earth nearby, hauntingly pointing to the sky.

This confirms what my nose had already told me: this is a garden of death. God knows what else is out here. I already saw his trophy collection in the shed.

My ears twitch as I hear something scrape against concrete. He's now moved to my rear, flanking me from behind.

He has home-field advantage. I'm just blindly moving through his snare.

I weigh the risk of simply firing my gun but discount the foolish notion immediately. The chances of hitting someone are almost zero—but that someone could be the child.

The child, I remind myself. I can't fail. It's all about him.

I keep moving toward the glow. I can hear the sound of movement getting closer to me.

I could kneel down and lie in wait, ready to fire my gun . . .

But my feet keep me moving forward. The television is getting larger, and I can make out a score on the screen.

Footsteps.

I definitely hear footsteps behind me.

I run forward, leap through the brush, and emerge onto the patio.

The child is no longer visible on the couch, but I see a foot in a white sock poking out over an armrest.

The noise behind me is much louder—like a wild animal running through the brush.

I race into the house, rip off the goggles, and slide the glass door shut. The first thing I see is the bright image of my own reflection.

I press my face against the glass and see a shape standing out there. Tall, powerful. Right at the edge of the patio.

I lock the glass door and run around to the couch. The boy looks to be about twelve. He's passed out with his head on a pillow.

The cup of purple liquid is gone.

Still gripping the gun and casting nervous glances at the back door, I peel open the child's eyelids. Yellow eyes look up at me.

His pupils are dilated.

I give him a slap on the cheek. "Wake up," I whisper.

"Are we gonna go see the fort now?" he asks dreamily.

"Kid, you don't want to go there."

I pull him into a seated position and take out my phone. I dial 911 and blurt the address to the operator, then set the phone down but leave the line open.

I ignore the dispatcher's pleas for more information as my entire attention focuses on the glass door.

He's out there . . .

What are you going to do now, Oyo? I have the kid and found this place.

Do you turn into a rage monster like Joe Vik? Or do you sneak away into the night?

I get an answer a moment later when a statue comes shattering through the glass.

Broken shards fly at me. I duck down and protect the kid. The stonework crashes into the glass coffee table and falls to the floor.

I stick my gun over the edge of the sofa and fire into the darkness.

BANG.

BANG.

BANG.

I squint through the opening and can see only the tops of the over-grown plants against the night sky.

If this were Joe Vik, I'd be worried that he'd be coming in through the front door.

But he's not.

He's something else entirely.

The Toy Man knows when to run.

In the distance I can hear the sound of sirens. I wait until they're right outside, then put my gun back into my holster.

I won't be needing it again tonight.

CHAPTER FIFTY-NINE
SURROGATES

I've been inside a holding cell for four hours, and nobody has even come to talk to me since the police brought me in.

The cops on the scene did their job. They treated me with an appropriate amount of suspicion, got the kid to the hospital, then let me lead them through the bone-strewn garden and the little shack of horrors—which was even more horrifying the second time.

Oyo must have freaked out and started ripping shelves from the walls.

There were body parts and noxious fluids everywhere.

One cop puked. I wisely kept my distance from the door.

When we arrived at the police station, I wasn't in handcuffs. But a lieutenant was waiting outside for us.

He said something to the cops who brought me in, and the next thing I knew, I was in bracelets and escorted to this holding room.

Somebody spoke to someone.

Now the question on my mind is who is going to be the next person to walk through that door?

Will it be Bill with a pistol and a silencer?

Will it be some rough ex-con "randomly" placed in my cell?

Or am I just getting too damn paranoid?

What I know is that Oyo the Toy Man is on the run and probably off to his next kill spot. My gut tells me it won't be in the United States. I'm not sure how far I can chase him. I barely made it this distance.

There's the sound of keys, and the door opens. A short woman in her midthirties dressed in a suit jacket and skirt enters the room and sits across from me. She's got dark hair and aquiline features. Her eyes give away the fact that she's intelligent.

After the door shuts, she drops a folder onto the table in front of me.

"Dr. Cray, let's go over your story."

"Am I making a statement?"

"No," she replies. "I'm going to give you your story. What you need to tell them. How you found the house."

"Pardon me? I thought I had that already."

She taps her fingernails on the metal table and assesses me for a moment.

"There are two kinds of facts, Dr. Cray. The ones that you can prove and the ones you cannot. What you *think* is irrelevant." She opens the folder and studies it. "You received an anonymous tip from someone in Atlanta that brought you to Mr. Basque's home."

"Basque? Who is he?"

She pulls a photo from the folder and shows it to me. Other than the fact that he's black, he looks nothing like Oyo. "This is Mr. Basque. He's the one that killed the people found at 437 Sweetwater Road."

"No, he's not. What is he? Some patsy you keep on standby?"

"His name is on the rental receipt. The child has already identified him as the one that picked him up."

"The kid is still high on the concoction Oyo gave him. He'd say Santa Claus did it. Why are you protecting this monster?"

"We're not. If there is a third party, they will be dealt with."

I can't believe this. "I know you guys do stupid things, but I can't believe you'd protect a child murderer. What am I missing here?" It hits me all at once. "Yourselves. Fuck. I get it. You had no clue, or you were looking the other way. This is how you try to cover your asses when it turns out you aided and abetted a murderous pedophile."

I let out a deep breath, finally glimpsing the whole picture. "This is fucking big. It's not just one agency supervisor that falls on their sword—this is the kind of thing that makes news for months and means congressional inquiries. Funding cuts and that kind of thing. Am I right?"

She has no reaction. "So are we clear on the anonymous phone call?"

I shake my head. "No. We are not. Lies are not how you fix fuckups."

"Dr. Cray, I have a copy of a document you signed explaining that you fully understood the penalties for exposing intelligence secrets."

"Yeah. And there's a part in there about the Constitution. And there are whistle-blower laws. Lady, it doesn't work like this."

"Then I'll have to take your actions as being hostile to the interests of the United States."

I try to raise my hands, but I'm stopped by the fact that they're locked to the table. "Whoa. You don't get to wave the patriot flag. That's what the Chinese government says to people before they send them off to the organ-harvesting van. That's what bad guys with badges say."

My mysterious visitor checks her watch, taps her fingers on the table again, then replies, "We're done."

She gets up, knocks on the door, and leaves.

I shout through the open door, "Can I have a phone call?"

It's slammed without a response.

Half an hour later, two deputies come to get me. I try to ask them when I get to speak to someone, but they ignore me.

We walk down a row of crowded holding cells and into another section where one cell sits empty.

They professionally push me to the back of the cell and uncuff one hand, only to have me put both hands behind me so they can cuff me to the back row of bars.

I glance at a name tag. "Deputy Henley, doesn't this seem a little unusual?"

"Just following instructions, sir," he says with genteel southern politeness.

Something fucked-up is happening here. I'm not sure if the kindly deputy has any clue.

"I'm supposed to get a phone call."

"You had your call, sir. You can talk to the judge tomorrow."

"But I was never even charged with anything . . ."

He and the other deputy back away and shut the door.

I can't get the fact out of my mind that the other cells were crowded, yet here I am in my own private suite.

Something seriously fucked up is going on here.

CHAPTER SIXTY

VIGILANTE

I don't close my eyes. I don't take my attention away from the door leading into this cell. If Cold War Bill was the Ghost of Christmas Past and Mysterious Woman is the Ghost of Christmas Present, then the next visitor is going to be the Ghost of Christmas Yet to Come, and something tells me I ain't going to like what he's bringing.

Whichever division fucked this up has probably decided, using whatever ethically damaged decision-making process they have, that the life of one disgraced loudmouth professor isn't worth their jobs or their freedom.

I was told to stay away, and I didn't. I was given the chance to play ball, and I refused. Now they're out of options and time.

From Birkett's histrionic phone call, I know she's not in on this. I'm not in *Six Days of the Condor* territory here—I hope. I'm just dealing with a couple of bad cops—who happen to work for an intelligence agency.

If this were an authorized operation, I'd probably be in a black helicopter on my way to some secret rendition site.

But that doesn't make them less threatening—only more so.

When the door to the cell opens, my skin shivers as adrenaline courses through me like water down the Amazon.

The deputies are bringing in two more guests. And shit, the first one is a skinhead with neck tattoos and an honest-to-goodness swastika on his arm.

He weighs in at about 160 and is already staring at me with hate in his eyes. Somebody told him something, because usually I'm a pretty likable guy at first glance.

The other man is more muscular and doesn't have any tattoos. He's got a flattop cut, not a full skinhead dome.

Skinhead is uncuffed and takes a seat right across from me so he can stare me down.

Flathead moves to the corner to my right, about five feet away from me. He crosses his arms and leans back as if he doesn't have a care in the world.

I wait to see how this show is supposed to start.

Clearly Skinhead has it in for me, but why is Flathead here? Are they a team?

As soon as the deputies leave, Skinhead gets up and stands in front of me. I already stretched my legs out so I could use them to protect my space.

"I heard you're a faggot that likes messing with little boys," he says, following it up with some spit. "I heard they found some dead little boys in your house. That true, faggot?"

"How much?" I reply.

"How much? What? You think I'm some faggot that's going to let you blow me?"

"How much did they say they'd pay you to do this? Did they say they'd get you a lawyer, too?"

"What the fuck are you talking about?"

"I'm Theo Cray. I hunt serial killers. I found one in Montana. I was just on the news because of the one I found in Los Angeles. His name is John Christian, and it turns out he's a CIA informant who's being protected by someone who wants me dead."

Skinhead shakes his head. "Jesus Christ. What the hell is that all about?" He turns to the man in the corner—who is now a foot closer to me. "You heard of this crazy faggot?"

Flattop replies, "I don't think he takes you seriously."

Skinhead is in my face. "You don't take me seriously? Faggot? How about I make you suck my dick, faggot?"

"I don't think either one of us wants that. I hope not."

He grabs his crotch. "What, my dick don't taste good enough to you? You need some little boy's dick?"

"I wouldn't take that shit," Flattop says to Skinhead. "Show that faggot you're serious."

Skinhead is getting himself worked up, but I realize he's not the one I need to worry about. Flattop is the professional here. He's getting Skinhead angry so he'll attack me. But Flattop is the killer. He's military. Maybe retired Special Forces or some DEVGRU wet worker they called in. This is Georgia—it couldn't have been hard to find one.

Professor Theo wants to turn to him and point out how transparent the tactic is. Someone called in an arrest on Skinhead. Skinhead is the patsy so that after Flattop bashes my skull into the ground, they'll have someone to take the blame.

Skinhead can say all he wants that there was another man involved, but if he's the one they find covered with my blood, it's not going to matter.

Skinhead is cracking his knuckles, getting ready to sucker punch me.

I speak as calmly as possible. "When they ask you what happened, just remember the name Oyo Diallo. That's the man they're protecting. That's who killed the children in Los Angeles and at the Sweetwater address. He's called John Christian here. Just remember that. They might make you a deal—if they don't try to kill you like me."

This breaks his concentration. It's also messing with Flattop. I'm telling Skinhead the thing that he was sent to keep quiet. Chances are, he has no clue what I'm talking about.

Flattop has stopped inching toward me for a moment as he thinks this over.

Then, just like that, his concentration is back. It's like he's a Terminator that's just rebooted. If Skinhead doesn't do something in the next minute, he's going to start the fight himself.

I have to wait for the right moment. I've got one crazy jailhouse neo-Nazi and a trained killer about to go for my throat . . . and my hands are still cuffed to the bars behind my back. As good as the instruction I've been getting from my MMA fighter student may be, it's all theoretical.

Beyond that, I've only got one thing going for me, and if I fuck it up, I'm dead.

"You say some weird shit," Skinhead says as he backs away.

Flattop knows now is the time to strike.

CHAPTER SIXTY-ONE
PARANOID

If I were where Flattop's sitting, my most devastating form of attack would be to use my heavy boots for a kick to the head. In one move he could knock me out and not worry about getting any bites or bruises from me. This is where I'm the most vulnerable with my hands cuffed to the bars.

His shoulders tilt to the side as he leans on his right leg, freeing up his left.

Fuck. He's a martial artist. He's about to kick me in the head from where he's sitting.

Now that Skinhead has backed off, I pull my legs in under the bench. I have to be ready to move fast.

Once Flattop knows what's going on, I won't get a do-over.

He takes a deep breath, and one arm grips the bench to his right. I try not to watch with my eyes directly at him—I need him off guard.

Skinhead is walking back toward me, deciding that he's going to go for it.

There's a flash of movement to my right as Flattop's powerful leg explodes toward my head.

But I duck before the boot smashes through the air and slams into the bars.

He has no idea how vulnerable he left himself.

My arms whip in front of me in a fraction of a second as I lunge forward and my left hand stabs the open end of the handcuff into Flattop's left eye socket before he can get his balance.

He screams and flails at me with his hands. I get another punch in—this one to his right eye, cutting a gash over it.

He falls to the floor, and I kick him in the head. His screaming stops.

Behind me, Skinhead is looking confused.

I swing my right arm around and connect the cuffs with the side of his head.

"Fuck no! Fuck no!" he yells with his hands up, pleading for mercy.

I give him three fast punches to the temple using the cuff as a brass knuckle, dropping him to the ground. He curls up in a ball and stops moving, stunned by the head trauma.

I rush back to Flattop and wipe the blood off the cuffs using his shirt.

His breathing is labored as he lies there unconscious. He may or may not live, but he'll definitely never see out of that wreck of an eye.

I back up to the bars and place the handcuffs just like they were before I picked them using the handcuff key I've kept on me since Joe Vik nearly took my life.

It takes ten minutes for the deputies to come to the cell. I don't know if this was planned or just really bad jail management.

Skinhead has picked his head up off the ground and is leaning on the bench at the far end of the cell.

The guards unlock the door and rush to Flattop.

One of them turns to me. "What happened?"

"He attacked the other one. But he wouldn't have it."

An older man in a suit pushes his way through the growing crowd of deputies. He singles me out. "Who are you?"

"Theo Cray," I reply.

"The guy that found that murder house?"

"Yes."

"What the hell are you doing in here?"

I just shake my head.

"We had a mix-up," says a deputy. "We thought there was a warrant for him, but there wasn't."

"So you put him in this jail cell with these animals?"

"Sorry," says the deputy.

The suited man reaches behind me and unlocks the cuffs. When he pulls his hands away, there's blood on his fingertips, but he just wipes them off on his black slacks.

"This way, Dr. Cray," he says. "Watch the blood."

Two paramedics are working on Flattop, trying to stem the flow of blood from his eye.

I should feel some remorse, I guess. But all I can think is how much I wish he were Oyo.

The man in the suit takes me gently by the arm. "I'm so sorry you had to see that, Dr. Cray. My apologies. This isn't the kind of jail we run here."

I glance backward at Skinhead. A paramedic is putting gauze on his bloody temple. I don't need to worry about him.

An unreliable witness works both ways.

My primary concern is making sure my next strike happens before whoever was behind this gets to me again.

CHAPTER SIXTY-TWO

Confessional

When I get back to my hotel room, it's almost four in the morning. I spent the last several hours spilling my guts about everything. While I was vague about the means by which I found Oyo's fingerprints on the DHS doorknob, the police didn't seem bothered. In all, I spoke to two detectives from the Douglas County sheriff's department, an Atlanta FBI agent, and a Georgia Bureau of Investigation agent—while a recorder caught everything.

They asked questions but were still trying to figure out what the hell happened at that house at Sweetwater. Throughout our conversation, deputies would come in and slide them notes.

At one point I asked, "What's the body count right now?"

An actual forensic investigation hadn't even started yet, but they were trying to quickly assess how serious the situation was.

Sheriff Art Duane, the man in the suit who pulled me from the cell, replied, "Fourteen, and that's only what's poking out of the ground."

One of the detectives asked me if I'd ever heard of anything like this—meaning how Oyo could get away with so many killings under the watchful eye of an indifferent government.

At first my answer was no, but then I remembered the story of Andrei Chikatilo, the Butcher of Rostov. He was active in the Soviet Union for more than two decades because the Communist Party didn't believe it was possible; they thought serial killers were a symptom of decadent societies like the United States, and moreover, they'd never have suspected one of their own party members.

In Oyo's case, his handlers couldn't accept the fact that they'd enabled a monster to rape and kill so freely. Now they're so desperate to cover up this fact that they tried to have me murdered—or at the very least, shut up. I don't know if Flattop was there to kill me. His goal may have been to put me in the hospital as a kind of warning. It's quite possible his beating wasn't going to involve the kind of maiming that I gave him.

I'm glad I'm realizing this now and not then, because I would have hesitated and found myself with a wired jaw and Mysterious Woman sitting in the corner telling me this is what happens when I don't play along.

Fuck her. Fuck them. Fuck Flattop.

I had every right to cave in his skull.

This seething anger is what's helping me stay awake as I sit in my hotel room with my back to the wall and eyes on the door.

I even put pillows under my sheets in case Cold War Bill decides to sneak in and shoot me. I'm 99 percent sure that's not going to happen now. I've already spilled everything the local authorities need to know. Going after me now would only add credibility to my story. And my story didn't involve Cold War Bill, Mysterious Woman, or Flattop. I kept them out because those are the kind of details that make me look crazy.

I try to focus on what's most important: my rage is fueled by how they tried to fuck with me and the fact that Oyo is still out there.

He's on the run, and I doubt they're helping him. If they are trying to assist, it's probably to set a trap. But he's too smart for that.

I'm sure he had a backup plan if things went south. Part of that plan has to involve getting out of the country. Would he do that right now?

I gave his description to the cops who showed up at the Sweetwater house. That probably went out to every state trooper within hours.

People on the run try to either get as far away as they can or find some place where they can wait things out.

Assuming the nursery was Oyo's only safe house in the Atlanta area, where would he go if he had to improvise? Checking in to a motel would be the quickest way to get caught.

Does he have an accomplice in the area that he could run to? Ms. Violet's assistant Robert was afraid of him, and I doubt Oyo would flee to his church.

Where else, then?

Maybe I already have the answer . . .

I take out the map I made from the tracking data. There was one house that I had ruled out as his killing room, but it might be a place he'd run to if he needed to stay out of sight for a few days.

It's the home in the nice suburb that belongs to the corporate attorney. While I can't see him willingly sheltering a fugitive, what better place for a wanted African war criminal to lie low than a Waspy home in a rich neighborhood?

CHAPTER SIXTY-THREE
HOUSE CALL

I pull up in front of the house in my rental car and hop out without a care in the world, holding onto a package like I'm here to make a delivery.

Cars are starting to pull out of driveways as people head off to work.

There's a Mercedes parked on the street near the mailbox—which seems odd, given that there's plenty of driveway space in front of the two-story home.

Made from gray stone and set atop a small green hill, the house was probably the model home builders showed to sell the neighborhood.

I walk up the steps and knock on the door. Through the glass on the side I can see a rug, a staircase, and the light coming through a glass door on the other side of the house.

No one answers.

It could just be a wild hunch, but I'm not ready to drop it and tell the cops to come check on the house—which maybe I should have done in the first place, but now I'm in hunter mode.

I go back down the steps and peer through the glass window at the top of the garage door.

There's a Volvo station wagon and a dark blue Toyota Corolla with tinted windows parked inside. One of these clearly doesn't belong.

I also spot something else suspicious: a big bag of dog food.

There are three cars here, but evidently the pooch is the only one that had to go to work?

I walk back up to the front door and ring the doorbell.

I know full well that he's not going to answer. He probably suspects that I'm a cop trying to see if there's anyone inside.

I peer through the side window again and catch sight of what might be blood on the staircase. Scratch that—a house this immaculate, it's got to be blood.

There's not a lot. It doesn't look like Oyo just blew the lawyer's brains out when he answered the door.

Oyo might have the man and his wife tied up in a bedroom closet, waiting to see if he needs them as hostages. It's what I would do.

Since kicking in the door isn't an option, I need another plan.

I flirt with the idea of calling the fire department and seeing what would happen if a fire truck came racing to the house next door. Then I realize that Oyo is definitely the kind of guy who would shoot his hostages before leaving a party.

I go back to my car. As I climb inside, I'm positive I spot movement in an upstairs window of the house. *There.* The curtains moved again. He's in there. No doubt about it.

As I pull away, I catch a glimpse of something in the backyard through the slotted fence—a children's playhouse.

Damn it.

I park just around the corner. In my rearview mirror, I notice that the house has the perfect view of cars coming toward it. The other end of the street is a dead-end loop.

Oyo is sitting upstairs in the master bedroom, watching to see who is approaching.

I should call the cops, but I know he's not the negotiating kind, and if I spooked him, he might be minutes away from leaving—which means killing the homeowners.

I race around the houses that border the backyard and come up the other side, opposite from where I was before.

Peering over the backyard fence, I see a wooden staircase leading to a wooden deck—this was what I saw through the front door.

To the left and over is a small balcony attached to the master bedroom. The drapes are pulled tightly shut except for a small gap at the top. They appear to have been pinned: this is how he watches the road that leads up to the house from behind.

Call the cops, Theo.

They'll send a patrol car. Maybe they'll roadblock him, but they'll want to contain him first. He'll know they're coming.

I move to the side of the fence not visible from the bedroom.

I need to get to the deck, but I can't do that while he's watching the backyard.

There has to be some other distraction that doesn't involve a siren and dead hostages.

Shit. There is. There's actually an app for that.

CHAPTER SIXTY-FOUR
SHARING ECONOMY

I take out my phone and order an Uber to the house across the street from where I'm standing. This is a terribly unethical thing to do to the driver, but I'd like to think he'd agree to do it if we had the chance to discuss what's at stake.

The eight minutes it takes for him to arrive feel like eighty. As his icon rounds the corner, I can hear the sound of his tires rolling up the incline.

I'm sure Oyo is watching, too.

I wait for the car to reach the far side of the house. Then I climb over the back fence.

I wait another moment for the car to come to a stop in front of the home directly in front of Oyo's other window.

I text the driver: Running late. I'll be 5 minutes. Start the meter!

He texts back: No problem.

I feel a twinge of guilt but bury it as I slide around the house and start to creep up the deck stairs, trying to keep my back as flat to the wall as possible.

I finally reach the sliding glass doors and poke my head around inside, making sure that Oyo isn't getting a glass of orange juice in the kitchen.

The inside is empty—except it's not—there's a figure standing at the front door, peering out into the street through the glass window.

Oyo.

Fuck.

This was not my plan.

I stand back, aim my gun through the glass door, and point it directly at him.

Neuroscientists say they can predict an action our mind has decided to take moments before our conscious mind has even decided what we think we're going to do. The function of consciousness, they argue, isn't to make decisions, but to rationalize them after the fact. It's our brain's way of explaining why we did things—a kind of public-relations office that turns our id into a rational actor and not some lizard monkey acting out of fear.

I would argue that my actions were based on a rational calculus. I weighed the risks and decided on the best solution.

If you'd asked me a minute ago if I were a killer, I wouldn't have known for sure. My reaction to Flattop and Skinhead should have been some indication, but even when I faced down Joe Vik, I was still looking for some other option besides proactive self-defense.

I scream his name, "Oyo!"

He spins around.

I squeeze the trigger twice. The first bullet shatters the glass door but, given the reality of physics, takes a slightly altered path rather than the direct one from my muzzle to his forehead.

It's the second bullet that I fired that goes straight. Straight into his head.

His neck whips back, and he falls to the ground as hundreds of shards rain down in front of me.

I step into the home, gun pointed forward, and approach his body. There's a pistol in his waistband. I reach down and grab it, tucking it into mine.

It'll be much easier to convince the cops that it was in his hand when I saw him and that I took it from him after—not that they will care.

I check for a pulse, just to make sure that the bullet actually did wipe out his brains and it's not just a bad scratch.

He's dead.

I move up the staircase with my gun still drawn. He's had accomplices in the past.

The door to the master bedroom is open. Inside, two bodies lie on the bed: the lawyer and his wife in their bedclothes.

His throat is slit and hers is dark purple.

I check the closet—empty.

I move down the hall and see a small doll lying in the middle of the carpet.

The first door is a little girl's room. I sweep inside and open the closet. Just clothes.

I move down the hall to another doorway. This is also a little girl's room.

I sweep it: also empty.

I move down to the end of the upstairs and come to a bathroom door. I push it open and see two blurry shapes lying in the bathtub behind a frosted curtain.

They're not moving.

My feet feel like lead, but I have to check. I step onto a frilly pink rug and stand directly in front of the curtain.

With my left hand, I grab the edge and yank it away.

Two pairs of frightened eyes stare up at me.

Tearful eyes. Alive.

CHAPTER SIXTY-FIVE
CLOSURE

Sheriff Duane is sitting next to me on the curb as law-enforcement officials tape off the house and go over every square inch.

He's keeping me company just like I did the traumatized little girls while we waited for the police to arrive.

Their names are Connie and Becca. They were scared because they couldn't understand why Mr. Christian was so angry. They'd never seen him like that.

They still didn't know that their parents were dead. God help the person who has to tell them that.

I finally left their side when a female cop with a soothing voice came into the bathroom. I then let the deputies escort me out of the house and into the front yard, where they bagged the guns I had on me and did their due diligence getting swabs from my hands.

Sheriff Duane arrived within twenty minutes. After he took an assessment of what happened inside, he sat down next to me to get my story.

Thankfully, nobody put me in handcuffs.

"So you had a hunch he'd be here?" asks Duane.

"More or less. I knew he had business with the lawyer. I thought it might be a likely spot."

"And you didn't think about calling it in?" There's only a touch of recrimination in his voice.

"Sheriff, people like you never take my hunches all that seriously."

"You'd think that would change by now," he replies. "But I can see your point."

"There's also the fact that I don't know who I can trust. You ever find out why I ended up handcuffed with those two animals last night?"

"Nope. And I can't find out why federal marshals checked the big one out of a hospital this morning and took off with him in an out-of-town ambulance. Fact is, I can't even find his arrest report."

"Mysteries," I reply.

"Yep. Like how so much blood ended up on the inside of your handcuffs." His eyes dart over to me.

"You should run a cleaner jail."

"Maybe. Maybe." He points a thumb at the house behind us. "How about this crime scene? How clean is that going to be?"

"Oyo's prints are on his gun." They should be, or someone else tucked it into his pants.

"Good. And I can tell the bullet went through the front of his head. So that makes things easier."

"And if it hadn't?"

"I'd make sure you had a lawyer right about now."

I've been asking myself what I would have done if Oyo didn't have a gun. Would I have still shot him? Would I have then tried to cover that up?

Ethically, I tell myself, I would have been fine with ending him— even though only circumstantial reasons led me to the house. And that's where it gets sticky. In principle, vigilantism is a horrible idea. There's a reason why we have courts and thresholds for evidence.

As much as the aftermath proves that I made the right choice, I tell myself not to be so arrogant. This wasn't as clear-cut as it now appears to everyone.

Duane looks down the street as news trucks start to pull up. "Here come the buzzards. We've already got a small carnival at Sweetwater Road." He shrugs. "At least we have closure."

"Do we? You heard my story about how I found Oyo. We don't have closure."

"We have the normal kind, son. The kind you're talking about, I don't think that's on the table."

"You know there's no way he did all this without some folks straining their necks to look the other way."

"Yeah. But this isn't going to be my problem."

"Maybe not. So when do I get my gun back?"

He chuckles. "You're from Texas. You might want to get a replacement. This one's gonna be in evidence for a while."

I nod to the crime-scene van. "But you and me, we're good?"

"I reckon. Unless the FBI shows me videotapes of you and Mr. Oyo dancing around in your birthday suits together laughing it up about the prank y'all gonna pull. We're good."

He leaves me on the curb. A detective approaches me and politely offers me a seat in his unmarked car so I can go back to the station and make a statement.

I ask if I can sit in the front seat so the reporters don't get wind of the fact that I just showed up at another crime scene when we pass by them.

The detective obliges and, for the second time in twenty-four hours, I let the police drive me off.

It's become frighteningly routine for me. All I can think of are the scared little girls and what led to this.

Oyo may be over, but this isn't. They've already fucked with my life several times, and I suspect that even if I run my mouth off to the press and anyone else who will listen, I may get more visits from ghosts before I have a chance to tell my story to someone who can make a difference.

If I really want to end this, I may have to make a compromise I never wanted to make.

CHAPTER SIXTY-SIX
RESPONSE

Never believe anything that's reported in the first twenty-four hours. In the age of social media, this is especially true. People are so quick to rush to Facebook or Twitter with their hot take on whatever headline just flashed across their screen that they don't even bother reading the article or waiting to find out if it's confirmed.

Watching the Toy Man story unfold is fascinating. I have the news on in my hotel room as correspondents rush to Sweetwater Road to cover the second gruesome house of horrors to be discovered.

What are the odds that there would be two serial killers uncovered in such a short span of time, they muse. Are we in a new age of super-serial killers? Well, I wouldn't call it a new age. And second, I remark to myself, wait until they find out the twist.

As soon as I got back to my room and bothered to turn on my phone, I found dozens of messages. Detective Chen called me six times—desperate to find out what was going on in Atlanta. Apparently local officials here are too busy trying to figure out what the hell all this is to brief other law-enforcement agencies.

The LAPD is going to be in a particularly hot spot, because they effectively closed the case on the Wimbledon house, calling Ordavo Sims the primary suspect. If they plan to stick with that narrative, they're fucked.

Because John Christian / Oyo Diallo was from California and even had his car from there here, the FBI is on this case now—which means they're going to be revisiting every witness in Los Angeles. Especially Artice.

I'll be real curious to see what happens when they find out what kind of pressure was put on him.

Plus there's the fact that there was another set of fingerprints at the Wimbledon house. I'm guessing they belong to Oyo.

Chen and company are going to look really, really bad over the one that got away.

I'd gloat if this were office politics. But lives were lost. Hopefully the kid from the nursery isn't going to have too much trauma. I'm not so sure about the girls in the bathtub.

Their frightened faces are going to stay with me.

I've seen terror in the rigor mortis expressions of the dead and even felt some of my own, but to be in the moment—to be right there—affects a different part of me.

I understand even more how people like Joe Vik and Oyo can function. That part of a healthy human that feels empathy and wants to ease the pain of someone suffering in front of them, they don't have. Or worse, they get off on it.

Something else I've noticed was the strong scent of death in Oyo's kill rooms and Joe Vik's victims. The part of the brain that processes chemicals like oxytocin—which helps us feel empathy—is related to our olfactory senses.

I've heard anecdotally about correlations between serial killers and peculiar olfactory functions, but I wonder if there might be something more to it?

Personally, I feel it's dangerous to start naming genes that serial killers have in common—it could quickly become a horrible new kind of profiling and lead to authorities ignoring outliers. But there might be something to studying the idea of which variations can lead to that kind of behavior. It may not be as simple as "If this is broken, then you're a killer"; instead, it may be more like a diagram of which intersecting mutations can lead to that behavior.

There's a knock on my door. I grab my pepper spray and move quickly to the threshold, but before I can check through the peephole, I notice an envelope on the floor.

By the time I realize it's not a hotel bill, whoever left it is no longer in the hallway.

I open the envelope and find myself staring at a photocopy of an arrest report.

It describes a black male who was arrested on suspicion of attempted murder of a minor he was accused of sexually molesting.

The name is Scott F. Quinlan, but the face is Oyo's.

Well, damn. The report is from 2005 and was made by the Baltimore Police Department.

I'm on my phone two minutes later, calling to get the full file.

It takes an hour to find out that no such case is in the system.

Well, double damn.

Who dropped this on my door?

I do an Internet search for Scott F. Quinlan and come up with nothing. I try two of the research portals I used to find Oyo, and still it comes up blank.

Finally, I look up the name of the arresting officer and get a number.

"Hello?" says a man with a gruff Baltimore accent.

"Is this Officer Kimberly?"

"Sergeant Kimberly. Who may I ask is speaking?"

"My name is Theo Cray. I have a question about a case."

"Are you a cop?"

"No . . . I'm an independent investigator."

"What the hell is that?" he replies, clearly short of patience with me.

"You see the story on the news about the house in Los Angeles with all the dead bodies?"

"Yeah? You have something to do with that?"

"Well, I found them. I'm here in Atlanta. Maybe you heard about that?"

"Something. What do you need?"

"Could you pull up a website and look at the photo of the suspect?"

"Hey, guy, I'm in the middle of dinner. Can this wait?"

"Trust me. Just do it."

"Hold on . . ." A minute later, "Fuck. Those motherfuckers."

"I take it you recognize that man."

"No fucking kidding. I pulled that piece of shit in after the kid's mother came running out to my squad car. He was two blocks away washing down his van without a fucking care in the world. Arrogant prick said that he had diplomatic immunity or some shit like that. Which he didn't. But apparently he had something just as good.

"We book him. Get the statement from the kid, even get a rape kit. A couple hours later, some assholes from the State Department show up saying they have to put him under their custody.

"Our captain wasn't having any of that. Next thing you know, they're sending in their lawyers and fuck all. We're like, you take care of him.

"When I tried to follow up on the case, there was no docket. Nothing. They just whisked him off and the prosecutors declined to prosecute. Fucking weasels.

"I cornered one of them at the courthouse after I was on the stand for something else. I asked her how the hell they let that one slide.

"Know what she said? 'It was a domestic dispute that got out of hand.' A fucking domestic dispute. A little boy gets raped and that monster tries to stab a blade between his ribs so he won't go tell any-body. Prosecutor somehow decided that never happened. Fuckers."

He takes a deep breath. "Jesus. Looks here like they shot that asshole. Good fucking riddance. Wish I could thank whoever did that."

"You just did," I reply.

"Fucking serious?"

"Yep."

"Well, good. People may give you shit, but you did the world a good thing. Anything I can do for you?"

"Yes, actually. Oyo killed a lot of kids after he was let go. While I don't think the people who got him out expected he would do that, they didn't seem to put too much thought into the matter."

"No shit."

"I need a name of one of the feds. Somebody you might have remembered."

"Jeez. That's going back. Like I said, the folks came from the State Department. But I'm not sure if they knew who the fuck he was. They were just flacks."

"Probably, but the suspect must have talked to someone to get him out."

"Yeah. Yeah. Can I call you back? Maybe I got something."

I sit by my phone waiting for his call. Half an hour later, he rings me back.

"Okay, this is all I can get. We keep a log of incoming and outgoing calls. While we can't listen in, it's legal for us to track who somebody called. One of our detectives has a database and it started a couple years before then. It doesn't list the name of who placed the call, but I know when they let that asshole make his call. So this is the number." He reads it off to me.

I type it into a search engine.

I check the number twice to make sure it wasn't a mistake. I'd been expecting some line to the CIA or the State Department. This is something else . . . this is the smoking gun.

"Did you look this up?"

"Yes. Right before I called you. Ain't that a peach. And it's the direct line."

"Damn," I reply.

"Good luck on that one."

No shit.

CHAPTER SIXTY-SEVEN
ROOM SERVICE

I sit back on the hotel bed, fully dressed, check my watch, and decide I have time to call Jillian.

"Is this the elusive Dr. Theo Cray?" she says after picking up the phone.

"Still elusive. Before I tell you what I've been up to, tell me something about your day . . ."

"Ha. All right. From the news, I can tell you that it's not as exciting. Carol and Dennis got an offer on the diner."

Carol and Dennis are her dead husband's parents. Jillian took over running their Montana restaurant after serving in the army. When I met her, I could tell her heart wasn't in the place and she was ready to move on, but her love for them was too strong to ever let them know.

"Are they going to take it?" My interest is a little selfish.

"I think so. Carol and I have been selling a lot of pies, and I think I'm going to help her spin that off into its own thing."

"Oh . . . that's cool," I reply.

"Yeah . . ."

Say it, Theo. Say it. "You know . . . Texas could always use more pie . . ."

"Oh, really?"

"Maybe you come back down and let me help you test recipes?"

"I'll consider it," she says. There's a warmth there.

"Please do. There's just one catch . . ."

"Another serial killer?"

"Uh . . . no. Not quite. I may be spending the rest of my life inside a federal prison—or worse."

"Worse?" she asks.

"I made someone very upset. He's in full ass-covering mode and may or may not be trying to get me renditioned to some black-box prison in the middle of nowhere."

"Fuck, Theo. Tell me what I need to know. I'm not going to let them do that."

There is nothing warmer to a man's heart than the woman he loves telling him she's ready to sneak behind enemy lines and rescue him.

"Don't go GI Jane just yet. I'm working on a solution. A little bird told me that I may be called to some secret intelligence-agency court where what they really do is put a gag order on everything and detain you preemptively."

"What can you do?"

I hear the sound of a key in a lock.

"Gotta run. If you don't hear from me again . . ." I blurt out, "I love you," before she can respond.

I pocket the phone as an older man with receding red hair steps into the room. Still sweating through his gym clothes, he stares at his key and then looks at me, confused.

"I think this is my room," he finally says.

"When did you know about Oyo?"

The man, Senator Hank Therot, head of a House counterintelligence committee and capable of green-lighting black-ops budgets in the hundreds of millions of dollars with a stroke of a pen, glares at me. Then the realization dawns. "You're that professor asshole. You're so goddamn dead. I'm going to have you buried in a hole, then lose the hole."

"When did you know about Oyo?" I repeat. "When did you know what he really was?"

I know for certain that by the time Oyo grabbed the kid in Baltimore, Therot was fully aware of what this man was and didn't care. In fact, I have evidence that Therot, who personally pushed to make Oyo an informant, did everything he could to protect the man, because exposing him meant damaging his own reputation.

Therot looks around the room suspiciously, searching for a camera or recording device.

"I don't know what the fuck you're talking about," he says, then turns for the door.

I could have predicted as much. There's no way in hell he'd ever confess to any connection. But it doesn't matter. The people that kept him in power, the recipients of that funding—the former politicians turned lobbyists and contractors—realized he was a liability.

I made a deal. I'm not happy about it. Cavenaugh is getting his terrorist-profiling lab from me, and I get Therot. It's a devil's bargain. I rationalize to myself that I'll be able to do some good on the inside, but deep down I fear that's what everybody thinks before they go down the slippery slope and start using phrases like *collateral damage* in order to sleep at night.

Therot collapses before his hand can reach the door.

I'd coated the outside door handle with a contact poison that knocks you out in small doses. Senator Therot, his pores wide open from a workout in the hotel gym, got the full effect.

While he dozes, I take out a bottle of sanitizer and spray every surface, ensuring that no trace of me remains.

I'm done by the time the expected knock comes at the door. With latex gloves on, I open it and wipe down the exterior doorknob while two men wait alongside a wheelchair.

I give them a thumbs-up, and they load Therot's unconscious body onto the seat and strap him upright.

They head for the service elevator as I step to the stairs. When I cast a backward glance, I catch William Bostrom's eye as he and Mathis push Therot through the door.

We exchange knowing nods, aware that this won't really end the pain, but killing monsters never does. It's just something you have to do when you see them for what they are.

When I reach my rental car parked three blocks away, I see a familiar figure leaning against the side, sipping coffee from a paper cup.

"Let me guess, you're here to tie up loose ends?" I say to Cold War Bill, only half joking as my left hand cradles a small canister while my right goes to my side, ready to pull the pistol tucked into my back belt.

He rolls his eyes and makes a groan. "That's not how it works. It's easier and less messy to just buy somebody off. Which is what I think we did."

I can't tell if there's a little bit of recrimination in his voice, or just a general bitterness at the world.

He continues, "I'm here to make sure nothing gets fucked up. Do you trust your people?"

"Not one bit," I reply. "But I trust their self-interest."

"Right answer. One more question, just for my benefit. Why?"

I look back in the direction of hotel. "It seemed like the most efficient way to eradicate the vector that made Oyo possible."

Bill strokes his chin, nodding. "Okay, Professor. So it's all just biology to you?"

"And mathematics. Don't forget the mathematics."

Bill mutters, "Goddamn. I think you scare me more than Oyo."

"I'm just following things to their rational conclusion."

"That's what scares me. How long before you decide people are the problem and cook up some kind of killer bacteria to wipe us all out?"

"A bacterium would be an inefficient way to do that." I glance down at the small canister I'm holding in my fist. "Now, a designer prion . . ."

Bill looks down at my hand, then stares at me for a long moment, trying to tell if I'm kidding. "Shit. Now I don't know who should be more worried about this deal you struck: you or them."

Which is exactly what I want them to think.

Cold War Bill tosses his half-finished coffee into a trash can as he shuffles off—probably trying to decide how to warn his superiors that Professor Cray might actually be some deranged genocidal maniac plotting the apocalypse.

I pocket the cylinder and get back into my car and head for the highway, unconcerned with Therot, Bill, or his bosses.

I have a lab to build.

About the Author

Andrew Mayne is the author of *The Naturalist* and *Angel Killer* and the star of A&E's *Don't Trust Andrew Mayne*. He is also a magician who started his first world tour as an illusionist when he was a teenager and went on to work behind the scenes for Penn & Teller, David Blaine, and David Copperfield. Ranked as the fifth bestselling independent author of the year by Amazon UK, Andrew currently hosts the *Weird Things* podcast. For more on him and his work, visit www.AndrewMayne.com.